BLACK DIAMOND

BLACK DIAMOND

JOAN WOLF

Los Angeles • Saltese, MT • St. Paul

Black Diamond

All Rights Reserved © 2003 by Joan Wolf & Cruzane Mountain Publishing

No part of this book may be reproduced or transmitted in any form or by any means, graphic, electronic, or mechanical, including photocopying, recording, taping, or by any information storage retrieval system, without the permission in writing from the publisher. Any similarity to persons living or dead is coincidental.

For information, address:
Cruzane Mountain Publishing
1 Wolf Road
Saltese, MT 59867
www.cruzanemountain.com

ISBN:0-9744465-0-5
Printed in the United States of America

For my husband, Fred, without whom I wouldn't have this book

To my sons,

Stephen and Chris, who greatly contributed in so many ways
Fred, who supplied a wealth of material
Eric, who kept me going

And to my daughter-in-law, Ann Wolf, whose help was invaluable

ACKNOWLEDGMENTS

Many thanks for all the information so willingly given by the LAPD, the office of LAPD Internal Affairs, Hollywood Homicide Division, and the LA County Children and Family Services. The authentic details you provided were much appreciated.

And in the Northwest, thanks to officials of the state crime lab of Montana, Marty Raap, Attorney-at-Law, who answered a lot of questions, and the sheriff's departments of Spokane County, Washington, Shoshone County, Idaho, and Mineral County, Montana.

Special thanks to Sergeant Larry Jackson, Deputy Sheriff in Missoula, Montana. Finding you was like finding a nugget of gold.

BLACK DIAMOND

PROLOGUE

IT was late when Police Sergeant Dominick Garcia let himself in the two-story white stucco house in Hollywood Hills. He walked into the living room, the familiar scent of musk filling him with pleasurable sensations. The room, heavily mirrored, was furnished in Art Deco. It was softly lit, with white tapered candles burning on the mantelpiece.

Julia, dressed in black lounging pajamas accented with a crimson silk scarf, was reclining on the couch, cell phone in hand. As Garcia approached her, she said her goodbyes and set the phone down on the glass end table.

"Business or pleasure?" Garcia asked with a sardonic smile. "Or were you making arrangements with one of the gentlemen who yields a little of both?"

Julia Townsend was a prosperous madam who possessed a stable of elegant, high-priced call girls. However, it was known that she enjoyed personally servicing a favored few, for fees ranging from $1,000 - $2,000 a night, depending on the scenarios to be enacted.

Julia offered a tinkly little laugh. "And to what do I owe the pleasure of this unexpected and unannounced visit?"

"Unexpected? What's that supposed to mean?"

BLACK DIAMOND

Garcia shot back. "It's the fifteenth of the month, isn't it?"

"What's so special about the fifteenth?" Julia asked innocently, patting at the sides of her swept-up hairdo. Her shining white-blonde hair was piled high on her head like a turban, exposing glittery diamond earrings.

"Something happen to your memory?" Garcia answered, with a hard edge to his voice. "That's been pay-off day for the last five years."

"And for the last five years, you were a member of the Los Angeles Police Department. I'm not paying any more protection money to a has-been cop."

" Let's get one thing straight. You'll be very sorry if you ever call me a has-been cop again," Garcia said in a steely voice. "I might be temporarily suspended, but not for long."

"So you keep saying."

"Shut your damn mouth!" Garcia yelled. "I'm still the boss here. You're no better than a two-bit whore, and you better treat me with respect."

"Or what are you going to do?" Julia drawled. "Arrest me?"

"You fucking whore bitch!" Garcia moved towards her, his dark face taking on a menacing look. His narrowed brown eyes were blazing. "Go get my money!"

Julia sat back and looked at him with icy blue eyes. "You're washed up, and I'm not paying you one more cent," she said coldly. "And don't be coming around here anymore looking for something free."

Garcia grabbed her roughly and pulled her off the couch. Blue veins were throbbing in his forehead. He yanked her close to him, breathing hard. "I don't think you better talk to me like that, Baby," he whispered hoarsely in her ear. "I said you should treat me with respect. Now call me sir! Say: Please let me kiss your ass, sir!"

"Let me go!" Julia screamed, trying to wrench herself away.

Garcia held her tight, his heavily muscled arms and shoulders bulging under his dark polo shirt. "Say it!"

Julia pulled one arm free and slapped him hard on the face. "Let me go! You're crazy!"

Garcia released his tight hold, putting a hand to his cheek. "Now you shouldn't have done that, Baby."

Julia was trembling all over. The iciness in her eyes had changed to cold fear. "Dominick, look. I'll give you your money."

"It's a little late for that, Baby. It's respect I want. Now say: Please let me kiss your ass, sir."

"Dominick, please!" Julia cried, realizing he was over the edge.

"SAY IT!" He yanked off her silk scarf and looped it tightly around her throat.

Julia's face had drained of all color. Her eyes were bulging with fear. She spoke in a whisper through her contorted mouth. "Please let me kiss your ass, sir."

Garcia pulled the scarf tighter. "Say it like you mean it, Baby. Beg me."

Julia's voice came out as a strangled gurgle. "Please, Baby, let me kiss your ass."

Garcia saw the naked terror reflected in her eyes. Now she respected him. Now she knew the power he had over her.

He smiled at her and tightened the scarf. "You forgot to say sir!"

BLACK DIAMOND

"Sir-r-r-r-r-r..."

Garcia pulled on the scarf, aware that his hands were shaking violently. Finally he felt her body go slack. When he let go, she slumped to the floor. He knelt and checked her pulse, realizing she was dead.

As he stood staring at the lifeless body, slowly his rage began to subside. Goddamnit to hell, he thought. Why'd she have to go and make me do that? Goddamn women.

It had all happened so fast, Garcia could hardly believe it. He had totally lost his cool, and there lay Julia dead. Now he had to figure out what to do next. He sank into a chair to think things over. Any fingerprints and DNA could probably be explained away by the fact he was a regular visitor here. Everyone knew he often availed himself of Julia's services. But why chance it? It would be much better if this crime did not become the subject of a major investigation.

He'd make it look like a robbery gone bad. The Division wouldn't spend any time at all looking for a random junkie. That would be like looking for a needle in a haystack, and everyone knew it. They'd just go through the motions. Suddenly the sound of footsteps entered his consciousness, someone running. Now a door slamming. He jumped up, not sure what he had really heard.

The girl. Heidi. Was she somewhere in the house? Garcia raced through the downstairs, looking in every room. No one. The girl wasn't home. His nerves were just on edge. To be sure, he dashed upstairs and carefully searched each room. Nobody was there. He had imagined the whole thing. With a feeling of intense relief he started back down the stairs.

But something was nagging at him. During all his

years on the police force, he had trained himself to notice small details. Something had caught his attention, but he wasn't sure what it was. Turning around, he went back up the stairs to take another look. He began with Julia's room, once again flipping the light switch that turned on the elaborate golden candelabra.

He stood studying the room where he had once found so much pleasure. The mirrored ceiling reflected the four-poster king-size bed with its tasseled red satin coverlet. Pillows in every size and shape leaned against the intricately carved mahogany headboard. Julia's dressing table held an ornate Chinese jewelry box, an assortment of perfumes, and an ivory and gold mirror and brush set. A chaise lounge upholstered in deep purple velvet occupied one corner. The walk-in closet was filled with her flamboyant outfits and high heels.

Feeling satisfied that this room was not the source of whatever was nagging at him, he turned off the light and walked down the hallway. As he entered Heidi's bedroom, he was overcome with the feeling that this was where something was wrong. What was it? The room, with its simple white pine furniture, was in perfect order. Her clothes were hung in the closet systematically in a straight row, shoes and slippers in pairs beneath them. The papers on her desk were neatly stacked, pens and pencils standing in a lead crystal container beside them. A corner cupboard held a collection of dainty glass figurines. A thriving ivy plant was hanging by the window in a shiny brass bowl. What could possibly be bothering him?

Garcia stood in thought, looking at the matching sprays of spring flowers that Heidi had painted on her twin headboards. He remembered the night he had seen her painting them, kneeling on the bed in her tee shirt and blue jeans. Her long blonde hair was spilling down her back. Her lithe, shapely body rotated seductively as she dipped her brush into the paints and stroked on the colors. He had walked up to the bed, startling her. Just as he had laid his hand on her shoulder, Julia had appeared and they'd had words. After that, Heidi's door was locked.

As he stood looking at the headboards, suddenly he saw it. The detail that had bothered him. Heidi's bedspread was rumpled. She never would have left it like that, unless....Garcia was seized with panic. He hurried over and put the palm of his hand on the chambray coverlet, feeling it. There was no doubt about it. It was warm. Warm from body heat.

He crossed to the other bed and felt it. Much cooler. Heidi had been in that room a short time ago. In that room, listening. Now she wasn't in the house. He walked back to Heidi's bed and ran his hand up and down her coverlet, feeling its warmth. Where are you, little girl? Why did you run away? His hand struck something hard under the pillow, and he reached under to grab it. MY DIARY.

So she had been on this bed writing in her diary. Garcia hastily opened it to the newest page and began reading what Heidi had written after the date... *I think Mother is entertaining one of her gentlemen callers in the living room tonight. I wish I had stayed at Cheryl's. I hate nights like this. Now something seems to be wrong. The guy sounds really mad. They're arguing about something, for sure. I'm afraid he's going to hurt Mother. I'm going downstairs and see what's going on...*

Garcia slammed the diary down on the bed in fury.

Did you see what was going on, little girl? Did you go back to Cheryl's? Is that where you are now? Cheryl who? He wrenched open the top drawer of her bedside table where the telephone rested. There it was. Little Miss Orderly had a small personal phone book filled with names and numbers, recorded in her beautiful script. Thank you, little girl. But I don't have time to look through it now. First things first.

Garcia picked up the diary and phone book and hurried out of the room, back down the hallway. A plan had begun forming in his mind. He took out his handkerchief and wrapped it around his hand. No sense going out of his way to leave prints.

He turned on the light and went to the big screen TV across from her bed. As images of flesh videos they had watched together flashed through his mind, he clicked on the remote and adjusted the volume. Next he turned back the red satin coverlet, arranged the pillows as if Julia had been leaning against them, and disheveled the silk sheets. Before he left, he opened drawers and spilled out the contents of the Chinese jewelry box. Mostly costume jewelry. All the good stuff was in the safe.

Carrying the diary and phone book, Garcia went back downstairs to the living room and stood over Julia's body, assessing it. She had fallen on her back, and lay staring up at him with vacant blue eyes. The crimson scarf contrasted with her pale white bloodless face. Garcia knelt down to yank off the diamond earrings, the same as any junkie would have done.

"It's too bad, Baby, you came down to investigate when you heard noises. You should've stayed upstairs and watched the rest of the movie. It had a happy ending."

Garcia found her purse in the hall closet and rummaged through it, finding a thick roll of hundred-dollar bills. "Well, well. So the fifteenth was payoff day, after all. It would've been so much easier if you had just handed it over."

He left the purse unclasped and tossed it on the floor. Before he finally went outside to break the window and open it, he walked back into the living room for a last look. Leaving on one dim light, he went around turning off all the others. Then, with two soft whooshes, he blew out the candles and left.

CHAPTER 1

SUSAN gazed up at the starry sky from her front deck overlooking the lake. It was a warm spring night with only a faint breeze stirring. She had one hand tucked in the front pocket of her terrycloth robe. The other was dangling over the arm of her lounge, idly scratching the wiry fur of her affectionate Airedale terrier, Fritz.

A loon circled and dipped low, its strange laughing call echoing over the lake. Her reverie broken, Susan reluctantly got up and went inside, leaving Fritz out to enjoy the night air. She shuffled into the kitchen in floppy open-heeled slippers, poured a glass of wine, and climbed the stairs to her study.

Sitting down at her oversized cherry wood desk, she settled her tall, slender frame into the swivel chair and hit the start button on her CD player. She sat back and took a sip of wine, its tang filling her with warmth. The melodic notes of Chopin's First Nocturne began floating from the dual speakers on her desk. With a feeling of inspiration, she went into the word processing program and opened the file of her current work, determined to straighten out her troublesome Chapter 12. For the past few days, the latest chapter of *Blood Money* had seemed plodding, the characters wooden.

BLACK DIAMOND

Susan Muir, best-selling mystery/suspense writer, had won an Edgar award with her first book, *A Time For Murder*, just over a year ago, a week before her thirty-third birthday. "Young and promising," the reviewers had agreed. "Susan Muir has written a real page-turner ... A compelling work."

Susan had quickly attained celebrity status. Although she was a confident, self-contained person, she'd admitted to herself she rather enjoyed her sudden fame. She found it fun to be recognized by fans on the streets, even being stopped to give autographs. And she took pleasure in the attention she received in shops and restaurants she frequented. But she was also sensible enough to realize that after awhile she might well tire of it, once again valuing the privacy she so basically needed.

As her favorite nocturne came to an end, she pressed the repeat button and leaned back to let the haunting melody sweep over her again. Her shoulder-length auburn hair was highlighted by the soft glow from the antique lamp on the desk. The thick wavy hair framed her pretty face, expressive with wide-set, lively brown eyes.

Susan's blue-shuttered colonial house was set in seclusion on the south shore of Loon Lake, and the moonbeams filtering through the window afforded the front room its only light from outside. The rear of the house was graced with two gas lamps that hung on ornamental wrought iron poles on each side of the driveway.

Susan clicked away on her computer, deep in thought. The echoing cries of the loons floated in through the partly open window, an orchestral accompaniment for Chopin. The ringing telephone startled her, and she stiffened in her chair. Reluctant to be interrupted, she scanned her caller ID. When she saw there was no number registered, she decided to screen. The beep came, then silence, then a soft hang-up. For a few moments, she sat wondering who the caller could have been, then went back to work.

Shortly the phone rang again. Seeing that the caller ID screen was once more showing no number, she curiously picked up. "Hello, this is Susan."

She was answered by silence. Some muffled static crackled, followed by another soft hang-up. Susan was unnerved, and sat wishing the caller would ring again, with a simple explanation of trouble on the line. She thought to herself wryly that first she didn't want the phone to ring, now she fervently hoped it would. Could the caller have been Richard, checking to see if she was home? As her mind ranged over possibilities, she couldn't help thinking of Bruce Fione, the boy who had paid a visit that afternoon.

Gus Woodbridge, her regular spa serviceman, was out of town, and had sent a young employee to make the scheduled monthly rounds. The twentyish boy had been friendly enough, but something about his manner had made her uncomfortable. First he had arrived late, indifferently tossing his black curls while he offered a lame excuse. Then he had been slow to get to work, making his way inside the house for a glass of water. When he made a comment about the fresh doughnuts on the counter, Susan felt as if she had to offer him one, which he quickly accepted, with a cup of coffee to wash it down.

Besides, Susan thought maybe she had imagined it, but while they talked, he seemed to be giving her lingering looks with his dark, long-lashed eyes. No doubt about it, his presence had been unsettling. And with her house set in such a remote spot, it was her usual practice not to let strange people know she lived alone.

Susan tensed as she heard Fritz barking in the back yard. He usually barked only to signal the arrival of a visitor, and she certainly wasn't expecting anyone at that hour. She dashed to her bedroom window overlooking the driveway. A pair of headlights swept down the road through the darkness. The road circled the lake, winding through stands of old-growth pines. Its main purpose was to serve the homeowners, and with just one other house on the far remote end of the lake where she lived, only an occasional vehicle ever went by.

Susan watched the car disappear from view, trying her best to recognize it. A dark four-door, maybe midnight blue or black. She couldn't be sure, but she thought it could be the same car she recently had noticed in the driveway of the old gabled house a mile or so down the road. She had been surprised to see it parked there because the house had been closed for the season.

Earlier in the year, when Susan had first moved in, she had made the acquaintance of the owners, Jack and Jocelyn Stone, who told her they would be summering in their beach house in the Cayman Islands. Susan remembered thinking it was an unusual time of year to be going to the tropics. In Northern Idaho, she expected most people would rather leave for the winter.

Then not long ago, while taking a morning walk down the road with Fritz, she saw the couple carrying suitcases to their Cadillac. She had quickened her pace, hoping to exchange a few words, but her neighbors had pulled out before she reached them, giving her a wave as they drove past. Since Susan hadn't seen them again, she presumed they had decided to leave for the islands early.

Susan ran downstairs to let Fritz in, quickly double locking the door behind him. With a feeling of uneasiness, she went into the kitchen and poured herself another glass of wine. She shook some mixed nuts into a small wooden bowl given to her by her friend Flora after a trip to Mexico. She suddenly wished Flora was there right now. Glancing at the kitchen clock, she decided it wasn't too late to call her. Flora was a night owl, and at least they could talk a few minutes. Maybe that would help her case of nerves.

She picked up the phone and punched the speed-dial. After three rings Flora's voice mail answered. "Hi! This is Flora. I'm not in right now, but if you leave your name and number, I'll call you back."

"Where are you?" Susan said into the phone. "Out with Brad, I hope. If you're not too tired when you get home, give me a call. I'll be up."

Susan and Flora Finney had grown up in the same neighborhood in Marble Point, and had been best friends for as long as they could remember. Having Flora close by was one of the main reasons for Susan's move back to Idaho when she decided to leave the big city life of Los Angeles. And it was a move she was glad she had made. Not only did she have family and friends there, offering a sort of haven, but also, in her opinion, Marble Point was an ideal place to live.

After college, while Susan had moved from place to place working for several newspapers, Flora had elected to stay put, and now owned Flora's Fancy, a popular upscale gift shop in the downtown area.

BLACK DIAMOND

Feeling a little grounded just from hearing Flora's voice, Susan again mounted the stairs to her study, where the Chopin was still softly playing. The night breeze was picking up, and the cord on the window's blue louvered shade was blowing gently. In the background, the loons continued to cry out over the water.

She was completely immersed in her book when the telephone rang again. Thinking it was Flora, she automatically reached for it. "Hi there," she said.

"Well, hi there yourself. It's Nan."

"Nan! I was expecting another call. What a nice surprise!"

"I hope I'm not interrupting you."

"Not at all," Susan answered. "I'm glad for a break."

"You're working late."

"So are you," Susan told her. "It's really late in New York."

"But I'm not working. I'm not calling in my official role as your literary agent."

"Oh? What's up?"

"Mary's set on making a trip out West this summer. I haven't been able to talk her out of it. She wants to spend a few weeks at a guest ranch."

"It's no wonder. I know how much that girl loves horses. But since she's only thirteen, I suppose you're reluctant to let her go so far from home."

"Exactly. So before I start searching on the Internet, I thought I'd ask you if perhaps there's something in your area. Then at least she would be near someone I know."

"You might be in luck. The Black Diamond Guest Ranch is about twenty miles from here. It's way out on a country road, and I've never had occasion to go there, but I'll be glad to look into it."

"Well, I would really appreciate it. How's the book coming?"

"Fine, I think. I had some problems in Chapter 12, but I believe I'm back on track."

"That's good. I'm sure it will be wonderful. Can't wait to read it."

Susan woke early the next morning. She felt completely refreshed, and was glad she had turned the telephone off the night before, without waiting for Flora's call. Now, in the light of day, with the reassuring sun streaming through the windows, she smiled at the memory of her nighttime uneasiness that had prompted the call to her friend. At least it hadn't kept her up all night. She remembered snuggling under the down comforter on her queen-size bed, giving a few more thoughts to *Blood Money*, then falling into a deep sleep.

As Susan arose, she looked around her cozy, comfortable bedroom. Colorful wool braid rugs accented the plain soft carpeting. A white painted pine garden bench with blue flowered cushions sat invitingly under the window. The set of rich, warm maple furniture was in the same country style as the charming collections throughout the house.

She pulled on a plaid flannel shirt and jeans, then went downstairs to let Fritz out and get a pot of coffee going. When it was ready, she carried her filled mug to the front of the wrap-around deck so she could look out at the lake. The lake that morning was slate blue, dappled with shadow. Knowing the cushioned furniture would still be wet with dew, she sat on a slatted cedar bench to enjoy her favorite time of day. The air smelled wonderful, rich with oxygen, and the birds were singing their cheery good morning songs.

Just as Susan returned to the kitchen, Flora called. "Hi! Sorry I didn't get back to you last night. You guessed right. I was out with Brad, and I got home really late. Did you want anything important?"

Susan chuckled. "It seemed important last night. Now it seems ridiculous."

"What do you mean?"

"My nerves got the best of me, and I just wanted to hear your voice."

"That doesn't sound like you. What happened?"

"I was working on my book, and I had a couple of hang-ups that set me on edge, for some reason."

"It could've been Richard, trying to get up his nerve to talk to you."

"Could be. But somehow it didn't seem like it."

"Well, you're entitled to an occasional case of the jitters, living alone in that secluded place the way you do." Flora laughed. "Maybe it was because you were sitting there at that late hour writing about nefarious dark deeds."

Susan laughed along with her. "Maybe."

"But then, I guess you're pretty hardened to writing about such things, after your last job in LA."

Susan knew Flora was referring to her days as an investigative reporter for the *Los Angeles Times*. With many revealing stories to her credit, her final investigation had uncovered racial prejudice, brutality, and corruption in the LAPD Hollywood Division. While four officers were suspended, and two more placed under suspicion, her scrutiny had extended into the police department's upper echelons, and the ensuing Internal Affairs investigation was ongoing.

Then, burned out and ready for a change, she had used her savings to take time off to finish the novel she had been working on during every spare moment. Its instant success had netted her over a million dollars, and she had returned to Marble Point to settle down and write her next book.

"How about if I come out and have coffee with you right now?" Flora suggested. "Could you still use a little company?"

"I sure could," Susan responded. "I'd love it. And I happen to have some wonderful Gruyere. Why don't we go all out and have a cheese soufflé?"

"Sounds great! I'm on my way!"

The two friends caught up with each other's news over their leisurely breakfast. Flora had brought along a half-dozen croissants, and before it was over, they had eaten every one. When they had finished and tidied up, Flora left for her shop and Susan set off for the Black Diamond.

When she pulled her silver Subaru out of the driveway, she took the route around the east side of the lake so she could drive past the Stones'. She was really curious to find out if the car she had seen the night before was parked there. As she reached the house, she saw the driveway was empty. Resisting the temptation to stop and take a look through the garage window, Susan continued on down the road.

Nearing the northern edge of the lake, she spotted a dark blue car turning off Loon Lake Road onto the two-lane

BLACK DIAMOND

highway, in the same direction she was headed. She was sure the car resembled the one she had seen last night. Maybe it had pulled out of the Stones' just before she got there, and had been right ahead of her ever since.

She quickly accelerated, hoping to get a glimpse of the driver. She wanted to see what the mysterious visitor to the Stones' looked like. Susan smiled, reminding herself she didn't even know if the car had been at the Stones'. Well, her old reporter's instinct was kicking in anyway, and there wasn't a thing she could do about it.

She sped along the macadam road, gaining on the car. As she drew close, she realized it was a dark blue Lincoln Town Car, with an out-of-state plate. Doing her best to get a look at the driver, she could only make out that he was a square-shouldered man wearing a gray touring cap. Her heart fell as the Lincoln whipped around a slow-moving van, and a rush of oncoming traffic kept her from passing. She helplessly watched the car speed off into the distance. Oh well, she thought. Nice try.

When she had driven about fifteen miles out of town, she exited onto a frontage road that ran along the edge of the woods. Keeping an eye out for deer, she proceeded at a slow speed, watching for the turnoff. After a few miles, she spotted the 'Black Diamond Guest Ranch' sign and, following the arrow, made a left turn onto Cedar Creek Road.

Susan drank in the beauty of the towering, feathery cedars that lined the road. She found herself hoping they would always remain safe from loggers. With chagrin, she remembered how much she had enjoyed the cedar bench on her deck that very morning. Frowning in thought, just then she reached the gate of the Black Diamond and drove through, her tires crunching over the loose gravel.

She lowered her window to get a closer view of the grounds. Beds of tulips and daffodils were scattered about, and bright yellow forsythia bushes were in full blossom. White-trimmed, red clapboard guest cabins were set back amidst stands of thick fir trees.

Thinking how idyllic it looked, she drove towards a good-sized log structure that she guessed was the main lodge. A railed-in porch ran along the front of it, with a large wooden plaque of a black diamond hanging over the entryway. On one side of the building was a chimney with beautiful stonework.

On the ground out front, a planter made of a hollowed-out log caught her eye. It was filled with a variety of blooming flowers, a profusion of harmonious colors. A teenage girl with long blonde hair was bent over it, sprinkling the flowers with a tin watering can.

But as Susan drove up and parked, her heart sank as she realized that though it had once been a charming lodge, it now was sadly in need of repair. Up close, she saw the foundation was crumbling, the porch was sagging, the logs were dull and flaky, in need of oil, and stones were missing from the chimney. The dirty windows did nothing to add to the appearance.

Two boys in their late teens were sprawled on the steps. Susan got out of her car and approached them. "Nice day," she began, taking in their gaunt, unhealthy appearance. They had an ashen pallor, dull eyes, and lusterless hair.

When neither one answered, Susan asked a direct question. "Are you staying here at the guest ranch?"

BLACK DIAMOND

One of the boys guffawed. "This ain't no guest ranch."

"Really? The sign down the road says it is."

"That sign's ancient history."

"I think it used to be a guest ranch," the girl spoke up, walking over with her watering can. "But it's not anymore."

Susan smiled at the girl, thinking how unhappy she looked. Her round blue eyes had a depth of sadness about them.

"The flowers are lovely," Susan told her. "Did you plant them?"

"Yes," the girl said. "I love flowers."

Before Susan could say anything more, a well-muscled middle-aged man of average height came out of the lodge. He was wearing a purple silk shirt and designer jeans, along with hand-tooled leather boots. In addition to the gold chain around his neck, a thick Rolex hung on his wrist, and he sported a glitzy diamond on his right pinky.

He greeted her, then brusquely tossed his head at the three teenagers, indicating they were to leave. The girl turned on her heel and hurried away, while the two boys got up and shuffled off.

Susan introduced herself. When no return introduction was offered, she went on. "My understanding was that this is a guest ranch, and I came to make an inquiry about it."

The man gave her a tight smile. "Sorry, but this is no longer a guest ranch. It's now a cattle ranch." He gestured past the horse corral towards a far field where some Herefords were grazing.

"Oh, in that case, I'm sorry I disturbed you," Susan said. "I've noticed the sign down at the foot of the road, and I was looking into it for a friend of mine back East."

"That sign's from long before my time," he responded with another tight smile. "I guess you drove up here for nothing."

"Well, actually I'm a writer, and I'm always interested in seeing different settings," Susan answered. "Since I'm here, I'd love to take a look around."

"You're looking at it," he said shortly. "There's nothing else to see."

A dark-haired bulky man opened the lodge door and stuck his head out. "Tony, I think you wanna take this call."

"You can see I'm busy," Tony said to Susan dismissively.

Susan got in her car and backed out. She saw Tony watching her through the window, phone in hand. As she drove off, she had the odd feeling he was watching to make sure she left.

CHAPTER 2

LIEUTENANT Charlie Martin, tall and handsome with rugged features, sat brooding at his desk in the Internal Affairs Division of the LAPD. The sun streaming in from the window behind him fell on his bent head. His thick blond hair revealed a few gray strands in the bright sunlight. He scanned the papers before him one last time, then returned them to a folder and placed it in his desk drawer. He got up and adjusted the window shade, slanting the louvers upwards, then punched in a number on his telephone.

"Hollywood Division," came the voice on the other end.

"Lieutenant Martin, IAD. Put the captain on."

"Certainly, sir."

Charlie tapped his long fingers on the desk while he waited. His brows were furrowed in thought over his deep blue eyes.

"Captain Dulhaney here," came the commanding voice.

"Charlie Martin. How's the investigation coming on the Townsend murder?"

"A burglary gone bad. Pretty much a closed case."

"Did you look through the madam's appointment book? Talk to any of her clients?"

"I'll have to go through the files," Captain Dulhaney responded.

"I just did. I got the files from Records and didn't find much," Charlie came back. "Maybe the files aren't complete for some reason. Did someone ask the neighbors if they noticed comings and goings that night? Has the missing daughter been located? Was the murdered woman's name passed along to Vice and Narcotics so they can keep an ear out on the streets?"

"Look, Lieutenant, some junkie goes in to steal enough for a quick fix. The babe gets unlucky, gets in the way, and ends up dead. Pretty common in LA. Why make it such a big deal?"

"Call it a hunch, if you have to. And don't forget, you've got four suspended cops, and two more under suspicion. It doesn't exactly inspire confidence in your division."

There was a silence on the line, then Charlie spoke again. "I want to see every report pertaining to that murder, Captain Dulhaney. Send them to me personally."

"On whose authority?"

"Mine, and the Captain's."

"Very well. I'll see that you get them, Lieutenant."

"Thank you, Captain. Good day."

Dominick Garcia paced the floor of his cheerless room at the Wayside Inn, a small motel on the two-lane highway leading into Marble Point. No one knew he was here. He had been careful about that. He had slipped out of LA and driven to Vegas, leaving his car in a lot downtown where it wouldn't be noticed. Then he walked to a rental agency and used his fake credentials and phony credit card to get a car that couldn't be traced to him.

Garcia had been assigned to the Los Angeles Hollywood Division for the past fifteen years. He had spent the first eleven years in the Vice Squad, and the last four in Narcotics. While he had been receiving medals for heroism and prestigious awards for the highest number of collars in his division, he remained busy extorting protection money, taking bribes, planting evidence, performing cover-ups, and thumping people for fun. He also had been involved in two questionable shootings, the second one of a Hispanic teenage boy with no prior record.

Now he was suspended from the force, pending investigation. The media had made sure of that. They just wouldn't let go of the story of the poor defenseless youth, camping outside the intensive care unit at LA General talking to family members, nosing around his South Central neighborhood for character witnesses, interviewing his principal and teachers. "A good kid ... hardworking ... reliable ... top student ... leadership qualities..."

Garcia was filled with rage at the thought of the bleeding heart coverage that had dominated the news. It made him furious that they didn't appreciate how the police force risked their lives, trying to keep scumbags off the streets. They had no idea what it was like dealing with lowlifes day in, day out. And not even get treated with respect. The continual jeers rang in his head... "Pig! .. I smell bacon! ... I'll sue your white ass..." Then, when maybe he made one mistake, the media wanted to crucify him.

Dominick realized he was getting off track. This wasn't the time to be thinking of all that. He needed to focus on the business at hand. He stopped pacing and grabbed up the TV remote. Stacking the pillows against the headboard, he leaned back and began flipping channels. Not able to concentrate on anything, he finally punched the remote off, picturing the images flowing through his head, creating his own personal movie for the bare screen as he recalled the night of the murder, and how he had found out where Heidi was. Or, damnit to hell, where he thought she was...

When he had left Julia's, he had gone straight home and poured himself a glassful of Jack Daniels. He was shaken, and needed to pull himself together so he could think. He had to devise a plan to find Heidi. He picked up the diary and personal phone book he had taken from her bedroom and carried them to the sofa along with his drink. First he re-read the last entry in her diary to check on the friend's name ... *I wish I had stayed at Cheryl's* ... I wish you had, too, little girl. Then I wouldn't have this fucking problem.
    Then he had turned to Heidi's personal phone book and begun looking for Cheryl's name. He found it about halfway through, on the O page. Cheryl Overman... 982 Genesee Avenue... 213-654-6015. Thank you, little girl. A good starting place.
    By that time, it had been past midnight, too late to call. He might be able to find out whether or not Heidi was there, but it would make her too suspicious. He had to take his time, play cat and mouse. He'd lure her out of her hiding hole tomorrow. Right now he'd cruise over there and check the place out, maybe get a glimpse of her through a window. Then at least he'd know for sure she was there.
    He really didn't expect her to go to the police. She

wouldn't trust them. She had the smarts to know if she spilled her story, she was dead. Sure, the Division might take him in for questioning, but he'd be back out in no time. Of course, since he had already found out she was a witness, she was dead anyway, but she didn't know that.

Garcia was tense at the wheel as he drove back to Hollywood. Avoiding Julia's street, he drove up Genesee Avenue past #982, relieved to see there were no police cars outside. He parked in the next block and walked down the sidewalk to Cheryl's house. Out front only the porch light was burning.

Staying in the shadows, he stealthily made his way around back. One room was lit, and the shades were open. Feeling sure it was Cheryl's bedroom, he positioned himself in the bushes to stand watch. For twenty minutes there was no sign of movement in the room. Then he saw her. All his muscles tightened and a smile formed on his face. It was Heidi, no doubt about it, standing by the window, backlit by glowing lamps. I see you, little girl. It's late, time for bed. Sweet dreams. I'll see you tomorrow.

Somewhat reassured, Garcia had driven home. He had poured himself another glass of Jack Daniels and begun carefully reading through the stolen diary, looking for any other useful information. After an hour or so, near the bottom of a page, he had hit upon the entry that the next day had proved to be so valuable. Heidi had written: *If my mother and father had gotten married, my name would be Heidi Stone. That's a nice name, I think.* And then she had dreamily filled up the rest of the page writing *Heidi Stone* again and again. Once more Garcia had gone to the personal directory, soon locating the name, address, and phone number of Heidi's father, Jack Stone, of Marble

Point, Idaho, who apparently lived with Jocelyn Stone.

The next morning, with several alternate schemes in mind, Garcia called the Overmans' number. When the telephone was answered by a teenage girl, he asked to speak with Heidi. Being told Heidi wasn't there, he quickly used the guise he had planned. Garcia claimed to be Heidi's father. He'd had a call from the police that something had happened, but he hadn't been able to reach Heidi and was terribly worried. He was hoping that Cheryl, the friend Heidi always talked about, would know where she was.

"Oh, Mr. Stone, there's nothing to worry about," Cheryl had answered without hesitation. "She's on her way to your house. She took the Gr..." And then her voice suddenly stopped.

Garcia smiled in triumph and hung up the phone. Easy as pie. She had realized what she was doing too late.

But when he had arrived in Marble Point, he had found the Stones' house empty, with no sign of Heidi. And here he was, still sitting on his ass in a fucking fleabag motel, waiting for someone to show up. "Damn!" he said out loud. He stood up and fished in his pocket to make sure he had his key. I have to get out of this lousy room, he thought. I'm going to go get a whiskey.

Unnoticed by Susan, Bruce Fione passed her on the frontage road as she left the Black Diamond. He was in high spirits because he had a day off from Oasis Spa. The CD player in his '95 Firebird was cranked up, and he was belting out *"Paradise City"* along with Axl Rose. The loud music might have caught Susan's attention, but Bruce had his car windows closed to afford better sound quality.

BLACK DIAMOND

Well, well. I wonder what the pretty lady's doing in these parts? Bruce mused as he took in Susan's classic profile and tumbling auburn hair. He thought how lucky he had gotten yesterday when Gus Woodbridge sent him to her house for the monthly spa servicing. He imagined Susan's exquisite face, her curvaceous body, her elegant bearing. Last night he couldn't stop thinking about her. He had called a couple of times just to hear her voice on the answering machine. The second time, when she picked up, it had been a special thrill to hear her actual voice. Then he had dreamed about her.

Even if Gus intended to send him to her house again, he didn't plan to wait for the next scheduled service call. A single woman living alone like that would be glad to have a little company, especially when it was a good-looking guy like himself.

As Susan's Subaru trailed away in his rearview mirror, Bruce inhaled deeply, readying himself for the refrain. *'Take me down to the paradise city, Where the grass is green and the girls are pretty.'* Bruce's eyes shone as he sang along with gusto. But I have my own idea of paradise, he thought. As soon as I can, I'm taking off for some far-off exotic place where the palm trees wave in the wind. Year-round beach weather. Dark-haired beauties walking on the sand, wearing nothing but thongs and leis around their necks. Once in awhile a short flowered skirt wouldn't be too bad, as long as it was easy to reach up.

I have to add to my savings so I can split this two-bit town, he thought in frustration. If Tony has a delivery for me today, maybe I can skim some off the top. He didn't seem to notice the last time, but with that guy you can't really tell. If he found out he was being double-crossed, he'd probably smile at you while he was pulling the trigger. I have to be careful. Better if I can talk him into putting me on full time.

Then I'll only have to take care of one little problem. Laura thinks she's coming with me. How could she ever be so dumb? You think she would've figured out I only used her to get to Tony. Sure, we've had a lot of fun the last month or so, but like I'm spending the rest of my life with one broad. Ha ha ha. I plan to have a tequila in one hand and a different titty every day in the other. Bruce began breathing hard at the thought of it. A smile of ecstasy spread across his face as he poured out the words. '*So far away, So far away...*'

As Susan drove home from the Black Diamond, she couldn't shake off the strange feeling Tony had been watching to make sure she left. Tony who? she wondered. She thought it was odd he had never introduced himself. And she couldn't help noticing all the jewelry he wore. It didn't seem typical of a rancher. Besides, what were those teenagers doing there? They certainly didn't have the ruddy color and rugged appearance of ranch hands. And the girl had such a forlorn look about her, Susan found she couldn't get her off her mind.

When she neared home, once more she chose the route around Loon Lake that would take her past the Stones' house. She felt she had to see if the Lincoln Town Car was parked there. As she drove along, Susan took pleasure in the picturesque view. The lake was shimmering in the full afternoon sun. Small craft skimming the water sent up silvery sprays, and soft waves rippled across the surface.

As she reached the Stones', she found the driveway

empty, and began chiding herself. What was she doing? Was she really following her reporter's instinct? Or was she simply using her writer's imagination to color the ordinary life around her? An amused smile was playing at her lips as she pulled into her driveway.

As soon as she went inside, she made a small fruit salad while she heated up the leftover soufflé. After she had eaten her lunch and given Nan a call to report her findings about the Black Diamond, she went upstairs to her study.

She sat down at the computer and checked her e-mail. She was delighted to find a message from her sister Lillian. She immediately opened it and read it on the screen.

"Tom's vacation date is set. We plan to descend upon your beatific Loon Lake home, utterly shattering your tranquility, on July 7. The kids are wildly excited, and as you cam see, so am I. Mom and Dad are planning to be home on July 1, so that gives them a week to recuperate before dealing with the "Terrible Two"! Do you think you'll be finished with *Blood Money* by then? Love and kisses, Lillian."

Susan's mother and father were on the around-the-world tour they had promised themselves for years. A month ago Susan had put on a gala celebration for them, a combination retirement and going-away party. Her father had founded the popular regional newspaper, *The Beacon*, and had published it for the past twenty-five years. Her mother was a retired high school English teacher.

Susan thought how joyous her parents would be to find out that Lillian and Tom were coming with the boys. She would e-mail them all about it as soon as she heard from them. They were due to arrive in Hong Kong any day.

Her mother and father had taken their laptops with them, and had been e-mailing from Cyber Cafes in all the major cities. Susan had greatly enjoyed the immediacy of their correspondence. She had to laugh about it. Both her parents had initially refused to have anything to do with computers, insisting they were for the younger generation. Now they couldn't go on a vacation without one.

Would she be finished with *Blood Money* before Lillian got there? It sure would be nice. She could throw herself into the sport of spoiling her beloved nephews with utter abandon. She did realize she had been progressing with her book faster since Richard had left. Always disciplined about writing during the day, she now often found herself writing in the evenings as well.

Was she writing in the evenings out of sheer loneliness? Did she want Richard to come back? She wasn't sure. She thought of his handsome features, the unruly shock of red hair, the beautiful light blue eyes. He was a musician, a guitar and piano player, and wrote beautiful songs. She thought of one he had written for her... "I want to hold you in my arms forever ... And never let you go."

Then why hadn't he been able to make a commitment to marriage? And children? Susan hadn't minded their lifestyle during the two years they had lived together in LA, scraping by in their small apartment on La Cienega. Newspeople didn't get paid much, and, as a struggling musician, Richard never had a steady income. But, looking back, Susan realized that, ironically, those had been their happiest times.

She remembered with nostalgia how wonderful it was the nights she was writing her book on an old computer that

BLACK DIAMOND

was squeezed onto a shelf in their tiny bedroom, while Richard sat in the living room picking out new songs on his guitar.

On Saturday nights, if he left to play in one of the rock clubs on Sunset, she would work on her book until eleven or twelve, then run a comb through her hair and walk down to hear his late-night sets. She loved watching him perform, gyrating around in his tight black pants and white satin jacket, its gold sequins sparkling under the spotlight. The crowds went wild, clapping and cheering, and Susan got caught up in the glamour and excitement of it all.

But after she had attained her new wealth, she wanted to settle down. Besides the money for her first book, she had already gotten a huge advance for *Blood Money*. If they invested wisely, they would have plenty of money to live on and raise a family, while Richard pursued his music.

Initially he had been excited to move to Marble Point and pick out the house with her. He had loved the idea of living in beautiful surroundings in a house large enough for him to have his own studio. At last he was going to have all the finest equipment. He would make the demo tape that would propel him to stardom. As soon as they had moved in, he had converted the basement into the state-of-the-art studio he had dreamed of. But the demo tape he had planned to make in it had never been finished.

He had quickly tired of working in obscurity. He missed performing on the stage. Before long he began moping around, passing the time by drinking six-packs and playing along with tapes and CD's. Seeing his dissatisfaction, Susan suggested he play some spot gigs in Spokane, Washington, an easy drive from Marble Point. He did play on a few occasions, but soon decided Spokane lacked the glitter and glamour of Los Angeles. He told Susan he felt as if life was passing him by. He envisioned being a rock star, and he was sure the best place to make it, after all, was LA.

So when Ian called to ask Richard to be the new lead guitar in a band he had put together, he was ready to go. The most recent HOUSE ON FIRE single had already gotten some airplay and was receiving record label interest. Richard was sure it was the break he had been waiting for.

And no, he didn't think Susan should go with him. Wasn't she all settled into her new Loon Lake home, writing her new novel? Besides, he was sure the band would be touring. They'd see how it went. He was really sorry. He cared about her a lot, and had tried hard to make it work out. Lucky her, she had already written a bestseller. He had been spending his life writing 'Poor Richard's Almanac.' Now he was going to make it big on his own.

Susan's eyes grew misty as she sat reminiscing. As usual, it made her melancholy to remember that last morning they had coffee together in the kitchen. He had reached into his pocket and pulled out all his recently acquired credit cards and the checkbook from their joint account, placing them on the table. Giving her a rueful smile, he said thanks anyway, but he wouldn't be using them anymore.

It made Susan fully realize how tormented he had been that he wasn't paying his own way. Her attempts to downplay the fact she was the breadwinner had been futile. As hard as she had tried to bolster his self-respect, she had known in her heart it was impossible. Self-respect could only come from within, from a sense of real accomplishment. Still she wondered if there was something she could have done differently.

When she thought things over, she always recalled what Richard had said during one of their arguments: "You were selfish to ask me to move to your hometown. All your family and friends are here. Who do I have? I notice you never suggested we could settle down in *my* hometown." Lone Star, Kansas wasn't exactly Susan's idea of a place where she wanted to spend the rest of her life, but she knew he had a point.

Well, she'd never get finished with *Blood Money* at this rate. She quickly e-mailed Lillian and went to work.

CHAPTER 3

WHEN Bruce Fione got home that evening, he went straight for his bag of crystal meth that was stashed in the back of the kitchen cupboard in a cracker tin. Walking into the living room, he shook some of the white powder onto the round glass end table by the couch. He made it into a line with his pocketknife, then held a rolled-up twenty to one end and snorted. Feeling the rush, he punched in Laura Finley's cell phone number.

"Hey, Babe!" Bruce said exultantly when she answered. "Get ready to roll. I have a place for us tonight."

"Oh, great!" Laura's heart began racing. "Where?"

"Out on Loon Lake Road. The McCullys have kindly invited us to be their guests."

"Way cool. What time are you picking me up?"

"Around nine. And don't forget your ticket for the night's entertainment."

"You know I won't," Laura breathed into the phone as the connection went dead.

In her cabin at the Black Diamond, Laura quickly began pulling out clothes. Her new roommate, Heidi, was stretched out on one of the twin beds, leafing through a magazine. "Big date?" she asked with a smile.

    The two girls had bunked together since Heidi had moved into the Black Diamond a few days ago. It had been about two weeks since Laura's old roommate, Josie, had abruptly disappeared. Laura didn't know what had happened to her, only that she had gotten into some kind of trouble with Tony. Laura hadn't been in love with the idea of having a new roommate, and she had no idea why Heidi was even there, but she knew enough to keep her mouth shut about it. All she knew was, Tony had given orders to treat her like an outsider. And around here, you did whatever Tony said. But, Laura had to admit, Heidi hadn't been any trouble. She pretty much kept to herself.

    And it sure was a bonus the way Heidi had spiffed the place up. The dingy one-room cabin actually looked cozy. Heidi had scrubbed and polished the scarred pine board floor until it shone. Then she had washed the old frayed braided rugs before she put them back down. After she had cleaned the knotty pine table and chairs, she arranged a colorful display of wildflowers as a centerpiece.

    "I'm going out with Bruce," Laura said, holding a loose-knit white sweater under her chin. "How does this look?"

    "Real nice," Heidi answered pleasantly. "What are you wearing with it?"

    "My tan suede pants suit. I'm sure Bruce will be picking me up on his cycle."

    Laura moved into the tiny bathroom to apply her makeup. She began by carefully assessing herself in the bathroom mirror. She wished her long, stringy brown hair was softer and shinier, her pale brown eyes brighter, her sallow skin creamier, her teeth whiter. Picking up her tube of blush, she determinedly set to work to make herself as attractive as possible for Bruce. She was wild about him.

When Laura was finally satisfied with her appearance, she riffled through the bottom dresser drawer and got out "the ticket" that Bruce required, a half-gram of pure crystal meth. Before she dropped it in her bag, she sprinkled some of the white powder on her hand mirror, lining it up with a nail file. "I better catch up to my man," she said to Heidi after she took a snort. "We'll really be tweaking later, but, if I know Bruce, I'm sure he'll give himself a little head start. Are you sure you don't want to join me?"

"No thanks," Heidi said. "Here comes Bruce now, anyway. Enjoy yourself."

The roaring motorcycle came to a stop on the road in back of the Black Diamond, and the headlight turned off. Laura grabbed her knapsack and ran to meet him, breathless as she leaned to kiss his lips.

"Ready to roll, Babe?" Bruce said.

"I'm always ready for you."

"Just the way I like it." Bruce smiled casually. "Now be a good girl and hand over your ticket."

"Here it is, Angel," Laura whispered as she handed him the package of meth.

"Climb on." Bruce turned on the engine. "We're going to party!"

The dark red motorcycle pulled out with a thunderous roar, spitting up gravel. Bruce made a turn and drove onto the blacktop, speeding towards the frontage road. A half-hour later, under a clear night sky, they were cruising along Loon Lake Road, both wearing knapsacks over their matching brown leather jackets. A sharp breeze blew off the lake, and the air was brisk. Their faces were glowing, and their eyes shone beneath their helmets.

Bruce felt free, confident. Everybody was used to him riding around at night on his Harley Sportster, and he often took the route around the lake. So there was no need to worry about being recognized. He only had to be careful when he pulled off the road, and he would be.

He had scouted the area out that afternoon, when he learned the McCullys were going over to the coast for a few days to visit their daughter. When he could get away, he had driven his Firebird out to their large Georgian style house overlooking the western side of the lake. Across the road, not too far from their property, he had spotted a narrow little path into the woods where he could easily hide his cycle. Maybe a hiker or two used that path on occasion, but no way would anybody be around at night.

Bruce smiled as he neared the McCullys' house. Luck was with him. No cars were coming in either direction. He turned off the road onto the path, driving a little way into the dense woods. Then he switched off the ignition and stepped to the ground, offering Laura a hand.

They crossed the road and made their way to the front of the McCullys' house. Standing with Bruce at the door, Laura watched over his shoulder as he studied the lock with a pen flashlight. Then he reached into his pocket and pulled out an assortment of tools, selecting a highly sophisticated bronze passkey. He had bought it off a buddy two years ago, and it had turned out to be one of his most valued possessions. Using deft fingers, he slipped it into the lock and slid it back and forth to get the feel of it, finally twisting slowly while he manipulated the doorknob. Then they were inside.

After they set down their knapsacks, Bruce reached into his pocket for his glass pipe and the packet of white powder that Laura had given him. He hurriedly dug in his other pocket for a lighter. With a flick, he held the flame under his pipe while he inhaled deeply, then handed it to Laura. Exhilaration flooded through them. As they stood in the marble-floored foyer smoking together, their state of ecstasy rose to dizzying heights.

They walked arm in arm into the parlor. The white plaster ceiling was high, lofty. The paneled walls were painted a warm blue, a charming backdrop for the richly upholstered sofas and chairs. The fine wood pieces with their ornamental carving were true works of art. Bruce mentally compared the house he had broken into with the pigsty that he called home. He imagined the two cramped rooms, the peeling paint, the rusty fixtures, the worn carpeting, the dime store furniture. The deep-piled plush carpet underneath their feet muffled their footsteps as they crossed the room to where elaborately carved stair balustrades rose to the second story.

"Come on," Laura said, starting up the steps. "I can't wait."

Bruce pulled her back. "Later," he whispered hoarsely. "Let's have a bottle of wine first. There's a wine rack in the dining room."

They passed through the central hall into the large formal dining room. Laura drew the heavy brocade draperies while Bruce lit a tall tapered candle on the sideboard. In the flickering candlelight, Laura began looking around at all the silver pieces in the room. She picked up a candelabrum off the massive mahogany table and ran her fingers over it admiringly. "Wow! This will be worth a lot. And there's two of them. I'll just run and put them in my backpack right now."

"What's the rush, Babe?" Bruce said, taking her by the arm. "We have all night. Come on, let's pick out a bottle of wine."

He guided her toward the wine rack and the two of them looked through all the bottles, settling on a Pinot Noir. Laura opened one of the drawers in the sideboard and found a silver corkscrew. Bruce uncorked the bottle with a flourish, then sniffed the spicy aroma. Smiling appreciatively, he poured the dark ruby wine into two crystal glasses.

They tapped their rims together in a toast. "To our nighttime fun," Bruce said in his husky voice. "With the man I love," Laura added.

They both took a deep drink of the slightly sweet, medium-bodied wine, then Bruce started out of the room, carrying the bottle. "Let's go. We'll have ourselves a refreshing little dip before we head upstairs. Their spa's right out back."

"Whatever you say, Angel," Laura breathed softly. "You're in charge."

Together they stepped outside onto the wide-planked, railed deck that extended the full width of the house. Matching sets of redwood furniture with wide-striped cushions were clustered around cedar planters filled with irises, gladiolas, roses, and other flowers that gave off an overall sweet scent. The stars blazed above them.

"This is the life," Bruce said, pivoting on the balls of his feet as he looked about. "This is exactly what I'm going to have."

Laura quickly put her arms around him, searching his eyes. "You mean, this is what *we're* going to have, right?"

"Right. Now get us a couple of towels."

Laura walked over to the open-shelved wooden cabinet that held stacks of luxurious, monogrammed towels. She took two back to the spa and handed one to Bruce. "Guess what?" she said with a giggle. "The McCullys had these towels monogrammed just for us. Mine and Mine."

"Right on," Bruce answered, flashing her a smile.

He removed the Jacuzzi cover and turned on the spa lights. Blue tiles shone through the clear shimmering water. "Looks like someone takes good care of this," he said wryly.

Together they undressed and sank into the water, setting their wine glasses on the edge of the spa. Bruce turned on the jets and they leaned back to luxuriate in the forceful flow of water and the streaming bubbles.

"Oh look," Laura said, pointing to a glass bird feeder hung in a pine tree next to the deck. "That bird feeder's empty. Someone forgot to fill it. The poor little birds will be starving. They'll be so sad when they come looking for food and find out it's all gone."

Bruce jumped back out, fired with energy. "I feel like a beer," he said. "Be right back."

"I'll go with you," Laura said, scrambling after him. "I can't sit still."

Wrapped in their terrycloth towels, they reentered the kitchen and Bruce began looking through the refrigerator. Laura noticed a bag of popcorn sitting on the microwave. She opened the door and tossed it inside, punching the popcorn setting.

"What are you doing?" Bruce asked Laura as she started up the microwave.

"Making popcorn for those poor hungry little birds," she answered. "Did you find a beer?"

"No, there isn't any. And now we have to wait for the popcorn to be done. Instead of standing around, we might as well get started in the dining room."

"Good idea, Angel," Laura answered. "I'm all for it."

They retrieved their knapsacks from the foyer and hurried into the dining room. Laura began by stuffing the two silver candelabras into her bag. Bruce picked up the sugar bowl by its fancy handle. Holding his head back, he shook some sugar into his wide-open mouth before he tossed it into his bag along with the matching creamer. They threw in all the costly pieces from the drawers, then left their sacks and returned to the kitchen.

By this time the kitchen was filled with the aromatic smell of freshly popped corn. While Bruce was opening the bag, Laura decided to run back and grab another bottle of wine. She had to rummage through her knapsack to find the corkscrew that she had already taken. Finally they went back outside and eagerly crawled back into the hot tub's enveloping warmth.

"Oh, I forgot to fill up the bird feeder," Laura said, noticing the popcorn bag on the edge of the hot tub where Bruce had set it. "I'll do it when we get out."

Bruce poured more wine into their glasses, and they drank greedily. They began talking to each other faster and faster. Their mouths were so dry from the meth, the wine stained their teeth and lips red, giving them a clown-like look.

They began pouring the wine carelessly, spilling it in the water. Laura knocked over the popcorn bag, and pieces of popcorn began floating all over the surface. "I'm afraid we're creating extra work for our friendly spa serviceman," Laura said with a smile, idly pushing at some popcorn with her toe.

Bruce sprang up. "I've had enough of this anyway. Come on, let's go upstairs."

Rewrapped in their terrycloth towels, they went inside and mounted the staircase in a high state of anticipation. They walked down the hall and looked through the doorways until they found the master bedroom. It faced east, toward the lake, and since Bruce thought it was unlikely there would be any boats out at that hour, he turned on the Tiffany lamp that sat in the center of the bedside table.

Laura pulled back the silk coverlet on the double bed and slipped underneath it. "I'm ready for you, Angel," she said in a throaty voice.

"Don't be getting all covered up," Bruce answered from across the room, where he was bent over the dresser, searching through the drawers.

"I'm just getting warm while I'm waiting for you," Laura said, leaning on one elbow to watch him. "Are you finding what you're looking for?"

"I always find what I'm looking for, Babe," Bruce responded, carrying four various colored scarves toward the bed. "And as soon as I get you tied up, I'll get you so warm you'll think you're on fire."

"I know, Angel." She spread-eagled on the bed.

BLACK DIAMOND

"Hurry. I can't wait."

As soon as Laura's hands and feet were tied to the four-poster bed, Bruce began looking around the room again. "Now we need a bedtime toy."

As Laura watched, he opened the drawer of the bedside table and pulled out a .357 Magnum. "Well, well," Bruce said excitedly. "Look what we have here."

He held the gun at eye level and looked down the barrel. "It's even loaded. I can't believe how nice the McCullys are to us."

He began to brush Laura's thigh with the pistol butt, running it up and down teasingly. "Getting warm, Babe?"

"Bruce! What are you doing?" Laura said, a note of alarm in her voice.

"Trust me, Babe," Bruce said huskily. "Relax. You'll love it."

Laura began to writhe on the bed, edging away from the gun. "Bruce! Stop!"

"Who's in charge here?" Bruce's eyes hardened, his pupils small from the meth. His face was flushed to a bright red.

"You are."

"You better remember that, Babe. Now open your legs for me."

He looked down at her face as he reversed the position of the gun and began rubbing higher and higher on her thigh with the barrel. Her mouth was twitching nervously as she resisted. She strained against the scarves on her ankles, trying to pull free. Bruce began working her with his other hand. "You'll be ready for it, Babe. Just relax."

As her moistness came, the straggly brown hair that

was fanned out on the pillow appeared to Bruce as soft wavy auburn. The pale eyes seemed to be a deep vibrant brown, set in milky white skin. The curvaceous mouth was full and generous. The sensuous face floating beneath him was Susan's. Susan Muir. She belonged to him already.

Bruce began breathing heavily. "I think I need a new partner, Babe."

"No! Bruce, no!" Laura screamed. "Do whatever you want."

"Are you opening up your legs for the gun, Babe?"

"Whatever you want. Go ahead."

"Just relax. If you make me nervous, I might accidentally pull the trigger."

Laura closed her eyes as Bruce opened her with one hand and began working the barrel up inside her with the other. "Our heads got spun, didn't they, Babe?" Bruce said in a thick voice. "Here we go. Just trust me."

Through his heavy breathing, Bruce heard loud moaning sounds. Were they from Laura...or Susan?

CHAPTER 4

AT the Black Diamond, Heidi was stretched out on her bed thinking. After Laura had left, Heidi put down the magazine she had been leafing through, no longer needing to keep up a pretense. She was lying on her back, with her hands clasped behind her head on the pillow. Now she could turn her full attention to making her decision. Or rather, finalizing her decision. Heidi knew what she had to do. She had to make the phone call. She couldn't let that horrible monster get away with murder.

Heidi thought back to that last night in her house in LA. She had been walking home from Cheryl's, her best friend who lived a few blocks away in the same Hollywood neighborhood up Nichols Canyon. Just as she had been approaching her house, she saw a man cross her front porch, open the door, and disappear inside.

Wanting to be unobserved, Heidi had entered the house through the kitchen door and crept quietly up the back stairs to her room. She had just begun her nightly ritual of writing in her diary, when she heard the beginnings of an argument downstairs in the living room. As the argument escalated, she thought she discerned panic in her mother's voice. Heidi grew terrified, remembering other nights when her mother would get yelled at and beaten, appearing in the morning with purple welts and bruises that had been impossible to cover up.

At last, filled with an uneasiness she couldn't squelch, Heidi stole down the back stairs and, with her heart pounding, sneaked along the hallway on silent feet to the living room. Remaining hidden in the hallway, she pressed herself flat against the wall while she slowly stuck her head out and peered into the room.

Heidi froze in terror. She was afraid her mother was dead. She was slumped on the floor motionless, her face ghostly white. Standing over her was Police Sergeant Dominick Garcia. There was no mistaking him. He had been at the house many times. Heidi saw his formidable brawny figure in nearly full profile, his thick neck, dark-complected face, prominent nose and chin, close-cropped black hair.

Heidi stood looking at the grisly scene, thoughts racing through her head. Was her mother really dead? Should she go in and see for herself? What could she do anyway? Did she dare try getting past Garcia?

The police sergeant straightened his shoulders and stepped away from Julia's body, starting towards a nearby easy chair. Heidi felt all the nerve draining out of her. She was overcome with the realization that when he sat down, he would be facing the exact spot where she stood. She jerked her head back in alarm. Weak-kneed, she leaned against the wall, fearful of being detected if she made a move. She was trembling all over as she stood trying to decide what to do. The house was so hushed, she felt sure that any second Garcia would hear the sound of her breathing, and would dart into the hallway and grab her.

At last she summoned the courage to move. Looking over her shoulder, she slowly made her way down the hall. As she turned into the kitchen, she was seized with panic when she realized the hallway would be out of sight. Her skin crawled with fear as she imagined Garcia following after her. Suddenly she lost all caution and made a dash for the door.

When she got outside, she cut through the side yard, then ran the entire way back to her friend's house. She called out her name as she wildly punched at the doorbell. Cheryl, whose parents were out for the evening, flung open the door, and Heidi fell into her arms, panting and sobbing. When she told Cheryl what had happened, the two set off on foot for a phone booth on Sunset to call 911. Even though Heidi felt there was no hope for her mother, she knew it was important to make the call. But she definitely didn't want it traced to Cheryl's.

There was one thing Heidi instinctively knew. If it was a murder, and Dominick Garcia found out Heidi was an eyewitness, she was as good as dead. He probably would find out anyway. After all, he was a detective. Maybe he already knew. He could have easily heard the back door slam and glimpsed Heidi through the window as she ran away. She broke into a cold sweat at the thought of it. She had to get out of LA.

She and Cheryl spent the rest of the night closeted in Cheryl's bedroom, working out a plan for Heidi. At six o'clock in the morning, the front page of the *LA Times* confirmed that her mother had been murdered. The newspaper also reported that Julia Townsend's seventeen-year-old daughter was missing, and was being sought by police for questioning. Heidi and Cheryl quickly put their plan into motion.

Cheryl's little brother had spent the night at their grandmother's, and her parents, unaware that Heidi had spent the night, weren't up yet. While the house was still quiet, the two girls slipped outside and walked to the bus stop. Heidi was carrying Cheryl's backpack, jam-packed with articles she would need, along with several of Cheryl's loose-fitting outfits. In her pocket was a wad of bills Cheryl had been saving up for a new portable CD player. A phone call to the station had assured them it was enough for a ticket to Marble Point, Idaho where Heidi's father lived.

She knew her father didn't want her staying with him, but she couldn't think who else to turn to. She didn't know anything about her father's family, and she only vaguely remembered the few relatives on her mother's side. Like Heidi, her mother had been an only child, and her parents had been so disapproving of her lifestyle, they had ceased all communication years ago. Heidi was hoping if she just showed up at her father's, now that her mother was dead, maybe he'd be willing to take her in for awhile, until she could figure out what to do next.

While they sat on a bench waiting for the number two bus that would take Heidi to the Greyhound terminal, they exchanged tearful promises and goodbyes. Cheryl wouldn't tell a soul where she went. Heidi would write to her as soon as she could. When the bus pulled up, the two friends embraced fiercely, then Heidi was on her way.

During the twenty-nine hour trip, Heidi hardly slept

at all. Every time she would start dozing off, vivid images of the murder scene would flash through her mind, jolting her awake. Inevitably she would start re-living everything all over again, imagining herself stuffing her diary under the pillow, sneaking down the back stairs, seeing her mother's body on the floor, hiding in the hallway, making her escape.

She wished she had her diary. Maybe when things died down, under one pretext or another, Cheryl could get it for her, along with a few other personal things she wouldn't want to lose. Her mind wandered to her picture album, her scrapbook, her cherished gold locket her mother had given her when she turned "sweet sixteen." Inside was a photo of Heidi and her mother, arms around each other's shoulders, smiling. Cheryl had snapped the picture at Heidi's birthday party, especially so she'd have it for her new locket. If only she hadn't already taken her locket off that night when she went downstairs. Then she would still have it. Heidi's thoughts turned to her sweet-sixteen birthday party.

Her mother had always had such fond memories of her own sweet-sixteen party, she had been determined to have one for her daughter. Heidi had tried to talk her out of it, telling her she didn't think her friends would come. Her mother said that was nonsense, that nobody would miss going to a sweet-sixteen party.

As her mother began making grand plans for the occasion, Heidi actually got caught up by the sheer force of her mother's enthusiasm. It was going to be a splendid party, with Heidi's favorite color, pink, the theme color. The table would be set with a fine pink linen tablecloth, with a centerpiece of pink and white carnations. Her mother could already imagine how beautiful the flowers would be, with a wonderful sweet, spicy fragrance. Heidi's birthday cake would be decorated with pink rosettes, pink ice cubes would be floating in pink punch in a hand-cut crystal bowl.

In the end, not wanting to hurt her mother's feelings, Heidi reluctantly gave out ten invitations to girls she hoped would come. But in her heart, she was sure the girls wouldn't be allowed to attend a party at the house of a madam. Except for Cheryl, Heidi hardly ever asked friends to come over. It had been her experience that they usually came up with one excuse or another. And she had gotten the idea long ago that Cheryl's parents preferred that Heidi go to their house.

Finally it was Heidi's birthday. She was wearing her new pink party dress and the locket her mother had given her that morning. Her mother looked striking in bright pink chiffon and matching heels. When the hour of the party approached, Heidi noticed her mother stealing nervous glances out the front window, obviously hoping for signs of guests.

At the appointed time, no one had arrived. Heidi couldn't help wondering if Cheryl was even coming. Minutes dragged by as they waited for the sound of the doorbell. The two of them sat wordlessly looking at the pink balloons and the pink and white streamers hanging from the ceiling. At length her mother murmured something about how it was a shame that people were always late, and look how the pink ice cubes were all melting, she should have waited to put them in the punch.

About fifteen minutes later, they both jumped at the

doorbell's shrill ring. Heidi rushed to answer it, her face flushed with hope. There stood Cheryl and Leslie, Heidi's friend from her art class at school. The two girls handed Heidi her presents, offering sincere apologies for being late. Leslie had arranged to meet Cheryl at her house and walk over together. She had waited and waited for a bus, and now she had made them both late, and she was really sorry.

Cheryl had realized at once that the house was unnaturally quiet, and asked Heidi if the others had come. Tears sprang to Heidi's eyes as she shook her head no. Heidi quickly brushed the tears away as she led the two girls into the living room, trying hard to put on a good show for her mother's sake.

Heidi knew her two friends were greatly embarrassed for her when they walked into the room so full of decorations and refreshments, so empty of guests. Her mother gushed over Leslie when Heidi introduced them, saying how wonderful it was that she could come, and she guessed it was just going to be the four of them, but that meant more pizza and cake and ice cream for everyone!

Her mother went about with frantic energy, lighting candles, leading the "Happy Birthday" song, helping Heidi cut her cake, spooning out ice cream, ladling punch, serving pizza, taking pictures as Heidi opened her two presents. Then her mother thanked the girls for coming and told them to go on enjoying themselves, not to worry about playing their music too loud, she loved to hear it. Then she retired to her room.

When Heidi went up after the girls left, she saw her mother's eyes were still red from crying, and there were wads of crumpled tissue in her wastebasket. She hugged her mother and thanked her for such a nice party. She told her she'd never forget it. It was too bad the other girls couldn't come, but it was fun just the way it was. Then her mother reached out and pulled Heidi close, holding her tightly, and they cried in each other's arms.

New tears ran down Heidi's cheeks as she remembered the scene. And now her mother was dead. She thought her heart was going to break with sorrow. As the bus rolled along, she kept thinking how different her life would have been if her father hadn't left. Her mother hadn't fought for child support, since they had never actually been married.

Instead, she had tried her best to support the two of them herself, but soon found she could only manage to buy the barest necessities, never able to afford even a small luxury. Neither could she accumulate any savings for the future. She had opened a college account for Heidi, but at the end of every month, she fell into a state of despair when she could put in only a dollar or two. Finally she had turned to the oldest profession in the world, and with a good body and a good head for business, she worked her way to the top rather quickly.

When Heidi began guessing how her mother made a living, and questioned her about it, they sat down and had a long talk. Her mother admitted she wasn't proud of what she was doing, but it was the only way she knew how to ensure their financial future. She felt guilty exposing Heidi to her lifestyle, not wanting her to get the wrong idea about men and sex. Heidi would fall in love with a wonderful boy and marry, then sex would be the most beautiful, joyous experience imaginable. Heidi avoided the men who came and went to see her mother, and, in spite of her strong adolescent stirrings, found herself usually avoiding boys as well. She didn't like having to rebuff continual unwanted advances.

As Heidi looked out the bus window at all the houses in the distance, she kept imagining happy families living in all of them. Children with mothers and fathers. Fathers who loved them and paid attention to them. Heidi had tried so hard to make her father like her. When he still lived in Hollywood, she would walk to his house, holding out fresh hope each time that he would be glad to see her. But he never once was. Either he would turn her away completely, or would act unfriendly and fidgety, not showing any interest in her at all. After five or ten minutes, he would announce that he had business to attend to, and Heidi would leave and sadly walk home.

Now she hadn't seen him at all for several years. After he moved to Idaho, she had sent him Christmas cards, school pictures, and a program from her eighth-grade graduation, but had received nothing in return.

What was he going to do when she showed up in Marble Point? When she called him from the phone booth, would he even come to the bus terminal to see her? What would she do if he refused? She didn't even have enough money to buy a ticket back to LA. But it didn't matter. She couldn't go back to LA anyway. Heidi nervously glanced at her watch. Only two hours to go. She finally fell into a fitful sleep.

The next thing she knew, she was jolted awake by the sound of the bus driver's droning voice as he announced their arrival at Marble Point. It was almost pitch dark outside, and Heidi's heart raced as she craned her neck to look at the bright lights of the bus terminal. She was really here.

There was the sign for Marble Point.

She got her backpack from above the seat and slipped it on. As soon as the bus came to a stop, she hurriedly made her way up the aisle. She said goodbye to the driver and descended the steps, taking in big gulps of fresh air. Then she entered the terminal and went straight to the phone booth. She set down her backpack and punched in her father's number with trembling fingers. When he answered, Heidi sagged with relief at the sound of his voice. She still remembered their conversation clearly.

"Hello." The voice was clipped, gruff.

"Hi, Dad. This is Heidi."

"Hey. How're you doing?"

"Fine, Dad. But there's something I need to talk to you about."

"Unfortunately, I can't talk right now. I'm expecting another call."

"But mother's dead. She was murdered."

"Yeah, I heard. It's too bad."

"So now I have no place to go." Heidi's voice was cracking.

"There's plenty of foster homes in LA. You'll just have to find one."

"But I had to leave LA. I'm here in Marble Point."

Her father began sputtering. "What the hell are you talking about, you're in Marble Point? You can't be in Marble Point. You know that."

"I know, but the police are looking for me in LA."

"You goddamn stupid moron! Don't you know this is the first place they'll look for you?"

Heidi had been choking back her tears, but now she

broke into sobs. "I don't have any money left to go anywhere else. Won't you please come and talk to me, Dad?"

"Jesus Christ. I just don't need this."

Heidi spoke through her sobs. "There's someone after me, too, Dad."

"What the hell do you mean, someone's after you?"

"The man that murdered mother. He's a policeman."

"Oh fuck! This isn't happening. Tell me it isn't happening."

Heidi waited, realizing her father was thinking it over, probably working his jaw muscles the way he did.

"I'll be there as soon as I can. And whatever you do, don't talk to anyone. And stay out of sight."

The phone slammed in Heidi's ear and she replaced the receiver. As miserable as she was, she still felt relief. At least he was coming. Wanting to look her best, she gathered herself together and went into the restroom. Her legs were shaky, and she supported herself by placing her hands on the countertop as she leaned over the sink.

The girl looking back at her from the mirror seemed a stranger. Her face was drawn and pale, her long blonde hair dull and tangled, her sad blue eyes glistening with tears. Startled by her appearance, Heidi washed her face with cold water, attempting to restore some color, then fished through her backpack for a brush and comb. Ten minutes later, feeling a little refreshed, she went out and sat on a bench to wait for her father. Remembering his instructions to stay out of sight, she kept her head lowered.

Heidi waited for what seemed like a long time, afraid her father had changed his mind, and wasn't coming after all. She kept her head down, but stole glances out the plate glass window, watching for a car that might be her father's. When a dark gray Cadillac pulled up, her heart started thumping. Her father always drove Cadillacs, and that had been the first one to pull in.

She jumped up and ran outside. She recognized her father at once, his angular, craggy face, a thin dark mustache. She opened the door and climbed in the front seat, resisting the urge to hug him. Hardly giving her a glance, he pulled out of the terminal and drove off.

First he demanded to hear all the information she had, then coolly related his plan. He had called a friend of his and made arrangements for her to stay there until things died down. He warned her to strictly mind her own business. She was not to ask any questions or give any answers. She was to keep her mouth shut. When the police came around looking for her, he wouldn't have any idea where she was. He'd probably go away for a little while himself. He did not want the police nosing around. And then he had left her at the Black Diamond.

Heidi's reverie was ended by a knock on the door, and she jumped off the bed. Before she had a chance to answer, Tony flung the door open and walked in. "Where's Laura?"

"She went out with Bruce." Heidi tried to smile and act natural, even though she was shocked by the way he had burst into her cabin. Her father had instructed her to act nice to Tony, and not cause any trouble.

"Tell her I want to talk to her when she comes in."
"Okay. I sure will."

Tony looked her over from head to toe. "You know, you're not a bad looking little piece. I've been keeping my eye on you. I think it's about time I got to know you better." He gave her a knowing smile. "But right now I have some business to take care of." He turned on his heel and left.

Heidi's face had turned crimson, and she felt weak all over. She recognized the look Tony had given her. It was the same one she had received so many times from her mother's gentlemen callers. She couldn't stay here. She felt as if she would be suffocated by the dark forces swirling around her. She had always been sustained by her mother's love. Now her mother was dead, and she was all alone.

She made up her mind quickly. When she slipped off to a phone booth to make her call to the LAPD, she was going to make another call at the same time. She was going to call her father and beg him to come and get her.

CHAPTER 5

AFTER his workday in Internal Affairs, Charlie Martin was in his West Hollywood apartment pouring himself a very dry martini. The clam sauce he had made was simmering on the stove in a cast iron pot, and its spicy aroma filled the neat little kitchen. He had stopped at Ralph's, his favorite neighborhood grocery, on the way home and picked up a dozen fresh clams and a loaf of French bread.

Spaghetti with clam sauce was one of his specialties, and he had considered asking Jessica Tate, the new tenant on the third floor, to join him for dinner. An attractive brunette in her mid-thirties, Jessica had made it obvious that she was interested in him. But, the problem was, he admitted ruefully, he wasn't interested in her, so why get something started?

They had met at the swimming pool in the apartment complex when they were doing laps, and since then had enjoyed several conversations at the poolside, sunning on chaise lounges. But when Jessica came up with two tickets for the Lakers game, Charlie had declined. Not an easy thing to do, as he was an ardent Lakers fan, but he didn't want to get involved. After that, Jessica had invited him to a party in her apartment, and he said he had other plans.

BLACK DIAMOND

Charlie took a sip of his martini and smiled in satisfaction. He stirred the clam sauce with a wooden spoon, then tasted it. It was just right. He picked up the basil on the counter and restored it to its place in the wooden spice rack beside the stove.

Once again it crossed his mind to give Jessica a call. The dinner would be superb, he had a bottle of Chianti on hand, and he could quickly set the table for two. He was sorry about turning down her invitations, and wanted to make a friendly gesture. But he knew how one thing would lead to another, and he just didn't want complications with someone who lived in the same building.

Anyway, he really wanted to be alone. He realized he felt like being alone quite a bit lately, probably too much. After two years, he and Carolyn Reeves had recently broken things off. Although they hadn't actually lived under the same roof, they had spent nearly every night together during their long relationship, either at Charlie's apartment, or hers.

Carolyn was the manager of the Tommy Hilfiger Department at Macy's. Charlie had met her when he was buying a new jacket, and the two had almost instantly become a couple. But Carolyn had wanted to remain a couple permanently, a couple with a marriage certificate and children, and Charlie didn't want to take that step. After the break-up, sometimes he thought about the good times they had together, but mostly, he realized that he missed Carolyn's Scotty dog, Bryce, more than he missed her. She had been too self-absorbed.

Charlie carried his martini into the living room and settled into his favorite, well-used easy chair, stretching out his long legs on the ottoman. The chair faced his floor-to-ceiling bookcase that covered an entire wall. He took great pleasure in surrounding himself with books, even if he didn't have as much time to read as he would have liked. He found the presence of books comforting, and when he sat in his easy chair, he derived joy from looking at all the familiar spines.

Charlie felt himself relax as he sipped his martini. The pungent smell of the clam sauce drifted into the living room, giving him a feeling of well-being. Life was pretty good. Then what was wrong? Why did he find himself more and more often sitting in this chair thinking? At forty, was he satisfied with his life? Or did he need to make a change?

Charlie Martin had proudly joined the police force upon graduation from USC at the age of twenty-one, after impatiently waiting most of his life for the moment. He had always wanted to be a cop. In kindergarten, he had been the first one in the class to raise his hand when the teacher asked the time-worn question: What do you want to be when you grow up? His fair, young face was glowing. His round blue eyes sparkled with joy. He had answered excitedly: "A policeman."

Now, as the years had passed, when someone asked him his line of work, he didn't really want to say. When he did answer the question, it was without any animation. Charlie pulled his legs off the ottoman and stood up. As usual, when he was contemplative, he was drawn to his music. He crossed the room, settled himself on the piano bench, and began improvising over some pleasing chord patterns.

Susan awoke at the break of dawn, and decided to begin her day with a jog along the lake. She pulled on a sweat suit and running shoes, and went out on the deck to do some stretches. It had rained during the night, and the air was washed and fragrant. Susan inhaled deeply as she ran down the walk, with Fritz eagerly dashing ahead.

When she reached the road, Susan made a conscious decision to turn right and jog along the western side of the lake. She was going to stay focused and think about her book while she ran, the way she usually did. She was not going to allow herself to play investigative reporter and check out the Stones' house.

Susan jogged along the roadside, maintaining a comfortable pace. Her blood was pumping, her mind and body were in harmony, she felt loose, free. She grew exhilarated from the rush of endorphins to her brain. She was clearheaded, able to think at a higher level. As she ran on, watching the slowly rising sun tint the lake, she excitedly worked out new scenes for *Blood Money*.

When she reached the McCullys' house, she realized they had returned from their trip to the coast. The garage door was open, and both cars were parked inside. Susan made a mental note to pay them a visit later in the day and inquire about their trip. She found the McCullys pleasant people, and enjoyed having them as neighbors. She was pleased to have a good reason to stop in, wanting to develop their relationship.

The McCullys were an intelligent, well-informed couple, and Susan remembered how she had enjoyed a lively discussion with them at a local dinner party when she had first moved to Marble Point. Thinking about it now, it flitted through her mind how Richard hadn't shown any interest in the conversation, and had kept putting out signals that he was ready to leave.

Refocusing on her book, she jogged another mile, then turned and headed back. By the time she reached home, she felt completely energized, suffused with a feeling of well-being. She planned to take a quick shower, have a light breakfast, and begin writing.

But while she was standing in the shower under the stinging needles of hot water, she remembered she had promised Nan to send the first twelve chapters of her book today. Susan had read through them the day before, and although she knew she would end up doing more rewriting, felt satisfied enough with the manuscript to let her agent take a look.

Susan smiled to herself, thinking she would get the errand out of the way before she went to work. Why not? The Fed Ex drop box was in the same block as Robin's Roost, her favorite little coffee shop that served fresh warm bagels and cream cheese. And there was no need for her to feel guilty about not getting right to work. She truly believed it was important to deviate from her normal routine, finding it freshened her spirit.

A half-hour later, after dropping off her package, Susan walked into Robin's Roost, reveling in the wonderful smell of freshly brewed coffee. Robin, a plumpish, cheerful woman in her late forties, greeted her warmly as she crossed the room to take a stool at the counter. It was still early, and Susan thought that Robin might find some time to talk. Living by herself, Susan usually enjoyed the chance for a little conversation, and liked to catch up on the local chitchat.

BLACK DIAMOND

As she climbed onto her stool, she took a sidelong glance at the man sitting at the far end of the counter. He had picked up his newspaper and was raising it so it blocked the view of his face. Now he had opened it, and was holding it in a tent-like position in front of him. Susan thought it was peculiar how he leaned forward, burying his face in it. It was like he was hiding. But he had only held the paper up when Susan sat down, as if he didn't want her to see him. But that was ridiculous. Why in the world would anyone want to hide from her in Robin's Roost? What a crazy idea. Now she was really getting carried away, creating a mystery around someone who just wanted to be left alone.

While she was waiting for Robin to take care of a customer at the cash register, she sat looking around the room. A few thirtyish people were sitting at the round pine tables symmetrically arranged on the plank floor, and several couples occupied the side booths that were softly lit by Tiffany-style hanging lamps.

Her gaze traveled to the area behind the counter. It had a nice homey look. Next to the espresso machines and coffeepots was a good-sized warming table. Big stainless steel pots of soup, with ladles sticking out of the lids, were set in its holes. An array of food was on display, fresh bagels, big pretzels, an assortment of rolls and small cakes.

Susan looked in the long mirror behind the display case trying to see the reflection of the man at the counter, but his head was still buried in the newspaper. She watched as he reached for his coffee mug with one outstretched hand, while he kept the paper clutched in the other. Susan finally gave up trying to get a look at him as Robin came and took her order for a bagel with extra cream cheese and a double cappuccino.

Susan turned her attention to Robin as she worked the cappuccino machine. She enjoyed watching the clouds of steam rising from the spout, accompanied by the pleasant hissing sound and rushing aroma of coffee.

"Did you hear about your neighbors?" Robin asked as she placed her order in front of her.

"Which neighbors?" Susan responded with a questioning look.

"The McCullys. Their house got broken into while they were over at the coast."

"Oh, no!" Susan gasped. "That's terrible."

"The poor things discovered it when they got home last night. The sheriff told me about it when he came in this morning. He's pretty upset. You know Wally. He acts like he's personally responsible for any crime in the county."

Susan knew what Robin meant. Sheriff Wally Woods was an ambitious ex-patrolman who had swept to victory on his campaign promise to stamp out crime. The incumbent sheriff had not been effective in dealing with the county's rising crime rate. Wally Woods pledged to work hard to make his jurisdiction crime-free. After the host of recent break-ins, he had begun making statements on local TV. Splendidly regaled in full uniform, down to his chin-strapped hat, he told the citizenry that he had not forgotten his promises. This new wave of crime would not be tolerated. Residents in his jurisdiction would be safe. Squad cars would be cruising around the clock. An emergency number was already set up. Citizens should immediately punch NO CRIME on their telephones ... 66-27463 ... if they noticed anything at all suspicious.

"It's no wonder Wally's upset," Susan said. "This is the fourth or fifth break-in recently."

"Fifth," Robin answered emphatically. "He was definite about that. And he thinks it's the same crazies. They're finding the same two sets of prints, and it's always the same pattern. They use the house for their own pleasure, then steal everything they can carry."

The man at the counter rose to leave, pushing aside his leftover Danish, and Robin went to take care of his check. Susan watched with rapt attention. Now she'd have a chance to see the mystery man who had stayed hidden behind his newspaper. But no. He seemed to be carefully keeping his face averted. Stretching out from her stool, Susan managed to get a partial glimpse of his profile in the mirror. As she caught sight of his closely trimmed black hair and prominent features, she stirred with a strange feeling of past remembrance.

She watched him make his way to the cash register, noticing his stocky build, the forward set of his head, the thick neck, the wide, muscular shoulders. No doubt, there was something familiar about him. After he paid the check, he pulled on the touring cap he had been holding in his hand. Shock waves shot through Susan. The touring cap! The gray touring cap! This man was the driver of the Lincoln Town Car she had followed.

Susan impulsively took a last gulp of coffee, threw some money on the counter, told Robin she had just remembered an important errand, and followed him out the door. He was halfway up the block, walking at a brisk pace. Susan's heart skipped a beat as she saw him approach a dark blue Lincoln Town Car parked at the curb, and she hurried after him.

Without breaking stride, Susan made a mental note of the license plate as she walked by. So it was a Nevada plate! She pulled her notebook out of her purse to jot down the number as soon as he drove away. She decided on the spot to call her friend Ed Holbrook at the *LA Times* as soon as she got home. He covered the police beat and would have the connections to get the license plate run through records. No stopping now, Susan told herself. But one thing seemed certain. In spite of her nagging feeling that she recognized the Town Car driver from somewhere else, she must be wrong. She was sure she didn't know a soul from Nevada.

Before she went to her car, Susan stopped in the Downtown Bakery and bought a dozen cookies to take to the McCullys. The bakery was famous for its chewy, spicy, dark molasses cookies, and she thought they would make a nice gift to take along when she made her visit.

When Susan got behind the wheel of her car, she decided to stop at the McCullys' on her way home. She was truly sorry about their misfortune, and was anxious to offer them any words of consolation she could. As she drove along, Susan's mouth began watering from the wonderful aroma of the warm, spicy cookies inside the bakery bag. When she turned onto Loon Lake Road, she smiled to herself ashamedly, hoping that when she presented the cookies to the McCullys, they would offer her one.

BLACK DIAMOND

When she reached their house, she parked in the driveway and walked around to the front. As soon as she rang the bell, both of the McCullys came to the door, greeting her cordially. Susan amusedly thought of the couple as living proof of the maxim that when people lived together for years, they often began to resemble each other. Both had round beaming faces, framed by short hair the same shade of gray. Their generous mouths turned up in the same cheerful way, they both had laugh crinkles around their lively blue eyes.

"We saw you driving down the road, and thought you might stop," George McCully said. "We figured you probably heard the news by now."

"Yes, and I'm terribly sorry," Susan answered.

Lisa McCully accepted the molasses cookies with gratitude, and the three of them moved into the kitchen where there was a fresh pot of coffee perking. They took chairs around the wooden table that was gaily covered by a blue print cloth. Sun was streaming through the southern window, throwing patches of light on the warm maple cabinets. Lisa put the cookies out on a plate, and Susan eagerly took one, finding it every bit as delectable as she had anticipated.

"I'm so sorry you arrived home under such dreadful circumstances," Susan began.

"Thank you," Lisa answered. "Yes, it was awful. As soon as we came in and turned the lights on, we realized our two oil paintings were missing from the living room wall. Then, while we were standing there in shock, George realized our antique mantel clock was gone. It was one of our most treasured wedding presents." Tears sprang to her eyes.

"There, there, Dear, don't get yourself all upset again," George said consolingly. "Wally told you he's sure they'll get it back."

The doorbell rang, and George jumped up. "I bet that's Wally now. He said he was coming by again to keep us updated."

Lisa poured more coffee, setting another mug on the table. "George and I have already arranged to have an alarm system installed. I think we'll feel much safer. I don't want to worry about this ever happening again."

George led Sheriff Woods into the kitchen, ushering him to a chair. The sheriff was a dark-haired, vigorous man in his early forties, tall and lithe, with a springy step and a firm handshake.

"There's no news yet," Wally Woods announced. "We're still waiting for lab reports. I just came by to assure you that everything's being done. All the pawnshops have been alerted. I'll let you know the second we have a lead."

The sheriff turned to Susan. "I'm glad you're here. I'd like to take the opportunity to caution you that you can't be too careful. It's so remote down there at your end of the lake."

"I agree with you, Sheriff," Lisa interjected. "George and I are worried about her, too."

The sheriff gave Susan one of his charming smiles the voters loved. "Be patient with me. I promise we'll catch these crazies, but until we do, please stay on your guard. If you notice anything suspicious, phone us at once. I've given orders that I want notified about all calls coming in on the NO CRIME line any time of day or night. I'm handling this matter personally."

"Thank you. I appreciate your concern," Susan

answered. "But I'm sure I'll be fine."

After the sheriff left, Susan visited with the McCullys awhile longer, learning more details about the break-in. Susan's heart swelled with sympathy as, with some hesitation and embarrassment, the couple revealed how their personal lives had been so disgracefully violated by intruders using their bed.

When Susan made her departure, the McCullys walked with her to the driveway. As she went to open the car door, George took her by the arm, looking straight into her eyes. "Susan, if anything at all happens to alarm you, give us a call. We'll keep the phone on the bedside table turned on. I can be over there in a few minutes. And I still have the Colt .45 they missed."

Dominick Garcia was seething in anger and frustration as he steered the Lincoln Town Car away from the curb and entered the flow of traffic. Why was everything going so wrong? He just couldn't believe that Susan Muir, the *LA Times* reporter who had brought him down, was sitting inside the coffee shop. The goddamn bitch that ruined his life. When he shot the dumbass Spic kid, of course the whole media had gone wild for a few days, but then as usual they dropped it and moved on to something else.

It would have all blown over, but Susan Muir just wouldn't stop. She had a real vendetta against him. She used every contact she had in Hollywood, nosing around digging up dirt. Before she was through, he and three of his buddies were suspended. Then she'd gotten tired of playing big time investigative reporter, made a crapload of money writing a book, and left town. He had just hoped wherever she was, she'd rot in hell.

He had recognized her the second she sat down at the counter. They had never met, but her image was burned into his mind, the way she used to strut around the station house in her classy outfits, interviewing the captain and watch commanders. Always carrying her precious fucking notebook.

So now she lived in Marble Point, Idaho, for God's sake. But he shouldn't be surprised. Anyone with lots of cash was getting out of LA, and he knew Marble Point was the new in-place for the rich. A nice friendly little mountain town, peaceful and quiet. Folks were neighborly. Its citizens were safe.

All except for one citizen, Dominick Garcia thought. The population of Marble Point, Idaho was about to be reduced by one. Susan Muir hadn't recognized him in the coffee shop. He had made sure of that. God, how he hated her. The nosy bitch. She had kept his nerves so on edge he couldn't even eat his Danish. He had felt her watching him, hoping he'd move his newspaper so she could get a look. The way she just wouldn't give up, she probably caught a glimpse of him in the mirror when he left. And he must have looked familiar to her. He could feel her eyes boring into him when he walked out.

No wonder he looked familiar. His picture had been plastered on the front page of the *LA Times*, along with the three other victimized cops she wouldn't let up on. Unfortunately, her memory could be triggered at any moment. That was the problem.

He still hadn't found Heidi Townsend, and for all he knew, by now she had called the LAPD and turned him in, thinking she was hidden away somewhere safe. The police might already be looking for him. As long as things went according to plan he wasn't too worried about it. Without Little Miss Orderly's direct testimony, they'd never get a conviction. And Little Miss Orderly wouldn't be around to testify, he'd make sure of that.

After he got rid of Heidi, he planned to dispose of her body very carefully. But what if something went wrong? If her body was found and anyone knew he had been in town, he'd be in deep shit. Too deep to crawl out of. And that wasn't a chance he was going to take. Dammit all to hell, Garcia thought. This looked like it was going to be so easy. Why did there have to be so many problems? He drove the Town Car towards his fleabag motel where he had some whiskey in his suitcase. He could always think better with a bottle of whiskey in his hand.

When he reached his room, he dug for the bottle he had carefully hidden from the maids. He didn't trust them not to help themselves. He took a swig, then picked up the telephone directory and sat down on the bed with it. The first order of business was to find out Ms. Susan Muir's address. He thumbed through the book until he came to the M listings, then located Mu and ran his index finger down the page. And there it was. Susan Muir, 134 Loon Lake Road. The same road the Stones lived on. So Susan Muir and Jack Stone both elected to live in the poshest part of town. The lucky oh-so-rich folks sitting on their choice waterfront property. Well, it was lucky for him, too. He could conduct all his business in the same neighborhood, and save on gas.

Garcia took a long draught of whiskey, and moved to a

cheap vinyl chair to think things over. He had already wasted three days waiting for the Stones to come back from wherever the hell they were. He had to take action. As he sipped on his whiskey, the idea came to him. If the Stones' house was still empty tonight, he'd break in and take a look around. Maybe he could find some kind of a clue that would point to their whereabouts. He wasn't a detective first class for nothing.

    Feeling good that he had a definite plan, he drained the bottle of whiskey. He let out a loud burp, then rearranged his mouth into a tight-lipped sadistic smile. While he was in the neighborhood tonight, he would get the lay of the land at 134 Loon Lake Road. He could start making preparations for the moment he and Susan Muir would finally meet face to face.

CHAPTER 6

THAT night Heidi pulled on her jacket and stuffed her hands into the side pockets to make sure all the coins were there. After fretful hours of waiting, at last she was leaving to make her telephone calls. She tiptoed to Laura's bedside and stood watching the slow rising and falling of the girl's chest as she slept.

Laura let out a soft snore, making Heidi smile. She felt a little guilty, as if she were eavesdropping, but was relieved to have confirmation that her roommate was actually sound asleep. She could hardly believe it. Laura was usually up until all hours, but tonight she had announced at nine o'clock that she was worn out and was going to crash. It was no wonder, the way she had stayed out so late with Bruce the last couple of nights. Heidi felt sorry for Laura, sure that Bruce was leading her on and taking advantage of her. She was afraid Laura would end up getting terribly hurt.

Heidi tiptoed across the cabin and slipped noiselessly through the door. Glancing all around her, she began making her way towards the tool shed on the far side of the lodge. She had seen an old rusty ten-speed bike in there the day she was looking for garden tools. When she decided to make her telephone call to the LAPD, she had gone back to check on the bike's condition. The tires had been flat, but an air pump was strapped to the bar. She had filled the tires and checked the pedals and brakes, deciding that, even though the light didn't work, the bike would serve to get her to a phone booth.

Heidi ducked behind the thick-trunked fir trees as she crossed the grounds, thankful that, except for the lights in the main lodge, the night was lit only by a small slice of moon. As she finally reached the door of the storage shed, she took a quick backward glance over her shoulder and went inside.

Heidi rolled the bike out and jumped on, pedaling hard towards the back fence. Her heart was pounding. She knew if anyone saw her and told Tony, she was in big trouble. He had made it clear she was not to leave the grounds under any circumstances. When she reached the fence, she unlatched the gate and rode through, carefully re-latching it behind her.

The gravel crunched under her tires as she took the road that ran behind the ranch. She hoped no one had stepped outside the lodge, fearful that the unexpected noise of crunching gravel would draw attention. She was relieved when she came upon the smooth macadam road. Now the only sound she heard was the soft whirring of the pedals. In spite of her fear, she felt a wonderful sense of freedom as she sped along through the darkness with the crisp air against her face.

When she reached the frontage road, she turned

BLACK DIAMOND

toward Marble Point, remembering from the night her father had taken her to the Black Diamond that there was an old gas station just a few miles away. As she biked towards it, a car and a few pickups passed. She did her best to keep to the far edge of the road, feeling vulnerable with no headlight or reflectors. After she had ridden about three miles, she sighted the gas station ahead. Approaching it, she realized there were no lights on inside the building, and that it must be closed for the night.

Her heart soared when she spotted a phone booth out front. She rode over, and leaning her bike against the booth, stepped inside. She gathered up the coins in her pocket and piled them by the coin box. A wave of emotion swept over her as she remembered how Cheryl had insisted she take the jar of coins she'd been saving. She missed Cheryl so much. How she would love to call her now, while she was at the phone booth, but she didn't dare stay away from the ranch any longer than she had to.

She fed coins into the phone to get the number of the LAPD from information, copying it down with the pencil and paper she had brought along. She took a deep breath and pressed in the number, her heart fluttering.

"Los Angeles Police Department. Operator 888."

Heidi almost hung up the phone. She was intimidated by the woman's cool, assured voice. But she gripped the receiver hard and forced the words out. "Hello. I'm calling to report that I know who committed a murder."

"Where was the murder committed?"

"In Hollywood."

"Do you have an exact address?"

"1753 Jalmia Street."

"I'll transfer you to Hollywood Homicide."

Heidi nervously waited through the silence, hoping they weren't trying to trace the call.

"Hollywood Homicide. Police Officer Mike Rivera."

"Hello. This is Heidi Townsend. My mother, Julia Townsend, was murdered last week. I'm calling to report I know who did it."

"Where are you calling from?"

"I'm sorry. I really can't say."

"How old are you?"

"Seventeen."

"When's your birthday?"

"September 18."

"And you say you know who murdered your mother?"

"Yes."

"Hold please. I'll transfer you to our nightwatch detective."

Heidi grew more nervous. She knew from the movies if you stayed on the line long enough, they could trace your call. The telephone receiver was damp from her sweaty palms. She kept changing the hand she held it with so she could wipe the sweat off on her blue jeans. She was about to hang up just when a voice came on.

"Detective Frank Russo."

"Hello. This is Heidi Townsend. I'm calling to report that I know who murdered my mother, Julia Townsend."

"What was the date of the murder?"

"April 15."

BLACK DIAMOND

"What was going on that night?"

"I really can't talk that long," Heidi said apprehensively. She felt sure he was trying to make her stay on the line.

"These are questions I have to ask you," Detective Russo stated with authority.

"Okay. My mother had a gentleman caller, and I heard them get into an argument. When I went downstairs, I saw him standing over her body."

"How far away were you?"

"I was by the living room door. He was standing halfway across the room near the couch."

"What color is the couch?"

"White."

"What was your mother wearing?"

"Her black satin lounging pajamas, I think."

As Detective Russo continued his line of questioning to determine if the caller was actually Heidi Townsend, and was a valid witness, the operator interrupted to request additional money.

"I'll be glad to call you back," Detective Russo said, after Heidi deposited more coins.

"That's all right," Heidi answered quickly. "I just want to tell you who the murderer was."

"So you know the name of the man you think was the murderer?"

Heidi drew in her breath. She couldn't get the words out. She didn't know whether to trust Detective Russo, or not. Maybe he was a friend of Dominick Garcia's. Maybe he would tell Garcia she called, and not tell anyone else. She shivered. She had already made up her mind. She had to go through with it.

"Yes I do. It was Dominick Garcia."

In the station house, Detective Russo's mouth dropped open. "Would you repeat that name, please?"

"Dominick Garcia."

The operator announced that time was running out. Heidi was determined to get off the line. "This is my statement," she said hastily. "Dominick Garcia of the LAPD murdered my mother. I'm positive. And I'm sorry, but I have to go now. Bye."

Heidi felt a rush of relief as the words she had practiced so long poured out of her. Drained of emotion, she thought about picking up her money and returning to the ranch. But instead she went through with her plan and pushed more coins into the slot, calling her father's number. She was filled with disappointment when she heard his machine on the other end, but decided to leave a message since she probably wouldn't have another chance to call.

"Dad, it's Heidi. Please come and get me. Let me stay with you for just a little while. I promise I won't be any trouble. I hate it here at the Black Diamond Ranch, and I'm afraid of Tony. Please, Dad. Bye."

She left the phone booth and walked to her bicycle. She stood looking up at the slice of moon before she climbed on the seat. She searched the sky for a wishing star, but there was none. The sky was dark and starless.

A sweep of headlights raked the entrance of the parking lot and drew her attention. A police car was pulling in. Waves of panic swept over her. How did they find her so

BLACK DIAMOND

fast? An electric jolt zapped through her. Of course, she had forgotten about caller ID. The Los Angeles Police Department had known the number she was calling from immediately. They had already tracked the number down and sent the Marble Point Police to pick her up.

Her first impulse was to jump on the bike and pedal away as fast as she could. Impossible. She could hardly outrace a police car. Her second impulse was to abandon the bike and run behind the gas station. But the policeman would follow her, and he had a flashlight and a gun. Thoughts of police chases on TV flashed through her mind. She would never get away.

"Everything okay, Miss?" came the booming voice through the rolled-down window of the police car. "Something wrong with your bike?"

Heidi made out the word SHERIFF on the side of the car as it came to a stop. "No, I'm fine, Officer," Heidi answered nervously, not exactly sure what was happening.

The tall uniformed man stepped out of the car. "I was afraid you might be having some kind of trouble, it being so late and all. I thought maybe you needed some help."

"Why thank you, Officer," Heidi answered politely. "That was very kind of you." Just as relief was flooding through her, Heidi remembered the bicycle was illegal, having no lights. She couldn't get on it and ride away. She desperately tried to think what to do.

"Did you stop to make a phone call?" the officer probed as she stood there.

"Yes," Heidi answered promptly, thinking she had no choice about lying her way out of the situation. "When I realized how late it was, I stopped to call my father so he wouldn't worry. The line's busy, so I'm waiting a minute before I call him again."

"Where do you live?" the officer asked.

"In Marble Point, out near the lake."

"Well, have a safe trip home."

"Thank you, Officer," Heidi said, filled with relief as she stepped back into the phone booth. "Good night."

Heidi waited until the police officer was out of sight, then began riding back. Her nerves were still on edge, especially since the police car had turned in the same direction she was going. If the officer saw her, he'd know she had lied about where she lived, not to mention the illegal bike. But she couldn't wait one more minute. She had been gone too long. She just had to get back to the ranch before she was missed.

Susan buttoned up her soft silk blouse, tucked it into her jeans, and pulled on a brown leather belt. It was 8:15 P.M. by the bedroom clock. She still had fifteen minutes before Flora was due to arrive. One of Flora's employees had called in sick earlier in the day, and Flora had to stay and close up the shop. Susan decided to use the time to check her e-mail. She hadn't heard back yet from Ed Holbrook about the license plate, and although she really expected a call, thought he might have e-mailed an update.

When she opened her server, instead of receiving word from Ed Holbrook, she found a message from her father in Hong Kong. She printed it out, knowing she would re-read it many times. She took great pleasure in her father's letters, marveling at his writing talent. She smiled as she leaned back in her swivel chair and read about his travels. His writing nearly crackled off the page as he described the sights, sounds, and smells of Hong Kong. Susan could vividly imagine every detail. She laughed aloud when she read the last sentence...How is my little girl enjoying her "retirement"?

If he only knew, Susan thought. In about two minutes she was leaving on an investigative reporting venture. She supposed when she answered his e-mail, she should admit she wasn't sure she was fully retired after all. If she told her father about all her suspicions, would he think she was being foolish? Was she just having fun playing at being an investigative reporter again, manufacturing a web of mystery and intrigue? Maybe, but she didn't think so.

Explaining her mission, Susan had invited Flora to join her tonight for beer and pizza at the Blue Moon, a local tavern on the frontage road out near Pinehurst, not too far from the Black Diamond. Susan hadn't been able to get Tony off her mind, and still had the strong feeling he could be up to something. She planned to strike up a conversation with the locals to see if she could uncover any rumors about the new people at the ranch. Then she'd go from there.

The doorbell rang, and Susan turned off her computer and hurried downstairs. Fritz was standing expectantly at the front door, and greeted Flora with tail-wagging enthusiasm as Susan let her in. Flora, wearing an ivory button-down shirt, looked attractive with sparkling hazel eyes and shoulder length light brown hair tied back in a green ribbon.

While Flora was making a fuss over Fritz, Susan got her jacket, then went around turning off all but one of the living room lights, as was her habit when she was going out for the evening. The sheriff's words of caution leaped to her mind...You can't be too careful. It's so remote down there at your end of the lake...Thinking better of it, she turned several lamps back on. Why not make it look as if she were home? It would discourage someone thinking about breaking in.

Susan opened the car door and climbed into the passenger seat as Flora got behind the wheel, and they set off for the Blue Moon, taking the route past the Stones' house. After Susan's identification that morning of the driver of the Town Car, she didn't want to miss a chance of seeing if it was parked at her neighbors'. She was still wrestling with the nagging feeling that she recognized the driver from somewhere else.

The Stones' house was dark as they drove by. An easy target for whoever was doing the break-ins, Susan couldn't help thinking. She wondered if the Stones worried about burglaries during their long absences. Maybe they asked the sheriff to keep an eye on their house while they were away. Wally was pretty good about lending the personal touch.

Before too long, Flora drove up to the Blue Moon, a low, rough-cut wood building served by a dirt parking lot full of potholes. As they entered, they emerged into a dimly lit space with an L-shaped bar, tended by a young man with long dark shaggy hair and a friendly smile. He was wearing a Mariners shirt and cap, in step with the baseball game showing on the soundless wall-mounted TV.

Susan and Flora received curious glances from the other patrons as they made their way toward two empty barstools. "Looks like you're a Mariners fan," Susan said as the bartender hustled over and stood before them.

"Big time," he answered with his friendly smile. "How can you tell?"

Susan and Flora laughed and ordered their beers and a pepperoni pizza. Their eyes began searching the room for the most likely prospects to engage in conversation. The customers, both men and women spanning the decades from twenty to sixty, seemed to be locals, some immersed in lively conversation, some staring at the silent TV screen.

A group of four was playing at the pool table that stood near the far end of the floor near the stone fireplace. The two sets of partners were bantering with each other in good-natured camaraderie. The square tables that filled most of the remaining floor space were occupied by a dozen or so people listening to the country western music coming from the jukebox. Two women were having fun singing along with the refrain. One couple, with drinks in hand, was half-dancing in a small confined area. A fortyish rugged looking man at the bar suddenly cheered about a play on TV, which he had clearly enjoyed without the benefit of sound. The bartender rushed over to catch the replay.

Susan plunged in and called across the bar with a smile. "What happened?"

The man, cheery faced with a full head of blond hair, smiled back. "The Mariners kicked some ass."

Flora had struck up a conversation with the woman on the stool next to her. The woman, in her fifties, had a bright lipsticked mouth and frizzy red-dyed hair. "Watch your language there, Artie," the woman called across the bar. She winked at Flora and Susan. "Art has a big bet riding."

"A good reason to take the game seriously," Susan answered with a laugh.

"Your friend here says you came out this way looking for horses to rent," the woman said to Susan. "She says you ended up driving for miles."

"That's right," Susan said, taking the cue. "We went up to the Black Diamond first. We thought for sure they'd have horseback riding, but we found out it's not a guest ranch anymore. The owner wouldn't talk to us at all. In fact, he was quite rude."

"I'm not surprised. He doesn't want anyone coming around the place."

Susan began tingling all over. "What do you mean?"

"When he got here, a few people went up to be neighborly, but he made it plain he didn't want to be bothered." The woman paused to take a sip of her drink, savoring the attention. "Since then one or two have gone up looking for work, but he just turned them away."

Susan leaned over conspiratorially. "I wonder why?"

"They're up to something. I hear there are comings and goings all times of day and night. Drugs is my guess."

"It sounds as if the sheriff needs to be alerted," Susan said.

"A couple of us have talked to Wally, and he says he's keeping an eye out."

BLACK DIAMOND

The TV commercial break began as the inning ended, and Art walked around the bar. "Can I buy you ladies a drink?"

"How about me, Artie?" the woman said with her lipsticked smile.

"Why, Elsie, I wouldn't leave you out," Art told her. "Hal, bring the three ladies a drink."

"Thank you," Flora said, introducing herself, "and this is Susan."

"Are you new around here, or passing through?" Art asked.

"Neither one," Flora answered with a smile. "We're from Marble Point. We came out this way to check on stables. We'd like to do a little riding this summer."

"They went up to the Black Diamond, and got the same treatment everyone around here gets," Elsie interjected. Art smiled. "In other words, you pretty much got thrown out. Here comes one of their guys now," he added, motioning over his shoulder.

Susan swiveled on her barstool, just in time to see Bruce Fione walk through the door. She took a quick intake of breath as he waved and walked toward them.

"Well, look who's here," Bruce said as he neared. "What brings Ms. Susan Muir out to these parts?"

"I might ask you the same thing," Susan retorted coolly.

"I came to shoot a little pool," Bruce answered. "Can I buy you and your friend a drink?"

"No thank you," Susan said promptly, before Flora had a chance to answer.

"I already took care of the ladies, Bruce," Art told him.

"Beat me to it, huh?" Bruce said sardonically, giving them all a broad white-toothed smile. "Lucky guy." He nodded towards the TV. "We'll see if your luck holds out for your Mariners tonight. I'm sure you have a little bet going."

As distasteful as he was to her, Susan directed her attention to Bruce, in an attempt to get information. "Do you live out this way?"

"Nah. I was up at the Diamond."

"The Diamond?" Susan questioned.

"The Black Diamond Ranch," Bruce explained, running fingers through his curly hair.

"Are you a friend of theirs?" Susan probed.

"You might say so," Bruce responded. "I play a little pool with Tony."

"Is Tony the new owner?" Susan went on.

"Yeah."

"I understand it's not a guest ranch anymore. What does he do there?" Susan queried.

"All I know about Tony is, he shoots a good game of pool."

"He must do something besides play pool," Susan pressed.

"I don't know. I never asked him." Bruce leaned close to Susan, giving her a long intimate look. "You look lovely tonight."

After all her years in LA, Susan would normally have a quick response to rebuff an unwanted advance, but something in Bruce's eyes chilled her. She looked away wordlessly.

The bartender walked out of the kitchen and came over. "Your pizza's ready. Do you want it here, or at a table?"

"Here's fine," Susan said, with Flora giving an affirming nod.

BLACK DIAMOND

"Hey, Fione!" someone called from the pool table. "Ready to get in the game?"

"Are we playing for drinks?" Bruce called back cheerily, walking over.

The bartender put their pizza on the counter, and Art returned to his stool to watch the game which had now resumed. The Mariners were up at bat.

As soon as Susan and Flora finished their pizza, they said goodbye to Elsie and Art and took their leave. As they began their drive home, Susan had a hard time shaking off the unsettling feeling Bruce had given her. "That guy really gives me the creeps," she said to Flora.

"I saw the way he looked at you," Flora agreed. "He's a real creep, all right."

"And now we find out he's connected to the Black Diamond," Susan mused. "Interesting!"

As they drove down the frontage road discussing it, Susan told Flora that before it was time for her next spa servicing, she was going to inform Gus Woodbridge she did not want Bruce Fione sent to her home again.

When they approached the turnoff to the Black Diamond, a sheriff's car was coming down the frontage road in the other direction. It slowed to make a turn, and under the road light that stood at the corner, they made out the figure of Sheriff Wally Woods.

"So Tony's getting a visitor," Susan commented wryly. "Whether he wants him or not."

"It looks like Elsie was right," Flora said, her voice shaded with excitement. "Wally's keeping an eye on the place, all right."

"Look!" Susan cried after a minute. "It's someone on a bike!"

"What in the world?" Flora exclaimed. She slowed down the car as her headlights illuminated a lone rider coming toward them in the darkness on a bicycle with no lights. As they passed, they could see the rider was a girl with long blonde hair. The way she was bent over the handlebars, they couldn't get a clear look at her face.

"Stop!" Susan cried. "I think it's the girl I saw at the Black Diamond! Let's see if she turns up to the ranch."

Flora braked to a halt and began backing up, while Susan twisted in her seat to look out the rear window. "Yes!" Susan exclaimed. "She's turning!"

"Very interesting," Flora remarked as she shifted gears and began moving forward again.

"Why would that girl be out riding in the dark?" Susan said in a tone of wonderment.

"On a bike with no lights," Flora agreed thoughtfully.

"And I'm sure she was trying not to be recognized," Susan added with a ring of certainty.

Flora smiled. "I get the strong impression our little adventure tonight has spurred you on to step up your investigation."

Susan smiled back. "Definitely." She had made up her mind.

CHAPTER 7

SUSAN sent her e-mails off to Hong Kong and shut down her computer. It was almost midnight, and she quickly figured it was 2:00 P.M. the following day where her parents were. She imagined them lounging at the poolside after lunch, luxuriating in the blissful comfort of the Regent Hotel, overlooking Hong Kong Harbor. Susan had been intrigued by her mother's glowing description of the famous five-star hotel. In Susan's e-mail to her father, she had mentioned her hunches of local wrongdoing, asking if he had any tips he had picked up during his newspaper days that he could pass along to her. She was anxiously awaiting his reply.

Undressing and pulling on her terrycloth robe, Susan picked up a towel and went downstairs, with Fritz running beside her. She carried a glass of ice water out to the deck and removed the hot tub cover. She could hardly wait to lean back in the hot bubbly water and think. Her mind was swirling with ideas, and she needed to sort them out.

It was difficult enough to plot a novel, especially working out all the changes that had evolved since her book had taken on a life of its own. She could barely keep up with the characters. She would plan for one thing to happen, and something else would happen. Instead of her being a master puppeteer pulling the strings, the characters would come to life and take over the stage, performing their own acts. It sometimes seemed as if she were merely a recorder of events. But how she loved it! How exciting it was! How fulfilling! She couldn't imagine not writing books!

Now, besides all the novel plotting that occupied her mind, she was trying to plan a course of action for her local investigation. Only loosely plan, of course. She knew from experience that, just as with the characters in her book, the investigation would take on a life of its own. But the next step was firmly charted. Earlier in the evening, on their drive home, she and Flora had agreed to go out to the Black Diamond Saturday night to see if they could find evidence of what Elsie had described as "comings and goings all times of day and night."

Tomorrow Susan was going to order the night vision scope she had seen in her Cabela's catalogue that afforded a clear picture within a hundred-yard range. She had been thinking of getting one for fun, to spot animals at night from her deck, and this gave her a good excuse. She knew that none of the shops in town carried them, but if she got two-day delivery, it should arrive in time.

Susan looked up at the sky. It was still dark and starless. She thought of the nights she and Richard had sat together in the hot tub under clear, bright skies, dreamily locating the stars and galaxies. But tonight was different. No stars, no galaxies, no Richard.

Even in the soothing water, thoughts continued to jump around in Susan's mind. Why did the driver of the

BLACK DIAMOND

Lincoln Town Car look so familiar? Why did she have the feeling she knew him from somewhere else? But she had searched her mind, and she didn't know one person from Nevada. And why had the Town Car been parked at the Stones'? And why would the Stones be spending all spring and summer at the Cayman's? Why had they suddenly left early? And what did Bruce Fione have to do with the Black Diamond? He did something besides play pool. She pictured his mocking eyes, the tiny pupils. He had to be on some kind of drugs.

She was glad she had decided to let Gus Woodbridge know she didn't want Bruce sent to her house again. But the way he had looked at her tonight, who was to say he wouldn't drop by to visit her after hours? Now she had that to worry about too, besides all the break-ins.

A glow of headlights on Loon Lake Road startled her out of her reverie. A dark outline of a car was moving slowly down the road from the direction of the Stones'. Was it the Lincoln Town Car again? Or was it someone looking for an isolated home to break into? As the car reached the front of her house, Susan couldn't see it from the angle of the hot tub. But she was sure the lights had stopped moving. Fritz picked up on her tension and stood up and growled. His hair was standing on end. Susan quieted him and turned off the jets, listening hard to the sound of the car engine.

The car had come to a stop. Its engine was idling, the headlights were on. Susan's pulse raced. Feeling vulnerable with no clothes on, she stepped out of the hot tub and slipped into her robe. Holding Fritz by his collar, she stealthily made her way along the deck to peer around the corner of the house. Under the light of her gas lamps, she clearly saw the Lincoln Town Car, stopped at the end of her driveway. She watched a lone figure who had been leaning across the front seat, reposition himself behind the wheel. He had been looking at the mailbox!

The engine noise picked up as the car moved off into the night. So the mysterious Town Car driver had been locating her address! Who was he? She shuddered, and hurried inside to the safety of the house. But did the house offer real safety? Maybe she should follow the McCullys' lead, and look into an alarm system.

Dominick Garcia had worked himself into a state of fury as he looked over Susan's house. So Ms. Susan Muir lives in a goddamn mansion. She screws up my life in LA and leaves me with a shithole to live in, while she takes off to live happily ever after in her fairytale home on the lake. Well, I have news for her. She might not like the lake so much when she's at the bottom of it.

He pictured how she had paraded down the sidewalk when she left the coffee shop that morning, just the way she used to parade around Hollywood Division. Like she was someone so big and special. In a hurry, on her way to do important things.

Then it hit him like a thunderbolt. She had been in a hurry. With a flash of realization, he finally knew what had been bothering him all day. She had left the coffee shop too soon after he did. She had been following him, hurrying to check out his car before he pulled away. She had noted his car model, gotten his license plate number, and kept right on walking, without ever turning her head. How could he have been so stupid?

He had been off his guard. He knew he had looked familiar to her, but who would ever expect her to get his license plate number? What the hell for? Well, it wouldn't do her any good, whatever she was up to. He'd get a different car the first thing in the morning. The fucking Town Car guzzled too much gas anyway. And he'd get out of that fleabag motel, too. He'd move down the road to the Sunset. It looked like the kind of place that wouldn't ask for ID if you paid cash up front. Besides, there was a bar right next door.

Satisfied that he was going to outsmart her, Garcia smiled and took a little drink. As the whiskey warmed him, he thought about how things were starting to go his way. On the drive back to his motel, he recalled with great pleasure how he had finally discovered Heidi's whereabouts.

He had stopped at the Stones' gabled house a little before midnight, and saw it was still deserted. Getting back in his Town Car, he proceeded about fifty yards down Loon Lake Road to a camping spot he had located earlier. He pulled into the small cleared area and parked at the furthest point from the road. Then, making his way through the bordering woods, he kept in a crouch as he veered off towards the Stones' house, set on a knoll across the road from the lake.

When he reached the back door, he inspected the lock with his small flashlight. Oh, so easy. Garcia smiled. Maybe they took his badge and gun, but he still had his entire collection of burglary tools he had picked up over his years on the force. And he was very good at using them. He was inside a few minutes later, standing in the kitchen, looking around in the dimness, getting his bearings.

A red blinking light caught his eye. The kitchen was set against the sequestered woods, so Garcia clicked on his flashlight, aiming the beam at a small square corner table that held a telephone and answering machine. Garcia's pulse quickened. A message might prove valuable. He crossed the room quickly. Three messages. With his hopes up, he hit the Play button...Mrs. Stone, it's Dorothy at Twin Oaks. Your order came in. It's here waiting for you. Thank you. No help there. He waited impatiently for the next message....Jocelyn, call me. You won't believe what I heard at lunch. You're going to die! ....She's not the only one, Garcia thought with a grim smile. Mrs. Stone, this is Dr. Phillip's office. You didn't keep your appointment today. Please call to reschedule. Interesting. Like she left all of a sudden. But, goddammit, where?

Seeing nothing else of interest in the kitchen, Garcia walked through the living room, dining room, and what seemed to be a small sitting room, before he came upon Jack Stone's office. A massive executive desk dominated the room, and Garcia headed straight to it. Aha! Another answering machine! Another blinking red light! So Hubby had his own telephone line. Four messages on this one.

Garcia's eye was caught by a lone piece of paper in the center of the desk, and he picked it up. A typed travel itinerary. He held it close under the flashlight's beam, thinking he had hit paydirt. He looked quickly for the final destination. The Cayman Islands. Fuck! His eyes scanned the top of the page and found it was an itinerary for Jack and Jocelyn

BLACK DIAMOND

Stone. Nothing about Heidi. He went to the departure date. June 5 had been crossed out, with April 18 penciled in. Goddamnit, so they had left in a hurry. The day after Heidi got here. So where the hell was she? Did she go with them?

His eyes returned to the answering machine. He drew in his breath and punched PLAY.... Jack, Rizzo has a problem. Call him.... Jack, Hernandez here. Where's that transfer? My men can't wait here forever.... Goddamn! Sounded like this guy was up to something. Next came a woman's deep, raspy voice... Jack, Julia's dead. Thought you might want to know.... And then, finally! Dad, it's Heidi. Please come and get me. Let me stay with you for just a little while. I promise I won't be any trouble. I hate it here at the Black Diamond Ranch, and I'm afraid of Tony. Please, Dad. Bye.

So they had gone to the Cayman's and left her behind. Dear old dad. Dominick let out a throaty chuckle as he hit the delete button. Gotcha!

At mid-morning, Lieutenant Martin sat in his office looking through the inter-departmental mail. He had just made a trip to the coffeepot, and a steaming mug was within his reach, along with two glazed doughnuts. Towards the top of the mail stack, he came upon a file from Hollywood Division. His body grew tense as he flipped it open. When he read through it, his face took on an incredulous look.

At 9:33 P.M. on April 19, a female claiming to be Heidi Townsend had called the LAPD long distance from an unknown phone booth and been routed to Hollywood Homicide. After being asked some preliminary questions to verify identification, she had spoken with Detective Frank Russo, relating events at 1753 Jalmia Street on the night of April 15, the date of the murder of her mother, Julia Townsend. The caller stated that she had seen Police Sergeant Dominick Garcia standing over her mother's dead body. The caller declined to disclose her whereabouts to Detective Russo.

The doughnuts and coffee forgotten, Lieutenant Martin re-read the report, then hit the number for Hollywood Division, asking to be put through to the captain.

"Captain Dulhaney."

"Lieutenant Martin, IAD. Are you following up on the Heidi Townsend call-in?"

The captain let out a little chuckle. "Lieutenant, you know as well as I do, the city won't let loose of the money for caller ID. To track down that number any other way would take hours and hours of manpower. We can't be spending that kind of time. We don't even know who the caller really was. It could've been Heidi Townsend herself, or it could just've easily been some Hollywood crazy. Do you know how many calls we get from crazies every day of the week?"

"I'm informing you, Captain, that I'm personally taking over the investigation of that phone call," Lieutenant Martin responded. "Good day."

As he hung up the phone, Charlie thoughtfully took a sip of coffee, then got up and walked to the office of Captain Mosely, the chief of Internal Affairs. He knocked on the heavy oaken door and waited. When he was admitted, he went in and handed the report to the captain, a white-haired sixtyish man of great stature. "Take a look at this," Charlie began.

When Captain Mosely finished reading, Charlie said, "You gave me latitude to look into the Townsend murder, because I had a suspicion it wasn't being fully investigated. Now I hope you can give me some manpower to help with this, sir, because I'm afraid Captain Dulhaney isn't moving on it. I'd like to subpoena the telephone company's records of all calls made from phone booths to the LAPD at 9:33 P.M. on the night in question. If you can assign me a couple of detective investigators to help with the paperwork, with a little luck it shouldn't take too long."

"Do you have a starting point?" the captain asked him.

"Not really. The only relatives that came up in Hollywood's search were grandparents back East, and they haven't been in touch for years."

"And the father?"

"No record of him," Charlie answered. "I thought we'd start in California, and work north and east, state by state. Hopefully Miss Townsend hasn't run too far."

"Well, you'll have all the help you need, Lieutenant. This could be just the break we've been hoping for."

"That's the way I see it, sir. If we can nail Garcia on a Murder One, I'm sure he'll roll over. When he's facing life, he'll be more than happy to break the code of silence."

The captain shook Charlie's hand and smiled. "Good work, Lieutenant. It looks like you were right about pursuing this case. Good instincts. Besides justice being served, it does seem as if it could give us the ammunition we need to blow the lid off Hollywood Division. Which would be very nice.

They've been getting away with their bullshit far too long." Captain Mosely clapped his hand on Charlie's shoulder. "I'm betting we'll have quite a case to present to the D.A."

Sheriff Wally Woods turned into the Black Diamond, slowing down his police cruiser to lessen the impact of the gravel against the tire wells. He believed it was his duty to preserve all the police equipment he was responsible for. He knew it was paid for with valuable tax dollars.

It was late morning, and the sun was still moving upward in a clear blue sky. As the sheriff pulled into the ranch, he saw a girl with distinctive long blonde hair watering the flowers in front of the lodge. She stood with her back to him, but at the sound of crunching gravel, she turned to see who was coming. The girl froze in place, then dropped the watering can and ran down the pathway toward the out-cabins.

The sheriff quickly parked and got out of the police car. He climbed the steps to the lodge, crossing the porch in long strides. When he reached the door, he flung it open and walked inside. The large room had an oversized slate fireplace, with mounted animal heads and antlers displayed on every wall.

"Greetings," he said to Tony, who was alone in the room, working at his desk in the corner.

"You ever hear of knocking?" Tony said in reply.

"I got news that wouldn't wait," the sheriff said.

Tony looked at him with interest. "Like what?"

"Like I was here just to make my regular rounds when I happened to spot that girl out front. Is she staying here?"

BLACK DIAMOND

"Yeah."

"Well, I saw her making a phone call last night from a booth by the Gas 'N Go."

Tony's face turned florid and veins throbbed in his massive neck. "What the hell are you talking about?"

"At nine-thirty or so, that same girl was at the phone booth up on the frontage road. There's no mistaking her."

"So what if she was?" Tony responded a little more coolly.

"Thought you'd want to know. Plenty of phones around here she could've used." The sheriff squared his shoulders and planted his hands on his hips. "Anyway, I need to have a little talk with her. She lied to me, told me she lived in Marble Point. And just now when she saw me, she ran away."

"I'll take care of it, Wally," Tony said. "You can count on it." He stood up, walked around the desk, and shook the sheriff's hand. "Thanks for letting me know."

Bruce Fione pulled into the alley behind Eddy's Pawnshop in Marble Point, inching past the delivery trucks parked haphazardly near the rear entrances to several stores. He squeezed his Firebird into a parking spot and jumped out of the car. He walked back and opened his trunk, retrieving two bulging duffel bags. He had phoned ahead, and Eddy was expecting him.

Bruce opened the small back door to the pawnshop and walked through to Eddy's office. Eddy, a potbellied, greasy-haired man in his early fifties, was talking rapidly into the phone he held between his chin and shoulder. "Yeah, yeah, yeah. Bring it in, and I'll take a look."

Eddy slammed the phone down, then got up and locked the office door. "Let's see what you got."

Bruce reached into the first duffel bag and pulled out the silver collection he and Laura had stolen from the McCullys, placing the things on Eddy's desk. The lovely shining pieces seemed markedly out of place on the scratched wooden veneer desktop. From the other bag, Bruce removed two oil paintings, several pieces of jewelry, and an antique mantel clock. He had decided to hang onto the .357 Magnum for awhile, it had been so much fun.

"Good stuff, huh?" Bruce began, as he folded the two bags back up.

"A couple of the silver pieces aren't too bad," Eddy countered.

Bruce's face flushed, and he planted his hands on the edge of the desktop, leaning over it. "Knock off the shit, pal. If you push me too hard, I'll take this stuff somewhere else."

"Go right ahead," Eddy said in a level voice. "But you better be real, real careful. Wally told me the McCullys are putting a lot of pressure on him to get this silver collection back."

Bruce took his hands off the desk and straightened his shoulders. "Look, Eddy. We've always been able to do business together. Why don't you just cut the crap and get to the point?"

Eddy took time to run a pocket comb through his black oily hair. Then he picked up the pieces of stolen property one by one, closely inspecting them. "I'll give you $500 for the lot."

BLACK DIAMOND

"What's that? Some kind of joke?" Bruce shot back, his voice rising. "$1,000 or nothing."

"My, you're driving a hard bargain today," Eddy said, sitting back in his swivel chair and crossing his legs. "I have to pay my cuts, too, you know. $700 is my top offer."

"This is goddamn highway robbery," Bruce responded hotly. "I'll settle for $800, and not a penny less."

Eddy clasped his hands over his potbelly and sighed heavily. Finally he reached into the desk drawer for his moneybag and counted out eight hundred-dollar bills. "This should buy you quite a bit of candy," he said as he handed Bruce the money.

CHAPTER 8

DOMINIK Garcia was pacing around his new room at the Sunset Motel, about to call Heidi. That morning he had driven out to the Black Diamond Ranch to look it over. Acting on instinct, he had stopped at the Gas 'N Go on the frontage road and made a discreet inquiry about the ranch, sensing it was possibly a front for some kind of illegal activity. He had learned that the old owners had sold the Black Diamond to Tony Rizzo two summers ago, and it was no longer being operated as a guest ranch. What Rizzo was doing up there was anyone's guess, because the guy pretty much kept to himself.

Garcia had gotten the telephone number, and now he was planning what he would say when Heidi came on the line. He knew he had to talk fast, and not give her a chance to ask questions....This is John Grenco, a friend of your father's. He got your message. He's busy, and he wants me to pick you up. Your father said to tell you not to say anything to Tony until he's had a chance to talk to him. I'll pick you up at the back gate tonight at ten and take you to the house. Your father should be there by then. I'll be driving a brown Ford Escort. Be ready, and remember, not a word to anyone....

BLACK DIAMOND

Garcia had made the trip out to the Black Diamond before he turned in the Lincoln Town Car, in case Heidi happened to spot him driving by. Tonight she'd see the Ford Escort for the first time. He didn't want to give little Miss Orderly any reason to become suspicious. The road behind the ranch would be dark, and by the time she recognized him, she'd be in the car, with the power door locks in place. And they'd be speeding away.

Yes, it would work. Garcia stopped pacing and went to the bedside telephone, hitting the number for the Black Diamond that was written on his notepad.

"Yeah," came the clipped voice at the other end.

"I'd like to speak to Heidi Townsend, please."

"Never heard of her."

"Oh, my mistake," Dominick said, instantly understanding that something was up.

"Who the hell is this?"

"John Grenco."

"Well, you've got the wrong number."

The phone slammed in Garcia's ear, and he raged into the dead receiver. "You lying sack of shit. Now I have another fucking problem to deal with."

Garcia went to his suitcase and got out his bottle of whiskey. As he took several long gulps, its heat spread through him, having a calming effect. Finally he smiled. Don't worry, little girl. You won't have to stay there. I'll find a way to get you.

Sitting at his desk in the Black Diamond lodge, Tony called through the open doorway to Butch Rivera, who was working on accounts in the small office off the main room. "Rivera, go get that fucking Heidi."

"Sure, Boss," Butch answered as he hurried into the room. Dressed in jeans and a silk polo shirt, he was medium height, in his late twenties, dark-skinned and dark-haired. "Be right back, Boss," he added as he went out the door.

Tony tensely flexed his arm muscles while he waited. His face was set in a deep scowl. Before long Butch opened the lodge door, ushering Heidi inside. "Here she is, Boss."

"Okay. Make yourself scarce."

"Sure, Boss," Butch answered. "I'll be right outside if you need me."

Heidi remained standing by the door, her whole body trembling. She was pretty sure the sheriff had identified her, and that meant big trouble.

"Get your ass over here," Tony yelled.

Heidi crossed the room on shaking legs and stood in front of his desk, looking down at the floor.

"Look at me, you little bitch!" Tony yelled.

Heidi jerked her head up and met his angry eyes. She fought back tears as she waited to hear her fate.

"What exactly were you doing last night?" Tony yelled. "You know goddamn well you had orders not to leave the ranch."

"I'm sorry," Heidi answered timorously, her voice quavering.

"I didn't ask you about sorry. I asked you what you were doing."

"I went to make a phone call."

"To fucking whom, if I may ask?" Tony responded

with dripping sarcasm.

"My father," Heidi answered, thinking it was only a small lie, since there was truth to it.

"Your father!" Tony shouted. "He's in the fucking Cayman's!"

Heidi was forcing back her tears. "I didn't know. I called his house."

"What for?" Tony bellowed.

"I wanted him to come and take me home," Heidi replied as tears overflowed from her eyes. "But he didn't answer the phone, so I left a message."

Tony stood up and walked around the desk, his big frame towering over her. "You expect me to believe that?" he said icily. "When someone just called here asking for you?" His eyes burned into hers. "Who did you tell where you were?"

"I didn't tell anyone," Heidi answered, her heart lurching. "Honest I didn't."

"Wait outside!" Tony thundered, pushing her away. He strode to the door and called to Butch Rivera, standing in the driveway. "Watch her."

Tony returned to his desk and lit a cigarette while he punched in the telephone number for Jack Stone's beach house in the Cayman Islands.

"Yeah?" was the answer through the trans-oceanic line.

"Jack, it's Tony. We got a problem here."

"Spit it out."

Tony's voice was hoarse with nervousness as he related the events into a silent telephone receiver. Finally Jack Stone spoke. "The guy that called, did he smell like a cop?"

"He could've been, Boss. He sure was the cool

type." Tony dragged on his cigarette. "Do you think maybe Heidi did call you? She said she left you a message."

"Listen, you dumb fuck, I retrieved my messages an hour ago, and I assure you there wasn't one from her!" Jack Stone yelled through the receiver. "You can't do anything right. You probably can't even wipe your own fucking ass."

"I'm sorry, Boss," Tony answered. "She had orders not to leave. She slipped off at night."

"Well, make sure she doesn't slip off again. Lock her up. I'll be home as soon as I can."

Susan had been working at her computer all morning, finalizing the notes for her speech that night at the Marble Point Arts Council's annual fund-raising dinner. As Brahm's Second Piano Concerto ended, she turned off the CD, realizing it was almost lunchtime. Before she closed her file, she read over her opening sentences.

"Good evening. I am very pleased to have been asked to speak to you tonight on 'The Role of the Artist in Society.' After some thought, I have decided to speak specifically to the responsibility of an author. I do believe that, when possible, authors' works should reflect contemporary issues that need to be addressed, attempting to effect reflection and change."

Feeling satisfied, she glanced through the rest of her notes, then turned off her computer. She had the whole afternoon ahead of her to assimilate her ideas. Later on she planned to take a leisurely walk along the lake, then relax in her sauna and hot tub before she showered and dressed for the evening. Right now she was going downtown to buy a gift for her sister Lillian. Her birthday was next week, and she needed to get her present in the mail.

She picked up the phone to call Flora, first checking her messages. Still nothing from Ed Holbrook. It was taking him longer than she had thought it would, and she felt sure he'd call this afternoon. She was anxious to see what he had learned about the mysterious Town Car driver, and decided to take her cell phone along with her. He had the number, and if he found out something particularly interesting, hopefully he'd use it.

She punched her speed dial for Flora's Fancy. When one of the employees answered, Susan straightened up her desk while she waited for Flora to come to the phone.

"Hello. This is Flora."

"Hi! Are you free for lunch at Emille's?"

"You've got to be kidding! Like I wouldn't make myself free for a lunch at Emille's?"

Susan laughed. "I'm leaving in a few minutes. When I get there, if you help me pick out a gift for Lillian, we'll get to Emille's that much sooner."

Flora laughed too. "In that case, I'll already have her gift picked out when you arrive."

Susan hung up laughing, and walked into her bedroom. She looked through her closet, deciding to exchange the blue jeans she was wearing for her yellow cords. She pulled on a black turtleneck to wear under the matching yellow chenille cardigan, and stepped into her new black suede flats. Her yellow outfit was one of her favorites, casual and comfortable, yet rather dressy. Perfect for a lunch at Emille's!

The unseasonably dry weather pattern was holding, and it was another fine spring day. Susan enjoyed the drive downtown, lowering her windows to let in a rush of sweet-smelling balmy air. Twenty-five minutes later she had found a parking spot, and was walking down the wide flagstone sidewalk to Flora's Fancy. It was in a block of Victorian type buildings, red brick with colorful wooden appointments.

Susan's arrival in the shop was signaled by a soft tinkling bell, and Flora rushed straight up to her. She was attractively dressed in an apricot mid-length cotton knit dress, accented with a hand-embroidered sash from India. "So sorry, but after you called I got absolutely swamped, and I didn't have time to come up with any ideas for you. Are you starving? Do you want to go to lunch first?"

"Not unless you do," Susan replied. "I'm fine."

"Okay. Take a look around, and I'll be with you in a minute. I'm just finishing up with a customer."

"Take your time," Susan said. "I could spend hours in here looking around."

Susan understood why Flora had been so busy. The shop was unusually crowded with customers, although it was beginning to thin out. Susan smiled to herself, thinking how Flora often ruefully remarked that shoppers never came in a predictable stream, but always in engulfing waves.

Susan loved Flora's Fancy, finding its atmosphere warm and cheery. The mixed fragrance of incense, coffee, and herbal tea permeating the little shop was pleasing and calming. The paned French window facing the street displayed delicate silk plants hung in gleaming copper bowls. Colorful rugs were scattered about on the polished hardwood floor, and decorative mirrors and clocks adorned the cream-colored plaster walls.

BLACK DIAMOND

Susan began by browsing through the china and glassware section, then looked at pewter bowls and candlesticks, wind chimes, antique colored bottles, scented candles, and dried flower arrangements. Next she entered a partitioned off section containing kitchenware, including dozens of specialty cookbooks. A blue patterned canister set caught her eye, along with an electric pepper mill, a fondue dish, and a hand-painted red rooster.

When she reached the coffee and tea corner, she appreciatively filled a deco-designed styrofoam cup with the 'flavor of the day' coffee Flora offered in a black carafe. On the surrounding shelves was a good selection of coffee beans, and a large silver grinder for those who preferred to take home a bag of freshly ground coffee. Smaller household grinders were also for sale. A wide assortment of herbal teas accompanied the display of several ceramic tea service sets.

"Have you found anything?" Flora asked, suddenly standing beside her.

"Have I found anything?" Susan laughed. "Now who's got to be kidding!"

Flora expertly steered Susan to the new line of stained glass window hangings, and she soon settled on a pair of bluebirds that she could just imagine hanging in Lillian's kitchen window. She wrote out a card and insisted on paying the usual fee for gift-wrapping and shipping. Finally the two friends eagerly set out to Emille's.

The French restaurant was nearby, and it was a quick walk. When they entered they were greeted by Emille himself, a dark beaming man of medium stature, wearing a white silk suit with a purple handkerchief in the breast pocket, and a matching bow tie. "Ah, Ms. Muir, Ms. Finney. So good to see you. I have just the table for you right over here."

Emille led them through the crowded restaurant, alive with tastefully muted conversation. The room held a rich aroma of tangy French sauces, and was softly lit by pencil light candelabras attached to the gilded framed mirrors placed about on the walls. The two women were seated at a small table set with a fine white linen tablecloth and napkins, heavy silver flatware, and crystal goblets, accompanied by a spray of fresh spring flowers in an amber vase.

They looked over the menus that were presented, passing up the offered special of boeuf bourguignonne, both opting for lighter fare. Flora settled on a salade niçoise, Susan on salmon mousse with sour cream and dill sauce. While they waited for their orders to arrive, they conversed over the soothing sound of flowing water from the white marble fountain in the center of the room.

"Are you all ready for your speech tonight?" Flora asked.

"Pretty much, but I'm glad I still have till seven o'clock," Susan answered. "Is Brad coming?"

"No, I didn't ask him. I'm going to go alone and make an early night of it."

Susan's cell phone vibrated and she pulled it out of her pocket. "This is Susan."

"Ed Holbrook here. I'm sorry it took so long to get back to you."

"That's okay," Susan said. "But I'm anxious to hear what you found out. I'm glad you called my cell phone." Susan spoke in low tones, not wanting her conversation to be an annoyance to the other diners.

"I think you'll find the report very interesting," Ed replied. "The problem was, the Lincoln was a rental car, so it took awhile to track it down. I just got a call with the information that it was rented on April 16 at an Avis agency in Las Vegas."

"Really?" Susan responded, trying to keep her voice down.

"Really. And there's more to come. The guy who rented it has a California driver's license."

Susan drew in her breath. "And the name?"

"Daniel Gallo."

"Thanks, Ed. I sure owe you one."

"Are you reentering the field of investigative reporting?"

"Sort of." Susan laughed. "I'll tell you all about it when I know what's going on myself."

"Well, keep in touch."

"Will do. Hey, I have an idea! Come on out here, and I'll pay you back by taking you to dinner at the place I'm in right now. I couldn't make you a better offer."

"Might take you up on it."

Susan hung up and related the news to Flora, her voice shaded with excitement. "So the plot seems to be thickening," she concluded.

Flora looked thoughtful. "Does the name Daniel Gallo mean anything to you?"

"Not yet," Susan answered. "But give me time."

Heidi was huddled on the dirt floor in a corner of the dark tool shed. Her long hair was rumpled and her eyes were red and swollen from crying. She couldn't imagine what was going to happen to her. According to her wristwatch, she had only been locked in the shed seven hours, but it seemed like endless days.

It was five o'clock in the afternoon, and she hadn't had a thing to eat or drink since breakfast. Her body was wracked with pangs of hunger. Her mouth and throat were parched, and she kept miserably licking at her dry lips. To make it worse, she had no idea if anyone was ever going to bring her food and water at all.

She had waited and waited, but no one had brought her anything to go to the bathroom in. A few hours ago, when she couldn't hold it any longer, she had carried an empty five-gallon paint bucket to the back of the shed and crouched over it in humiliation. She could hardly believe Tony could be so cruel. Even a jail cell had a toilet.

She felt so alone. The shed had no windows to look out of, and the only light in the fifteen by twenty-foot structure was the bare single bulb that hung from a cord near the door. And she was sure Tony planned to leave her out here. He had sent two boys to town to buy a new set of hasps and a padlock, ordering Butch to watch her until they got it all installed. At the end, Tony's last words to her had been, "You can stay in that shed till you fucking rot."

Heidi imagined starving to death, slowly turning into a skeleton, lying in the shed amongst the jumble of debris. She instinctively reached for her sweet-sixteen locket, to open it and look at her mother's picture, but of course it wasn't there. She fervently wished she had it with her. She missed her mother terribly. Every time she thought of her mother's kind face, her soft voice, her warm touch, and her lovely musk scent, the tears began anew. She longed for her mother to hold her in her arms and comfort her, to whisper soothing words. To tell her it was only a dream.

Without her mother's help, what would become of her? She was a prisoner, defenseless, helpless. What if Tony came into the shed to "get to know her better"? She shuddered. What about the teenage boys that hung out at the ranch? They were so high all the time, there was no telling what they would do, either.

Was she really going to be locked up here forever? When her father got her message, would he come and get her? Now he was in the Cayman's. Heidi didn't know exactly where the Cayman's were, but she knew they were far away. Was her father on vacation? Could it be a business trip? She had no idea what her father did for a living. She just knew he didn't have a regular job like other fathers.

Before he had moved out, he had always been secretive about his affairs, and had kept irregular hours. Heidi remembered how he had ordered her to leave every time any of his friends came over, telling her they had to talk business. She had decided long ago that he probably did something illegal, so it wasn't surprising to her that he was so worried about the police coming around now.

Since this happened, if he did come back and get her, there was no chance he'd let her stay with him. He was going to be really, really mad. He'd send her to live in a foster home in LA for sure. Heidi's thoughts turned to a girl in her eighth-grade class, Cassie Grant, who had been so unhappy in a foster home. Cassie and Heidi had become good friends, and Cassie told her stories of how the brother and sister in the family made her life miserable because they didn't want her living there. One Saturday morning she suddenly called Heidi to say goodbye, tearfully telling her what had occurred.

The brother and sister had taken a large sum of money out of their mother's purse and hidden it in Cassie's room under her mattress. When the mother found it missing, the two reported they had seen Cassie with a bunch of money. The parents searched her room, and when they found the money under the mattress, immediately called the authorities. When Cassie phoned Heidi, she was waiting to be taken away. Heidi often sadly wondered what had become of her.

Well, no use thinking about that now. She felt bad enough already. Heidi knew her mother would tell her to stay busy, and try to keep her mind off her troubles. She looked around the cluttered shed. All sorts of things were haphazardly thrown about. Empty paint cans, pieces of rolled-up carpet, some battered furniture, a broken lawn mower, some moth-eaten horse blankets, an air pump, and myriad other things. The tool shed had obviously become a catchall shed over the years.

She thought she'd try to put it in some kind of order. First she went to the workbench and found a hammer and nails. Using an old milk stool to stand on, Heidi pounded nails into one wall and hung up the old horse harnesses, a worn saddle, and some wickless lanterns. Encouraged by how much better it was looking, she continued on. She decided to carry the horse blankets to the corner to use for bedding. Next she began rearranging, pushing the most unsightly things to one wall, hiding them behind some empty kegs as best she could. She unrolled a piece of flowered carpet, covering a section of the dirt floor to make it the center of a sitting area. She pulled over a cushioned platform rocker, a round wooden table, and a couple of kitchen chairs.

Pleased with her efforts, she sat down, leaned back, and rested, admiring her little sitting room. As her physical activity ended, her dreadful worry returned. Then she asked herself the same question that had haunted her all day. Who had called the ranch looking for her this morning? Could it have been a policeman? Maybe the LAPD had traced her call to the phone booth, and had sent a detective to search around the area. Now she wished the police would find her. But, of course, Tony would say she wasn't there.

She could no longer drive the other thought out of her mind. What if the caller had been Dominick Garcia? Somehow he could have tracked her down. Then she was done for. If Dominick Garcia knew she was at the ranch, nothing would stop him. He'd find her. And she'd have no hope left. Heidi started shaking uncontrollably.

CHAPTER 9

ARRIVING at the Marble Point Inn, Lieutenant Charlie Martin turned onto the cobblestone drive that curved around the entryway under a wooden portico. Dressed in an open-collared shirt and tweed jacket, he glanced at his watch as he alighted from the car. Five o'clock. Well, maybe he was getting old, but he felt like having an early dinner and calling it a day. He'd either pick up a book or just flake out in front of the TV. His flight from Los Angeles to Spokane, Washington had been tiring, with several delays and a long stopover in Seattle. After he rented a Chevy Caprice at the Spokane airport, he still had a lengthy drive ahead of him. He was delighted to finally be at his destination.

The Marble Point Inn, built of old russet brick, was one of the town's most beloved landmarks. The six-story building stood on beautifully landscaped grounds shaded by stately fir trees. Charlie walked through the intricately carved wooden door into a welcoming lobby that was both cozy and elegant. Mounted antlers of an eight-point elk hung on the gas-burning stone fireplace, and cheery orange flames leaped in the hearth. In front of the fireplace stood clusters of couches, chairs, and small square tables holding polished brass lamps. Thumbed-through newspapers and magazines were invitingly spread out on the glass coffee table.

Charlie walked up to the wood-paneled reception desk. Greeted by a friendly clerk, he signed in on his advance reservation and was given the key to Room 605. On his way to the elevators, he located the entrance to the lounge and restaurant, passing a stuffed grizzly bear standing on its hind legs in a glass case.

Charlie smiled to himself, realizing he was actually in the West, away from the big city. Out of Tinseltown, with all its pollution, killer traffic, unbridled mass violence, and random drive-by shootings. And so far, he loved it. He found Marble Point a very pleasant town.

Reaching his door, Charlie inserted an oversized brass key into the lock, considering it a nice change from the modern disposable slip-in cards. When he walked inside, he was pleased with the ample size of the room, with its large, serviceable desk and two queen-sized beds. A round table with two chairs sat in front of the sliding glass door to the small balcony overlooking Marble Lake.

He stepped onto the balcony and looked out at the lake across the hotel's boat basin, enjoying the mild spring weather. He realized right away where the town of Marble Point had gotten its name. A huge whitish-gray rock that looked to be about two-hundred feet high was jutting out of the water near the edge of the lake. As he leaned on the railing looking at the rock, Charlie began to think about the mission he was on.

They had gotten pretty lucky locating the phone booth Heidi Townsend had called from. It could have taken a lot longer. Charlie smiled with pleasure as he recalled Denny Brown shouting out: "Bingo! ... 9:33 P.M. ... April 19 ... to LAPD ... from a phone booth to the north of Marble Point, Idaho!" Cheers had gone up in the room. While Charlie was booking a flight, two detective investigators had been dispatched to the crime scene to get the framed picture of Heidi off the living room table so copies could be made.

The eight-by-ten glossy prints of Heidi were in his briefcase, and he'd begin showing them around tomorrow morning. He hoped his luck would hold, and someone who recognized her and knew of her whereabouts would quickly emerge. His starting point would be the Gas 'N Go next to the phone booth she had called from, and then he'd take it from there.

As he stood on the balcony thinking, Charlie realized he had a good feeling about being here. He had a hunch things would go his way, and he couldn't wait to get started. It was Friday evening, but he hadn't minded at all sacrificing his weekend of leisure. He hadn't had any big plans, and Saturday was as good a day to get started as any. Besides, it would be nice to have a change of surroundings and see something new.

He only hoped this venture wouldn't all be for nothing. Not because he wouldn't be successful in finding Heidi Townsend and getting her testimony, but that the investigation might mysteriously get called off along the way. A few months ago, just as he had been ready to hand over an open and shut case to the D.A., he had been bitterly disappointed when the police commissioner had sent down orders to call it off.

Charlie had moved up from the force into Internal

BLACK DIAMOND

Affairs hoping to make a difference in what he perceived to be wrongdoing in his chosen profession. But now he often wondered if he had merely left a world that revolved around a seemingly impenetrable code of silence for a world that revolved around equally impenetrable high politics.

However, as he stood breathing in the refreshing lake air, Charlie admitted to himself that, although IA hadn't been able to entirely stamp out crime within the force, it had certainly curtailed it. He smiled as he walked back inside. He would just have to think of it all as a big apple pie. He had learned the hard way he couldn't eat a whole apple pie at once. He had to be reasonable and have it one slice at a time.

Charlie hung his jacket in the closet and unpacked his suitcase, setting out his shaving gear and toothbrush. He approved of the good-sized tiled bathroom that was outfitted with brass fixtures and stacks of plush towels and washcloths. He carried his empty suitcase to the closet, then finally sat down with the *Marble Point News* he had picked up earlier. He always enjoyed reading the local papers when he traveled, to get a feel for the town.

After he looked through the national and local news, he turned to the Arts and Leisure section. The lead story featured the Marble Point Arts Council. The public was welcome to attend its annual fund-raising dinner to be held this evening at the Marble Point Country Club. The gala event began at seven o'clock and included a buffet dinner priced at $100 a plate, and musical entertainment performed by local talent. The works of local artists would also be on display in the country club foyer, through the courtesy of art patrons allowing pieces from their private collections to be shown at the benefit.

The scheduled after-dinner speaker was best-selling author Susan Muir. Charlie's heart almost stopped. Susan Muir! So she ended up in Marble Point, Idaho after she left LA. Small world. Charlie suddenly realized he wasn't the least bit tired anymore. In fact, he had become instantly energized with a high charge. A hundred dollars a plate, but what the hell? He was going. Anyway, it was for a worthy cause.

Charlie had met Susan during her investigation of Hollywood Division when she was with the *LA Times*, and had found her quite attractive. He had talked to her outside Captain Mosely's office for ten minutes or so while she was waiting for an appointment, and afterwards had wished he could get to know her better. He thought she was very interesting and intelligent, and appreciated her sense of humor and easy laugh.

A week or so later Charlie had been on his way to the open-air market across the street to grab himself a double latte, just as Susan left the captain's office. When she reached the elevator, on impulse he asked her to join him, and she had smilingly accepted. Over their lattes and bran muffins, they had enjoyed a lively discussion, on topics ranging from city politics, through changing weather patterns, to music and literature.

Charlie had ended up staying away from the office much longer than he had planned, taking great pleasure in their conversation. Susan's underlying sense of caring and keen interest in things especially appealed to him. He felt as if sparks of electricity were flying between them, and realized he was very drawn to her. But before they parted, he had learned she had a steady boyfriend, a fiancé really, and so he hadn't made a move to ask her out. Was the guy still in the picture? Had they gotten married? Her last name was still Muir, but these days, that didn't mean much.

But Charlie knew one thing. It was worth a chance, and it would be great to see her, no matter what. His mission in Marble Point would give them common ground to renew their acquaintance. After all, Susan was the one who had gone after Dominick Garcia in the first place, and nailed him to the wall. She was also the one who opened up the whole can of worms at Hollywood Division, keeping the pressure on until the matter reached Internal Affairs. Charlie was sure she would be very interested in hearing about the turn of events.

Checking his watch, he decided he had time to shower and shave. He didn't know where the country club was, but in a small town like this, nothing could be very far away. His face broke into a boyish grin. He couldn't wait to see her!

The same lead article in the Arts and Leisure section had also attracted the attention of Bruce Fione. But for a different reason. To him it meant that scheduled guest speaker Susan Muir would be out tonight, so he would be free to visit her home. He couldn't pass up an opportunity like that. Ever since they met up at the Blue Moon Wednesday night, he'd been having wild fantasies about her.

A copy of Friday's *Marble Point News* had been on the table in the Oasis Spa lunchroom, and he had been looking through it while he distastefully chewed on his peanut butter sandwich. As soon as he saw her name, a plan began forming in his mind. The dinner began at seven o'clock, followed by musical entertainment. The pretty lady would never get home until at least ten, and probably a lot later than that.

He would have to come up with a good excuse to break his date with Laura, so she'd hand over the meth he needed. But that wouldn't really be a problem. He knew she'd give him anything he wanted. He'd tell her he had gotten into a big pool tournament at the Blue Moon, and stood to win a lot of money. He'd be able to add it all to his savings they were using to go away. That would do it, and she'd never check on him. She'd be too afraid he'd get mad at her, and she'd lose him. Bruce smiled to himself. It was convenient to have somebody so crazy about you.

Before he went out to get the meth, he'd stop at Pet Heaven and get some chewy treats for Fritz. The little dog had been friendly enough the day he had been at Susan's, but he might as well carry along an insurance policy. Anyway, it would be helpful to get the dog on his side right at the beginning. He knew there were going to be many nights to come.

Bruce had taken note of the lock on Susan's kitchen door the day of his spa visit, and it would be a piece of cake. He imagined slipping into the house and going through her personal things. He would be able to find out all about her, what kind of bath soap she used, what her favorite perfume was, what kind of underwear she wore. Bruce closed his long-lashed eyes and began panting. In a few seconds he realized he was aroused. His eyes shot open, and he slid down in the chair in case someone walked into the lunchroom.

BLACK DIAMOND

As he held onto his engorged penis, he considered making his way into the restroom to take care of it. He could drape the newspaper in front of him while he walked through the store. But he decided to wait. It would make it all the sweeter tonight when he was doing it in Susan's bed.

On the mountainside behind the Black Diamond, Dominick Garcia sat amidst a clump of bushes looking through his new 7X35 binoculars. He had picked them up at Barney's Sports yesterday in preparation for his vigil. He had also picked up a few ham and cheese sandwiches and a pint of whiskey that fit nicely into the pocket of his windbreaker.

But goddamnit, so far his plan wasn't working. He should have spotted Heidi by now. Where was she? Was she staying in the lodge, or one of the other buildings? He knew she was down there somewhere. He could almost smell her. But after two straight days, all he had to show for it was an aching ass. And a lousy empty bottle.

He wasn't going to stay much longer. The liquor stores in this godforsaken town closed at seven, and he had to get stocked up for tomorrow morning. They didn't open till eleven, and he planned to be up here long before then. Yesterday, after his plan to call Heidi was thwarted, he had gotten set up about three o'clock, and today he had arrived at mid-morning. He was afraid it was too late, and he had missed her. Maybe she was an early bird. Dominick chuckled. Except the worm was going to catch her.

Garcia was pretty sure he had spotted Tony today. In the early afternoon, a big dark-haired guy had flung open the back door of the lodge and gone over to one of the flashy pickups parked out back. He seemed to play the role of head honcho, with his swaggering walk and the cocky set of his head, a cell phone tucked to his ear. He had returned about an hour later and reentered the lodge, not making any more appearances.

A few teenagers had sauntered back and forth between the lodge and the small red cabins that were set back on the fringes of the grounds. Dominick had peered through his binoculars closely, watching them every step of the way. Heidi was not among them. One had been a girl with the same length hair as Heidi, but it was dark brown. He couldn't get a clear view of her face, and he knew the hair could be dyed, but Dominick was confident she was shorter than Heidi as well.

Several times, two beefy men in their early thirties had walked from the lodge to the biggest of the eight out-buildings. Dominick noticed they seemed to lock and unlock the door with an air of secrecy, and he strongly suspected some kind of illicit activity was housed inside. He could see from his spot on the mountain that the building had windows, but was fairly certain they had some type of interior covering.

From his experienced eye, he would bet it was a drug lab, probably meth. Meth labs were the most common because all the materials were easy to get. It was a perfect set-up, in an isolated spot, set apart from the other buildings in case there happened to be an explosion. He also knew meth labs had become a big thing in the Northwest.

If something didn't break for him pretty soon, he'd go into the building and take a look. If he was right, and he found out they were making drugs, it would give him great leverage to deal with Tony. He was sure the asshole would rather give up Heidi than have the feds on his case, especially since it looked like a big time operation. Dominick Garcia could play hardball with the best of them.

He came to stiff attention as the two meaty guys came out the back door and headed towards a dark blue van. He watched them carefully through the binoculars as they backed out and turned towards the same building they had been in and out of all day. They drove the van along the road of beaten-down grass, and pulled up to the front of the building. Delivery time.

Unlocking the door as before, they disappeared inside, soon returning with armloads of small boxes to load into the van. After three trips, they closed up the van, re-locked the door, and drove away from the ranch, taking a left on Cedar Creek Road. Damnit, it was tempting to go down there right now and find out what was going on. But he had to be careful. It was still daylight. He'd give this lousy stakeout one more day. If he hadn't found out where Heidi was by tomorrow night, he'd make his move as soon as it got dark.

What was that? Dominick cocked his head toward the noise of an approaching engine. He squinted through his field glasses in the direction of the roaring sound, and before long saw a red motorcycle drive past the main ranch entrance and continue up Cedar Creek Road. He watched it through the trees as it turned onto the forest service road that ran behind the ranch before it crisscrossed up the mountain.

It was the way Dominick had gone to reach the old logging road he was now parked on. The logging road had given him a bumpy ride, but it would be a sporting ride on a cycle. He hoped he wouldn't have a visitor. But to Dominick's relief, the motorcycle pulled up to the back gate of the Black Diamond. As the driver yanked off his helmet and wiped his face with a handkerchief, Dominick got a good look at his fine facial features and dark curly hair.

As he watched closely, the same brown-haired girl he had seen earlier came bursting out of a far cabin, and dashed up the path. She pushed through the gate and flung her arms around the boy, giving him a long kiss. Then Dominick saw her reach into her jeans pocket and hand him a package. The boy grinned, blew her a kiss, and peeled out. The girl followed him with her eyes until he was out of sight, then returned to her cabin.

One more possibility, Dominick thought, as he watched the girl walk away. He could always visit her cabin. She undoubtedly knew where Heidi was staying. And he had ways to make her tell. This waiting game was getting on his nerves. Tomorrow night, if he was still in stalemate, he was going to play a different game. An action game.

At the Marble Point Country Club, Susan was flushed with excitement, relishing a pleasurable feeling of success. The audience in the full-to-capacity banquet room had been very attentive to her speech. She thought she had presented her thoughts well, and the laughter she had received from several anecdotes was resounding in her mind. Making people laugh was a heady experience! At the end of her speech, people had asked a wide range of questions, and

BLACK DIAMOND

Susan thought she had fielded them well.

Throughout the hour, Susan had sought out Flora's smiling face at the table next to the dais. It had given her renewed confidence, affirming her own feeling that she was doing fine. Now, as the audience was dispersing, Flora was the first one at her side to offer congratulations before she took her leave. "I'm proud to be your friend," she told Susan.

"What a nice thing to say!" Susan responded, giving her a warm hug.

"And let me tell you one more time, you look stunning tonight."

"Thank you," Susan answered appreciatively. She wore no make-up, and her auburn hair fell loosely around her shoulders. She was dressed in a classic emerald green silk suit, with the jacket buttoned to the neck. Her only jewelry was a silver pin on her lapel and an emerald ring.

After Flora left, Susan spent time speaking with all the other people waiting to meet her. Just as the well-wishing throng around her melted away, one last person approached. Susan caught her breath and felt her heart racing. It couldn't be!

"Charlie Martin!" Susan exclaimed. "What a surprise! Where did you come from?"

"LA," he answered with a grin.

"I mean right now," Susan said, her face lit up in a smile.

"The corner table way in back."

"Well, you sure know how to surprise a girl!"

"I was pretty surprised myself," Charlie said. "It's just that now I'm way ahead of you. I found out you'd be here a couple of hours ago."

"What are you doing in town?"

"That's what I want to tell you about. Could I persuade you to have a drink in the bar?"

"It will take no persuasion at all."

"Your speech was great," Charlie said as they walked out of the banquet room. "And it's great to see you again, I must say."

"Thank you. It's really good seeing you, too."

They went down the hallway towards the bar, engaging in small talk about Marble Point. Charlie learned it was her hometown, and Susan learned he was staying at the Marble Point Inn. When they walked into the bar, they realized quite a few people had decided to have a nightcap to prolong the enjoyable evening. The buffet had been well presented, and the food delicious, from the lobster bisque to the fresh tropical mousse. The musical entertainment that followed had been very well received. A string quartet had played two short selections and a chorale had presented three lively songs.

Susan and Charlie made their way to a table by the wall that was being vacated by an elderly couple. Square tables made of rich dark wood were scattered throughout the lounge, with some pulled together to accommodate larger groups. Each table held a brass candle lantern that gave off a soft glow, creating a warm, homey atmosphere. The long mirror behind the bar reflected the gentle radiance. The barstools were almost filled, and there were only a few empty tables. As they crossed the room through the buzz of conversation, Susan pleasantly acknowledged the friendly remarks people made to her.

BLACK DIAMOND

When they were settled at their table, they each decided on a margarita. One of the bartenders took their orders, soon returning with the drinks and a bowl of snack mix. Charlie began explaining to Susan about his purpose in Marble Point. When he told her about Heidi's phone call to the LAPD, the nagging feeling of recognition Susan had been having about the mysterious Town Car driver suddenly gave way to full realization. Her mouth dropped open in shock.

"Dominick Garcia is in Marble Point!" she burst out. "And he's after Heidi!"

"How do you know?"

"He's Daniel Gallo!" Susan responded. "I can't believe I didn't realize it before. Now that I think of it, he even kept the same initials."

Charlie listened intently as Susan told him about her encounter with Garcia at Robin's Roost, and how Ed Holbrook had gotten the Town Car's license plate run through records for her. By the time she was finished, Charlie's face had a grim set to it.

"That was two days ago," he said somberly. "You know Garcia hadn't found her yet, or he would've been long gone." Charlie thoughtfully rubbed the salt around the rim of his glass. "Let's hope he hasn't found her since then. As soon as I get back to my room, I'll start checking all the motels to see if there's a Daniel Gallo registered, and go from there." He let out a long sigh. "That goddamn Hollywood Homicide."

Susan's face had taken on a reflective look. "You know, there's something really strange here. I'm almost positive that was the same Town Car sitting in my neighbor's driveway last week, and the same one that drove by their house a few times. So if the driver was Garcia, what in the world do you suppose that could be all about?"

"Good question," Charlie responded. "On Monday, I'll get the office to run a background check on your neighbors. What are their names?"

"Jack and Jocelyn Stone," Susan told him. "I think they're in the Cayman's right now."

The bartender came back in a few minutes to see if they wanted another drink. Charlie deferred to Susan. "Would you like another one?"

As much as she was enjoying herself, and sensed that Charlie had been too, Susan could see that now he was anxious to begin his search for Daniel Gallo, and so she suggested they leave.

"Please tell me you'll have dinner with me tomorrow night," Charlie blurted out. He had noticed that at least she wasn't wearing a wedding ring.

"I'm sorry, I can't," Susan answered. She saw Charlie's face visibly fall, like an underbaked soufflé. "I have other plans," she quickly added.

"Sunday night then?" Charlie plunged on.

"Absolutely," Susan said with a radiant smile.

"How about that guy you were with in LA?"

"What about him?" Susan asked teasingly.

"Where is he?"

"He's gone."

CHAPTER 10

BRUCE peeled away from the Black Diamond in a state of elation. It was Friday night, he was off on an adventure, and he had a bagful of crystal meth in his pocket. As an added bonus, Laura would miss him tonight and be gladder than ever to see him tomorrow. And that meant she'd be more than ready to show it. But right now he had something better to do. He was going to visit the pretty lady. She might be out for the evening, but she would be there in spirit.

His leather motorcycle jacket was zipped to the neck against the nip in the air. Underneath he was wearing a silver chain over a sleeveless V-neck tee shirt, tucked into tightly belted black jeans. As he sped towards Loon Lake, the wind whipped against his face. He felt physically charged, leaning into turns in harmony with his roaring cycle. He felt powerful, in control, ready for anything. As he turned onto Loon Lake Road, he accelerated, his state of anticipation growing higher and higher.

By the time he reached the south shore, he felt as if he couldn't wait another minute. Instead of leaving his cycle in the small campground along the way as he had planned, he drove straight to Susan's house. The roadway was empty of vehicles, so he turned into her driveway and rode around to the lakefront. Parking next to the steps, he pulled off his helmet and left it on the bike.

He knew he might've made some tire tracks on the lawn, but they'd be gone by morning. At least he was safely out of sight of anyone who happened to drive by. If someone accidentally showed up at the house, it would make it harder for him to escape, but he felt supremely confident tonight. There was nothing to worry about.

Bruce smiled as he listened to Fritz barking by the front door. Nice dog, protecting the pretty lady. Fritz didn't realize yet that Bruce was a new friend. He climbed up the steps and walked around the deck to the kitchen entrance. Fritz followed the same route indoors and stood barking by the kitchen door. Bruce talked to him soothingly through the door while he used his bronze passkey to pick the lock.

When he felt the lock give, Bruce pulled a bag of liver treats out of his jacket pocket. The clerk at Dog Heaven had assured him they were a special canine favorite. He confidently held one in an outstretched hand while he opened the door with the other. Recognizing Bruce, and smelling the liver treats, Fritz stopped barking at once and took it from his hand, chewing eagerly. Bruce knelt down to pet him, playfully fingering the little dog's bushy beard. By the time Bruce had given him several more treats, he was sure he had won him over.

Then he got out his meth and glass pipe. Deciding to smoke on the deck overlooking the lake, he went back through the open kitchen door, Fritz tagging along. Bruce looked at the hot tub wistfully, wishing he and Susan were going to share it together tonight. He imagined them luxuriating in the flowing bubbles, enjoying each other's nakedness. Not tonight, but very soon.

He walked to the front of the house and got settled into a cushioned chair and filled his pipe. He lit it, inhaling greedily, and was instantly suffused with pleasing sensations. He had snorted a line earlier, but its effect had been only a prelude to this higher state.

He took in the view of the lake. Evergreen mountains made a picturesque backdrop for the dark blue water. Off in the distance, a few white sails were bobbing around in the dusk. A haunting cry rang out over the lake, and a pair of loons swept past. Bruce drew deeply on his pipe, heightening his already intense sensual feelings.

He imagined Susan sitting out here alone in the evenings, sipping on a glass of wine. He closed his eyes and pictured her in a white filmy robe, held only at the waist with a sash. He imagined untying the sash, receiving her welcoming smile as the robe fell open. He began panting. His breath came faster and faster. No, not yet. He had to wait. He wanted to savor every moment until the end of the evening, when he was finally in her bed. Then he would have his awesome release from this sweet pain.

He jumped up and walked inside. Feeling thirsty, he took a look in the refrigerator and found a six-pack of Heineken. He helped himself to a bottle, took a few swallows, then carried it into the living room.

Bruce was struck by the magnificence of the large, high-ceilinged room, softly lit by two burning lamps. The cherry wood furniture was rich and lustrous, and the room's warm colors blended together harmoniously. A grand piano stood near one wall, at the end of a long wooden planter that effectively dvided the room into two sitting areas. An oil painting with bright colors dominated the beautiful stone fireplace, with built-in bookcases lining both sides. Bruce walked in and stretched out on a white sofa, propping his head with two throw pillows.

He drank from his bottle of beer as he looked around. The pretty lady had a pretty house. Suddenly he jumped up again. He was forgetting the music. He went to the entertainment center and looked over the stereo system. Top quality. He began leafing through her racks of CD's, approving of her choice of music. That would be one thing they would have in common right away. She had all his favorite old groups. Led Zeppelin, The Doors, Supertramp, The Who. Racks of classical, too. That was okay. He'd listen to anything she wanted to.

He looked through all the jazz, and some blues, eventually picking a selection of pop music. He read over the titles, then started the CD on the fourth band and returned to the couch. The opening strains of 'Our Day Will Come' floated through the room. As the words began, Bruce sang along in a husky voice... 'Our day will come and we'll have everything ... We'll share the joy falling in love can bring ... No one can tell me that I'm too young to know ... I love you so...' Bruce's voice was strong and passionate... 'and you love me ... Our day will come if we just wait awhile ...... Our day will come.'

Bruce jumped to his feet and dashed into the kitchen for another beer, then came back and played it again. This time, feeling surer of the words, he sat straight up on the couch and sang out in a vibrant voice ... 'I love you so ... Our day will come ...' Yes, our day will come, pretty lady. When you discover my charms.

He lay back again and closed his eyes, imagining Susan in his arms, her sweet-smelling, soft hair brushing against his face. The two of them would smile into each other's eyes as they listened contentedly to the music, a warm fire crackling in the hearth. Yes, their day would come. But he had to be patient. He remembered the angry flash of her eyes at the Blue Moon when he had moved too fast. Now he had to give her time to get over it. And when they did meet again, he had to move slowly, let her set the rhythm.

He was too used to girls falling all over him. Susan was a real woman. She wanted to have some of the control. When the time came, she would make pleasurable demands of him. He'd give her what she wanted, and he'd show her a few things, too. He smiled to himself. He'd have her begging for it. His sexual stirrings became so strong, he couldn't prolong the exquisite moment any longer. He left the couch and went upstairs.

As he stepped into her bedroom and flipped on the light switch, he was overcome with awe. This was where the pretty lady undressed for bed, where she walked around naked, looking at herself in the mirror. He was breathless, rooted to the spot. He stood taking everything in, then all at once rushed across the room to her dresser and began yanking open the drawers. Her lingerie was delicate, sheer, lacy. There lay her panties, so soft and dainty. He picked up a handful and buried his face in them. Oh, the sweet scent. He felt himself giving in to his need. No, no. Not yet.

He haphazardly went through her other undergarments, touching them, inhaling their fragrance. The silky softness of her pantyhose made him giddy. The pantyhose that covered her long slender legs. He dropped the things back into drawers, keeping one pair of black lace panties. He carried them to her bed and hurriedly stripped. He turned down the coverlet and lay on the fine chambray sheet. Oh, the scent of her was all around him! He nuzzled the pillow, breathing it in. He was in agony.

He turned onto his back and lay her panties on his face, taking hold of his erection. He began licking the panties at the crotch, moaning with pleasure as his hand stroked his erection. As he slowly moved his tongue, he imagined the soft, sweet flesh beneath the crotch. Something startled him. What was that? Was it lights flashing in his reeling mind? Or was it headlights?

He jumped up and looked out the window facing the road. It couldn't be! Susan's car was pulling into the driveway. He looked at his watch. It was after eleven o'clock! He had gone crazy. And now his motorcycle was parked out front. He was caught. Suddenly he was drenched in sweat, and his heart was beating wildly. The Subaru stopped and backed up. She was leaving. She had noticed the bedroom lights on!

He watched her pull onto the road and turn towards the western side of the lake. She was probably going for help, and someone would be here any minute. He had to get away. He realized he was holding Susan's panties. He'd take them with him.

Susan had been a bundle of emotions as she drove home from the country club. What a guy this Charlie Martin was! He was so affable and kind-hearted, and had such a warm, genuine smile. Besides, he had a rock-like stability about him that greatly appealed to her. She knew she had been attracted to him in LA, and had thought at the time she felt return vibes coming from him. If it hadn't been for Richard, things might have gone differently.

Now, here he was back in her life. And it seemed as if the vibes were still there for both of them. Or was she imagining his feelings for her? She knew she had a vivid imagination. Otherwise, she couldn't be a writer. But still, he had been very anxious to invite her to dinner. Susan's mouth turned up in a wry smile. And after all, he had been willing to pay a hundred dollars to see her again!

Her initial opinion of him had been reinforced this evening. Belying his occasional boyish grin, he was a serious-minded, dedicated professional with lofty ideals and sound values. He was clearly troubled by his perception of the gross mishandling of this investigation by Hollywood Homicide. And he was extremely worried about Heidi.

As was she. Besides, she couldn't help thinking about the night the Lincoln Town Car had stopped at her mailbox. If it had been Garcia, it must mean he had recognized her at Robin's Roost. Had he found out where she lived only out of curiosity? Or did he have a reason? Had he realized she had gotten his license plate number? She shivered. Well, right this minute, Charlie was trying to track down Daniel Gallo, alias Dominick Garcia. And hopefully the license plate number would be enough to lead Charlie straight to him.

Susan had a live Bob Dylan sixties concert playing in the car's CD deck. As she turned onto the lakeshore drive, her favorite song on the CD, "Visions of Johanna," ended, and she impulsively hit the selector button for Dylan's "Planet Waves." She suddenly wanted to hear "The Wedding Song." When its guitar opening floated from the speakers, Susan readied herself for the emotional impact of the words she knew so well. To her, the song was an ode to true love, the kind she was hoping to find.

Tonight the words stirred Susan's soul even more than usual as Bob Dylan sang in his low, gravelly voice. 'This tune that is yours and mine to play upon this earth... we'll play it out the best we know, whatever it is worth... because I love you more than all of that, with a love that doesn't bend... and if there is eternity, I'll love you there again... you're the other half of what I am, you're the missing piece... and I love you more than ever with a love that doesn't cease...'

That's what I want, Susan thought. She always knew in her heart that Richard and she had never had that kind of love. The lasting kind. It was as if she had finally made up her mind tonight when Charlie asked where he was. She realized she didn't want Richard back. She knew she had made a mistake. She had been slow to admit that her attraction to him had been greatly influenced by his dazzling stage performances.

Then too, for her it had been the heigth of exhilaration when he came to sit with her between sets. She had been aware that all the female eyes in the room were on their table, and she had tingled with pride. She could actually feel their envy, and had basked in it. This handsome star the girls all adored belonged to her, and the two of them would be going home together. A heady experience, but nothing to base a marriage on. Being honest, she had to admit that she felt Richard had lost much of his luster as soon as he stepped out from under the LA spotlights and moved to Marble Point. Deep in thought as she neared home, Susan faulted herself for having been so completely blinded by the stage lights.

Even in her pensive state, when Susan pulled into her driveway, she recognized at once that something was wrong. What was it? Fritz was running to greet her, the same as usual. But, wait! She had left him inside, she was sure of it. How did he get out? She brought the car to a halt and opened the door. Fritz jumped onto the front seat, nuzzling her excitedly.

Something else was wrong. What was it? She sat looking at the house while she kept one restraining hand on Fritz. The bedroom lights were on! She distinctly remembered turning them off. She had left a few lamps on downstairs, and that was all. Now there was a shadowy figure at the bedroom window! Someone was inside! A stranger was ravaging her home.

Her heart thudding, she backed out onto the road. Her legs were shaking so hard, she could barely keep her foot on the gas pedal. If only she had her cell phone with her! She'd go to the McCullys' and call the sheriff. She hoped they were home by now. They had attended the dinner at the country club, but Susan hadn't seen them in the lounge, so there was a good chance they had left right away. She sped down the lake road and, as she approached the McCullys' house, saw with relief that their lights were on.

She parked in the driveway and jumped out of her car, running up the steps.

George and Lisa both responded to the urgent

ringing of the bell, and rushed to the door. George looked through the peephole that had been put in as part of their new security system. When he saw Susan's distraught face, he quickly dismantled the alarm and flung open the door.

"I'm so sorry to bother you," Susan said breathlessly, as they led her inside. "There's someone in my house, and I don't have my cell phone with me."

"Oh my!" Lisa gasped. "Come on out to the kitchen phone." She saw how hard Susan was shaking. "Do you want me to make the call for you?"

"Thanks," Susan answered. "I think I can do it."

While Susan punched in NO CRIME, Lisa put a kettle of water on. George had still been in a suit and tie, but Lisa had changed into a warm robe upon returning home. "You look dreadful," she told Susan as she hung up the receiver. "You're white as a ghost. I'm making you a hot cup of tea."

"That would be wonderful," Susan said. "But I might not have time to finish it. Wally's on his way."

The two women heard the back door slam. "Oh no!" Lisa exclaimed. "George must be going to your house. I bet he went upstairs and got his gun."

They both rushed to the door, opening it just in time to see George spewing up gravel as he backed out of the drive. Susan dashed to her car. "I can't let him go alone!" she called over her shoulder.

"Oh mercy me!" Lisa cried. "Wait till I turn the kettle off. I'll go with you."

When Lisa returned seconds later, Susan was already gone, speeding after George down Loon Lake Road. She caught up to him as they reached the southern end of the lake, and they pulled up to the house together.

As they got out, Susan saw he was carrying his Colt .45. "If those lowlifes are in there, I'm nailing them," George declared with conviction. "Was there any kind of a vehicle here before?"

"No," Susan answered. "Either they hid one somewhere, or they came on foot."

The two of them hurried to the door and Susan tried the knob. "It's locked."

"Please unlock it," George said. "I'm going in."

"George, you have to be careful," Susan told him, taking hold of his arm. "They probably have a gun, too."

"Don't worry," George answered. "I'm sure those druggies are too high to shoot straight. Just unlock the door for me. You stay out here."

"Wally's on his way," Susan said. "Please wait till he gets here. If they're still inside, we can make sure they don't get away."

"We can't cover all three doors," George answered tightly. "I'm going in after them."

Susan reluctantly unlocked the back door, and George went through, holding his gun out in front of him. Susan followed behind him, leaving Fritz outside.

"You're not coming in here," George insisted, pushing her back towards the door. "There's nothing you can do."

"I'll get the fireplace poker," Susan answered firmly. "If you're doing this, I am, too."

Armed with their weapons, the silent pair crept up the stairs into the hallway. When they reached Susan's bedroom, they immediately saw its state of disarray. Susan's face drained of color. "Someone was in my bed! And they went through all my drawers."

"Just like they did at our house," George said bitterly.

Sensing that the intruders were gone, they nevertheless set off to check the rest of the house, going through every room carefully. When they reached the living room, they found three empty beer bottles on the coffee table. "They sure know how to make themselves at home," George observed grimly.

"Those beer bottles will be full of prints," he added. "But a lot of good it will do. They'll be the same prints they found in the other houses, and with no match in the police files, they won't mean a thing."

Susan darted into the kitchen to look in her refrigerator, then went back to report her findings to George. "They actually helped themselves to three of my Heinekens," she said in dismay. "I just can't believe it."

"I don't blame you," George said consolingly. "But at least you didn't get robbed. It looks as if you got home just in time to scare them off. I guess you can count your lucky stars for that."

"That's true," Susan responded, knowing how upset the McCullys still were over their missing family silver. But she really didn't feel very lucky. She was devastated that her sense of personal privacy had been shattered.

"I'm going to leave as soon as the sheriff gets here," George said. "I'm afraid to leave Lisa alone with those crazies prowling around."

"Definitely," Susan answered. "You should go right now. The sheriff will be here any minute. It looks like I called him the whole way out here for nothing," she added. "I guess there's not much he can do now."

"He'll be very personable and go through all the right motions, like he did with us," George responded, a trace of bitterness in his voice. "He gave Lisa every assurance he'd get our silver back, and we haven't seen one piece of it."

"I'm sure he's still trying."

"Yes, of course," George answered. "Please forgive my little outburst."

They went to the door and, as an approaching police cruiser came into view, Susan accompanied George to his car. "I can't thank you enough for coming over," she said.

"I can't thank *you* enough for calling on me," George responded. "I only wish I had gotten here in time to put an end to all this."

As he got in the car, he gave Susan an intense look. "Please consider staying with us tonight. Lisa and I will be terribly worried about you."

"Thank you," Susan replied. "I might take you up on it. I'll see how I feel after Wally leaves, and give you a call."

Inside the sheriff's car, Wally Woods was fuming. Not even the drive out here had calmed him down. This was all he needed. Susan Muir was a national figure. That meant big news coverage. Thank the good Lord he had given orders that he personally wanted to handle the calls coming in on NO CRIME. Undersheriff Casey Drews was on duty tonight, and had reached him on his cell phone the minute the call came in. The sheriff had told him immediately to keep this matter under wraps.

The investigation had to be handled very quietly. If the press got wind of it, he was dead. What a sensational story it would make. Best-selling author Susan Muir had been the guest speaker tonight at the Marble Point Arts Council's society dinner, and had returned home to find her house had been broken into. And the intruders had still been inside. She had fled to a neighbor's for help.

Regional TV would eat it up. He wouldn't be surprised if the networks showed up, too. Newspeople would be falling all over themselves to interview her. Had she moved to this idyllic little town to escape the crime of the big city? How did she feel about it now? How did she like gathering material for her suspense thrillers from real life experience? Would this delay the publication of her eagerly awaited new book?

And Sheriff Wally Woods would look like a fool. This had happened in his supposed crime-free jurisdiction. And, of course, all the other break-ins would be brought up and rehashed. He could imagine the damaging headlines. **CRIME WAVE WASHES OVER MARBLE POINT.** He would lose votes. And losing votes meant losing elections.

As sheriff, he had no job security. Every four years, his fate was at the whim of the voters. And anybody who ran for office knew how fickle voters could be. Especially if you didn't give them everything they wanted, all kinds of favors and special attention. They expected him to do things from fixing tickets to looking the other way when their kids got in trouble. All his former classmates expected the same Wally Woods personal touch that had gotten him elected as Marble Point High's class president two years running. They wanted him to enforce the law, but only for everyone else.

Well, he couldn't be thinking about all that now. He was here. There was Susan Muir, waiting at the scene of the crime. The crime that he had to keep hush-hush. He parked his cruiser, got out, and walked up to Susan solicitously, his black fingerprint kit in hand.

"I'm so sorry," he began, stooping to give Fritz a rub on the head. "What a dreadful thing."

"Thank you, Wally," Susan replied. "And thank you for coming."

"I see George McCully took good care of you until I got here."

"Yes. The McCullys are wonderful neighbors. Won't you come in?"

Susan led the sheriff inside and took him through the house, pointing out everything she and George had noticed. The sheriff's more experienced eye observed the two red glowing buttons that signaled the stereo system was turned on. He requested that he be allowed to dust for fingerprints before Susan touched it. He realized it was late, and he could get started right away. Yes, he would certainly enjoy a cup of coffee. He would take the prints in the kitchen first, and then get out of her way.

Just as the sheriff finished his work, Susan carried a tray into the living room, setting it on the coffee table. "I think coffee will taste good right about now," she said with a smile as they got seated. "Please help yourself to some cookies, too."

"This is very kind of you," the sheriff said. "Especially given what you've just gone through."

"I think it always helps to keep busy," Susan responded.

The sheriff stirred his coffee thoughtfully. "I'd like to talk to you about an important matter."

"Of course," Susan said. "Go right ahead."

"You are a national figure, a celebrity. If word gets out about this, I'm afraid there could be quite a bit of press coverage."

"I see what you mean," Susan answered after a moment's thought. "The press might see a human interest story in it. A writer of suspense thrillers gets material for her books from a harrowing firsthand experience."

"Exactly. And they'll dredge up anything else they can to go with it."

"And you don't want that kind of publicity for Marble Point."

"No I don't. The citizens are already quite concerned about all the break-ins. Until the perpetrators get caught, if the whole thing gets blown out of proportion with a lot of news coverage, it could reach panic proportions." He gave her a sincere Wally Woods smile. "I care foremost about the citizens' safety. But I also care about their state of well-being."

"I certainly see your point," Susan said. "So what is it you want me to do?"

"Be as tight-lipped about this as you can," the sheriff answered. "And maybe you can ask the McCullys to do the same thing."

"I will certainly do that," Susan said, rising to indicate their meeting was over. "As a matter of fact, I'm about to call them now, as soon as you leave. I'll pass your request along."

"Thank you, Susan. You're very civic minded. If we work together, I think we can keep this from leaking out until the culprits are nailed."

When the sheriff left, Susan put in her call to the McCullys. She told them she wasn't as frightened anymore, as she was angry. She was going to begin cleaning the house right that minute, and wash away all the evil traces. At that hour? It needed to be done, and her anger needed to be worked off. She doubted she could sleep tonight anyway. As Susan replaced the receiver, she silently vowed that whoever did this was not going to get away with it.

CHAPTER 11

HEIDI awoke with a start and sat bolt upright in the pitch dark shed. Her heart froze. There was a rat inside! She heard it scuttling across the floor! And now it was close to her. She could hear it scratching in the dirt. Scrrr-itch, scrrr-atch ... scrrr-itch scrrr-atch. It smelled the cheese in the piece of sandwich she had hidden under her blanket! It was going to crawl in after it and rub against her. Then bite her! She shrieked and jumped up.

She never should have turned out the light. She stumbled over to the bare bulb through the darkness, and yanked the cord.

She stood looking around the shed, but saw no trace of a rat. After awhile she walked cautiously back toward her bedding, keeping an eye on her bare feet. She bent down and took hold of the blanket, bracing herself to pull it back and look underneath. She couldn't force herself to do it.

From her stooped position, she intently studied the blanket for any sign of movement. It remained still, and at last she got up enough nerve to pull the corner back, a little bit at a time. Instead of a big gray long-tailed rat, there was her same piece of cheese sandwich, right where she had put

BLACK DIAMOND

it. She couldn't believe her eyes. Relief flooded through her. At least the rat wasn't in her blankets. But he was somewhere in the shed. She'd never be able to sleep again.

She looked at her watch. 6:00 A.M. She had slept for a few hours, anyway. The night before, she hadn't slept at all. She realized she was starving, and decided to eat a little part of the sandwich. She was afraid to finish it, for fear they wouldn't bring her anything else. On Thursday afternoon, Vince Bartel, one of the teenagers that hung around the ranch, had brought her a small jug of water and four thin sandwiches, two ham and two cheese. He told her that Tony said that was all she was getting, so she better not eat it all at once.

Now it was Saturday, so that had been two days ago. Her stomach was in knots. She longed for a juicy hamburger smothered in onions and pickles, with french fries, and a giant Coke. She fantasized it would be topped off with a triple-scoop chocolate fudge ice cream sundae.

She was so thirsty, her mouth was a thick cotton ball. She had used a little water from the jug to wash her grimy hands, but as much as she had wanted to splash some on her face, she hadn't. She knew she needed to conserve every drop. She forced herself to take little sips, and swished the water around in her mouth before she swallowed, hoping it would cleanse away some of the film on her teeth. Her hair was matted and tangled. When she looked at her hands, she couldn't believe the dirty fingernails were hers. She was beginning to feel like a wild animal.

The odor from her waste bucket had spread throughout the shed. She had desperately tried placing another bucket over it to act as a cover, but it hadn't really worked. And even worse, she lived in constant fear that the lone light bulb would burn out, leaving her in total darkness. That was why she had reluctantly decided in the middle of the night to turn it out. But with the rat at large, she wouldn't do that again. She'd just have to take her chances.

Pulling on her shoes and socks, she picked up the water jug and a little hunk of sandwich and carried them to the sitting area she had created. As an afterthought, she went and got the shovel, deciding it would be a good weapon against the rat if it came near. She already had the hammer she had found on the tool bench, but the thought of hammering the rat to death was repulsive to her. Maybe she could keep it at bay with the long-handled shovel.

She kept the hammer at her fingertips every minute. If Tony or someone else came in to do something to her, at least she could try to fend them off. The teenage boys that stayed at the ranch really worried her. They were so high all the time, there was no telling what they would do. She had kept away from them as much as possible because they always tried to put moves on her. At least they were scrawny, and if only one of them came after her, she might have a chance to fight him off. But she knew Tony was so strong, he'd probably just laugh at her while he grabbed the hammer away. She could imagine his jeers. Look, the little girl has a great big heavy hammer... Oh, I'm so scared... Give Daddy the hammer. Of course, it would never work.

What if Dominick Garcia came through the door? Heidi shivered all over. Maybe she could hide in the corner under the horse blanket. The light in the shed was dim, and if she lay really still, he might not know she was there. But maybe he

BLACK DIAMOND

would see the lump under the blanket, and steal over softly to take her by surprise. He'd reach under the blanket and grab her by the throat, squeezing the life out of her.

This was no good, thinking like this. Her mother would be ashamed of her. She always told her to have courage and look on the bright side. When Heidi was beset with problems that seemed insurmountable, her mother reminded her that after every storm, there was a rainbow, and if she survived the storm, she would find it. But it seemed impossible that a rainbow could ever be appearing for Heidi now. She felt so forlorn, in a state of utter despair. Everything seemed hopeless. She missed her mother so much, her heart ached. She could still hardly believe she would never see her again. And she hadn't even gotten to tell her goodbye.

This wasn't getting her anywhere. She was just sinking into a deeper state of despair. Imagine a rainbow. Heidi thought about how she had often painted pictures of rainbows, as a child. Arcs of bright shining colors in a blue sky. So full of hope and promise. What kind of rainbow could there be for her now? What could possibly happen to make her life bright and shining?

Heidi's eyes took on a wistful look. Her father. Her father would get her message and come to get her. When Tony told him what happened, he'd be a little mad at first, but when he saw how pitiful looking she was, any anger he had would turn towards Tony. My poor little girl, how could he have done this to you? Her father's heart would swell with love, and he would sweep Heidi into his arms. Don't worry. Now you have me. I'll take care of you. Nothing like this will ever happen to you again. You're my own little girl.

We have found each other at last.

Heidi began smiling. His wife Jocelyn would like her living with them, too. Heidi would help her with everything. She would clean, cook, do the laundry, and whatever else she could. In time, Jocelyn would grow to love her. They would go shopping with each other, bake cookies, maybe even ride a boat around the lake. And sometimes all three of them could go places together. They would be a happy family.

Heidi had such a feeling of well-being, she decided to go back and lie down on her blanket. She had to stay on the lookout for the rat, but she was very tired. She would just lie there with her eyes open and think about her rainbow. At least she would get a rest. She picked up the hammer and shovel and walked to the corner of the shed.

Scrrr-itch, scrrr-atch...Scrrr-itch, scrrr-atch. Heidi swung around in alarm. Looking up at her from a spot nearby was a bushy-tailed gray squirrel, with big, bright eyes. "Oh, you cute little fellow!" Heidi cried. "You're not a rat at all!"

Heidi dropped to her knees on the blanket, making little beseeching sounds to lure the squirrel up close, but he just sat staring at her. Moving very slowly so as not to scare him away, she reached for the remaining cheese sandwich and broke off a piece of bread. She stretched out her hand and set the bread down on the floor, thinking he'd be more likely to take it that way.

She talked to him in a low, soothing voice. "If you were a rat, you'd like cheese, I think. But I'm pretty sure squirrels like bread. Why don't you come over and take a bite? I won't hurt you. I want you to be my friend. I'll name you Jeremy. That's a nice name, I think. And we'll be good company for each other. I'll be real nice to you, and save you bread all the time."

Jeremy sat unmoving, except for the blinking of his eyes. "At least you're not running away from me," Heidi went on. "That's a good start. I know you have to get used to me. You can take your time. Just don't go away. I love having you here with me."

The squirrel left the bread and ran off, scrambling up the wall to a hole near the eaves. As he made his way through to the outside, Heidi watched his tail disappear behind him. For a long time, she kept her eyes on the hole, hoping he would run back through. She imagined holding him and cuddling him close, her heart full of love. She would have a friend. Then she wouldn't be so lonesome. Finally she lay down and closed her eyes, listening for the squirrel to come back.

On Saturday morning, Susan woke up at 9:15. It couldn't be! She looked again at her bedside clock, thinking she had read it wrong. She hadn't slept so late in years.

Charlie! What if she had missed his call? She sprang out of bed and ran to her study in pajamas and bare feet to check her answering machine. It showed she had two calls. She hurriedly pressed the Play button, and found the first call had come in at 8:45. It was from Flora, sounding a little surprised Susan hadn't answered the phone... Hi! It's me. What are you up to? I'm just calling to confirm our after-dark date tonight. Since you're closer to the Black Diamond than I am, how about if I bring Chinese to your house around six? Let me know. I'll be leaving for the shop at 9:30. Bye for now.

The sheriff had phoned at 9:00... Susan, this is Sheriff Woods. I'm calling to give you a preliminary report on the fingerprint findings. As we suspected, the prints appear to be the same as the ones found at the other five break-ins. I can safely assure you these criminals will be caught. Thank you again for your understanding of this matter. I'll check back with you soon. Good day.

The horror of last night came flooding back. Susan had been up until the wee hours, trying to cleanse her home of the intruders' essence. She had begun by washing all her bedding twice, going on to launder every article in her ransacked drawers. Although the sheriff had been considerately careful in removing all traces of the fingerprint powder, Susan had washed and polished the dresser and the inside of the drawers.

After she had cleaned the rest of the house to her satisfaction, she poured herself a glass of wine and took it outside to the front deck and sat down with Fritz. She petted the little dog fondly, thinking the evening's experience had probably been quite unsettling for him. The lake was starlit, beautiful and peaceful, and as she sat gazing at it, the lurid images in her mind gave way to the uplifting effect of its grandeur. Slowly she regained her inner equilibrium. Her thoughts turned to her book, and she began framing new scenes. After a time, giving Fritz a final loving rub, she had taken him inside and gone to bed.

And slept, Susan remembered thankfully. And she was not going to start dwelling on last night's events again. After spending almost two days preparing for her speech, she was anxious to get back to her book today. She'd return Flora's call right now, but she'd wait until dinnertime to tell her about what happened last night. Starting with the sudden reappearance of Charlie Martin in her life! She picked up the phone and hit Flora's number.

Flora answered on the third ring, a little breathlessly. "I'm running late. I couldn't decide what to wear."

Susan laughed. "So did you make a decision?"

"Yes, my standard 'when in doubt' outfit, my blue linen suit. But don't worry, I'm coming home at five to change into full nighttime adventure regalia, complete with a flashlight on my belt."

Susan laughed again. "It sounds as if you're getting into the spirit of it."

"I am. It's reminding me of the Nancy Drew-type escapades you talked me into when we were in grade school. I will say," she added, "life is never dull with you as a friend."

Susan's call waiting signal sounded. "I have a call coming in," she said. "Give me a second."

"Hello. This is Susan."

"Hi! It's Charlie Martin."

"Charlie! I'm on the other line. Hold on. I'll be right back."

Before he had a chance to object, Susan reconnected with Flora. "It's a call I have to take."

"Oh?"

"I'll tell you all about it tonight. The Chinese sounds terrific, and six o'clock is perfect. Have a nice day at work, and I'll see you then."

She went back to Charlie. "Sorry. Thanks for waiting."

"I could've called you back. I didn't mean to interrupt you."

"Not at all. It's nice to hear from you."

"Well, I have a little information."

Susan caught her breath. "Oh, what?"

"Our Daniel Gallo checked out of the Wayside Motel on Thursday morning, the day after you saw him. And he also turned in the Lincoln Town Car at Avis the same day."

"Wow!" Susan responded. "But that doesn't necessarily mean he left town," she added slowly.

"My thought exactly. So I went over to the sheriff's office this morning and got lucky. Sergeant Mike Mercereaux was the watch commander, and he was great. Very cooperative. He put a patrolman on it for me, to check out local car rental agencies. I'm sure if Garcia's around, he's changed ID's, so the patrolman will try to find out if anyone with a California driver's license rented a car on Thursday."

"Good thinking!"

Charlie laughed. "Well, I am a detective, you know."

"So, I was an investigative reporter, and I didn't think of that."

"You didn't have all night to think about it, either."

"Were you up all night?" Susan asked anxiously.

Charlie laughed. "No. It was a manner of speaking. But, I do think it's been proven that you think while you sleep."

Susan laughed back. "So anyway, if your patrolman comes up with a rental, he'll begin checking motels again for someone registered with the new license plate number, right?"

"Right. It's a long shot, because if Garcia thought you were on to him, he'd probably follow my same line of thinking, and claim he didn't have a car when he checked into the new place."

"So that means taking his picture around," Susan responded.

"Right again. When I get pictures, which will be on Monday. The office is closed down for the weekend, and so is DMV."

"Well, you've certainly been busy," Susan said. "I'm glad to hear our local sheriff's office treated you right."

"Yes, that Mercereaux was a very likeable guy. I'm planning on paying a courtesy call to the sheriff on Monday. I'll take Heidi's picture along, and maybe I'll get some help with that, too."

"If you haven't already found her," Susan responded.

"Thank you for the vote of confidence. By the way, I made seven o'clock reservations for tomorrow night at the Marble Point Inn. I hope that's okay."

"More than okay. I love that place."

"Great, because it so happens they're serving my most favorite meal in the world, and I don't want to miss it."

Susan laughed. "The Marble Point Inn Sunday night pot roast!"

"You're right, but only partly right."

Susan began laughing again. "And what else?"

"They're also featuring their famous homemade apple pie. Evidently, they keep enough apples in cold storage to make pies all-year-round."

"I take it you're an apple pie enthusiast?" Susan asked in amusement.

"I would say so. In my younger, dumber days, I

actually tried to eat a whole apple pie at once."

"And found out you couldn't do it?"

"Right," Charlie answered. "But I put forth a gallant effort."

Susan found herself laughing again. "Well, the Marble Point Inn's apple pie is wonderful, and I certainly think that after all your hard work, you deserve to have at least two slices."

"You wouldn't make fun of me?"

"Absolutely not. I might have two myself to keep up with you!"

"This is sounding better and better. What time should I pick you up?"

"Would you like to come by for a drink first?"

"I'd love it."

"Is five o'clock too early?"

"Perfect. If I have any exciting developments, I'll keep you posted. So if you don't hear from me before then, you'll know I'm just busy wearing out my shoes."

Susan laughingly wished him luck and gave him directions to her house. She purposely didn't tell him about the break-in because she was pretty sure he'd be worried and want to be protective. Even with all the spare bedrooms in her house, she wasn't sure it was a good idea for him to stay overnight. She believed it might be better to let things move along at a natural pace. She thought things were going just fine.

After Charlie hung up, he drank down the rest of the coffee in his cup, his thoughts still on Susan. He wished he was going to see her tonight. What was she going to be doing? And, more important, who was she doing it with? When she had given him directions to her house, he realized he would be going right past the Loon Lake turnoff this morning when he went out to the Gas 'N Go. He had been tempted to ask her if he could stop in, but had refrained, realizing that, since she hadn't invited him, it probably meant she was busy. He didn't want to push things. He thought they were going along very, very well.

Or maybe she hadn't invited him because she knew he had a lot of work to do. And she was right, of course. He better get going. He set down his coffee cup and headed for the shower. When he got out, he dressed in a fresh shirt and the same tweed jacket he had arrived in, having brought along no others. He had already treated himself to an early room service breakfast of sausages and scrambled eggs, so within an hour he was pulling off the frontage road into the parking lot of the Gas 'N Go. He picked up his briefcase and went inside.

A sixtyish man with short gray hair and glasses was behind the counter, not appearing to be too busy. "Howdy," he said. "What can I do for you?"

"I'd like to show you someone's picture, if I may."

"Go right ahead," the man answered amiably, leaning over the counter.

Charlie got an eight-by-ten of Heidi out of his briefcase, and handed it to him. "Do you recognize her?"

The man held the photo carefully by the edges and peered at it through his glasses. "Pretty thing. But, no, I don't recognize her. Don't get too many people in here since the highway went through. Just enough to keep food on the table." He handed the picture back. "Is she in some kind of trouble?"

"No. Not at all," Charlie answered promptly. "I just need

to locate her. Thank you very much for your cooperation."

Charlie filled up his gas tank, glad to give the man some business. When he left, he continued on down the frontage road, thinking he would scout out the area while he was here. After a mile or so, when he hadn't passed a single house, he was beginning to think he was wasting his time. It was just then that he spotted the 'Black Diamond Guest Ranch' sign. His hopes up, he turned onto Cedar Creek Road, admiring its beauty as he drove along.

Before too long he reached the ranch and drove through the gate. Sighting a log building that appeared to be the main lodge, Charlie drove up to it and parked, noting its poor condition. He mounted the steps with his briefcase and knocked on the door. Tony called out a gruff admittance and Charlie walked inside.

"Whaddaya want?"

"I'd like to ask you if you recognize someone," Charlie answered, crossing the room to his desk. Tony stayed in his chair, offering no greeting or introduction.

Charlie looked at the man's dark, scowling face, instinctively not liking him. As he was sizing him up, he noticed Tony's biceps straining against the rolled-up sleeves of his silk shirt. Charlie reached in his briefcase and pulled out Heidi's picture, holding it out to him.

Instead of taking it, Tony just gave it a cursory glance. "Never saw her before." His facial muscles showed no flicker of recognition, or even interest.

"Maybe you should take a closer look," Charlie said, irritated by the man's rudeness. "At a guest ranch, you must get quite a few people."

"This isn't a guest ranch."

"Then you should damn well take down your sign."

"Yeah, I'll do that. Now will you get the hell out of here, because I'm very, very busy."

Charlie insultingly planted both hands on Tony's desk and leaned over it, baiting him. "Doing what?"

"None of your goddamn business. And now will you please leave?"

"I don't think I'm ready to leave," Charlie said. "And I don't think I like your attitude, either."

"Look here!" Tony yelled. "Who the fuck do you think you are?"

"I know fucking well who I am. I'm Lieutenant Charles Martin, LAPD." He pulled out his badge and held it up.

"Jesus Christ! I'm sorry, Lieutenant. I'm Tony Rizzo," he said, reaching out to shake hands. "I had no idea. I get so many bums coming through. They either want to sell me something, or they're looking for a handout."

"So you'll take a closer look at the picture?" Charlie said.

"Of course I will, Lieutenant. I'll cooperate any way I can."

Tony took Heidi's picture from him and looked at it carefully. "Nice looking girl," he commented. "Is she in some kind of trouble?"

"None of your business," Charlie shot back. "Your business is to tell me if you recognize her."

"No I sure don't," Tony said slowly, emphasizing each word to make it sound more convincing. "I'm sorry, Lieutenant."

"What do you do here?" Charlie asked in a steely voice.

"Mainly raise cattle," Tony replied. "But I'm thinking of expanding, maybe pick up some pigs and chickens."

"How many people do you have working for you?"

"Three full time. Three part time. But I might put on another one full time if I expand."

"I'd like to show the girl's picture to all of them," Charlie said.

"Of course, Lieutenant. There's only one here right now. Two are off today, and the rest are in town picking up supplies. But you're welcome to come back anytime."

"Where's the one?"

"Back there in the office," Tony answered, making a move to walk in that direction.

"Call him."

"Butch! Come on out here!" Tony called loudly.

Butch Rivera appeared in an instant. "Yes, Boss?"

"Lieutenant Martin here wants to show you a picture."

"Sure, Boss."

Charlie held the picture up for him, closely watching his reaction. "Do you recognize this girl?"

"No way, Lieutenant. Never saw her before."

"Do you know that if you're lying, you could be arrested for obstruction of justice?"

"No, I didn't know that," Butch said. "But it don't matter, because I ain't lying."

"You never saw this girl even once in your life?" Charlie pressed. He thought he might have detected a faint flash of recognition, quickly disguised, in Butch's eyes.

"No, Lieutenant. Not once."

"What do you do here?"

BLACK DIAMOND

"I do the accounts for Tony."

"Are you pretty good with figures?"

"I guess so." Butch gave him a little grin. "If I wasn't good, Tony would let me know about it."

"Well, thank you," Charlie said, returning the picture to his briefcase. "You better get back to work."

"Thanks, Lieutenant. I'm sorry I couldn't help you."

Tony smiled as he showed Charlie to the door. "As you can see, Lieutenant, you're barking up the wrong tree here."

Charlie smiled back. "Be glad I'm just barking. As you may find out, my bite is worse than my bark."

As soon as Charlie left, Tony lit a cigarette and punched in Jack Stone's number at the Cayman's. His face had turned ashen, and his hands were trembling.

"Yeah?" came the familiar voice.

"Jack, it's Tony. Now we have a *real* problem."

"I'm listening."

"A detective from LAPD was just here showing me Heidi's picture."

"Fuck. So that little bitch did call LAPD."

"It sure looks that way, Boss."

"Was this the same guy that was looking for her the other day?"

"I don't think so. He sounded different."

"Shit. Fuck. So do you think this guy was satisfied she wasn't there?"

"Maybe. But he's coming back. He wants to show her picture to everyone. Butch was the only one around. Johnny and Phil are over in Montana putting something together, and the kids are out on deliveries. When he comes back, I know the guys will be cool, but I'm worried about the kids playing it right."

"You dumb fuck!" Stone yelled. "Get the kids out of there, for Christ's sake. Send them somewhere till the heat's off. Sometimes I wonder if you can even blow your own fucking nose."

"Sorry, Boss. You're right. I should've thought of that. Johnny and Phil can handle the deliveries for now."

"You can use Rivera, too."

"Right, Boss. He's a good man."

"Is that little bitch behaving herself?"

"Perfectly, Boss."

"Where do you have her?"

"In the tool shed. It doesn't have any windows, and it's locked tight as a drum."

"Make sure she stays nice and quiet. Tell her if she makes any more trouble, she'll find out we're not playing games."

"I sure will. When do you think you'll be home, Boss?"

"As soon as I wind up this deal down here. It just has a few loose ends."

"Sounds good. One more thing, Boss. What if this guy gets a search warrant?"

"I'll give Wally a call."

CHAPTER 12

WALLY Woods, casually attired in a sport shirt and slacks, sat in his den on Saturday night looking through the 1974 Marble Point High Yearbook. His mouth was set in a trace of a smile, and his eyes were shining. It was the yearbook from his senior year, his greatest year. There was the picture of him as King, happily waving to the adoring crowd from atop the festooned homecoming float, with head cheerleader Joyce Thurman, his Queen and steady girlfriend, at his side. Marble Point High's golden couple.

Here was the prominent single picture of him as captain of the football team. He was jauntily holding his helmet by the strap, his cleated feet in a spread-apart position. There he was featured as class president, now wearing a serious smile. Next was an informal snapshot of him and Joyce at the Valentine dance, dreamily coupled in a slow shuffle under hundreds of red and white balloons. Another informal shot of him and his buddies horse playing on the lawn. Now he was shooting a bow and arrow at a round target of hay in P.E., over the caption "Wally hits another bull's-eye."

He finally reached the pictures of the senior prom. A splendid occasion, he and Joyce both radiant and sparkly-eyed, she in her flowing satin gown, he in his red-boutonnièred tuxedo. The band had been sensational, and amidst the dazzling decorations, they had lightheartedly danced the night away. Then came graduation, and it had all ended.

Wally's glory days were over, never to be matched again. The popularity, the stardom, the adulation. The cheers in the football stadium still rang in his head. He yet relived the heady experience of walking around town on Saturdays after a win, with so many people telling him, "Great game last night, Wally." He kept running the plays in his mind. Best of all was the time they were running an eight-three pattern and he had broken four tackles to carry the ball in for the winning touchdown. The crowd had gone wild. After the game, the team had carried him off the field on their shoulders. He was a hero, a star.

What had he become? Somebody living in a tract house in the north side of town who had worked himself up from beat patrolman. As sheriff, he made a decent salary now, while it lasted, but it didn't make up for all the years he had received paltry paychecks. The others in the old high school crowd he had run with had soon begun traveling in different circles. They lived in five-bedroom lake view homes, drove BMW's, and belonged to the country club.

Of course, most of those classmates had earned college degrees that gave them tickets into high-paying fields. He had gotten a college football scholarship and given it a try for two years. It was football he cared about, not academics, and he had soon learned that the star of Marble Point High did not shine as bright in a constellation made up of top players from big schools nationwide. After two years of warming the bench, lucky to have five or ten minutes playing time in games already

BLACK DIAMOND

won, he had gotten discouraged and dropped out.

Joyce had remained in Marble Point waiting for him, and they had quickly gotten married. Two daughters came along in the first three years, and they had been blissfully happy. When their old high school crowd came home on college breaks, Wally and Joyce proudly showed off their babies, sure they were the envy of everyone. Then doting grandparents had gladly taken over while the young folks hit the rounds of parties together like old times.

But when those former classmates graduated from college, it was a different story. Some moved away, but quite a few returned to Marble Point and established themselves in illustrious careers. Others went to big cities and made a quick fortune with dotcoms and other ventures that allowed them to live wherever they wanted. A lot of them wanted to live in their hometown, and they came back.

Discontent had gradually settled in, as Wally and Joyce realized they had been left behind. They couldn't begin to keep up. Their old friends dined at Emille's. They went to McDonalds. Wally had been excluded from Saturday rounds of golf, Joyce from spa sessions and country club lunches. The golden couple had disappeared, imprisoned between the covers of Marble Point High School yearbooks.

After enjoying her position of popularity for so many years, Joyce couldn't handle being left out of everything. When she had no more tears left, she had turned to sweets. She spent her days furtively eating chocolate cookies, slabs of fudge, boxes of maple creams, jelly-filled doughnuts, and anything else she might have hidden around the house. Last year she had suddenly come to her senses, and Wally had been greatly heartened when she joined a weight-watchers club. But so far, her mountainous body had been stubbornly resistant to all her efforts.

Wally prided himself on remaining physically fit, and he was disgusted. He had married a size eight. Now he was married to a hippopotamus. He couldn't help feeling sorry for her, but he felt sorry for himself, too. Sometimes he thought if he could've looked in a crystal ball twenty-five years ago, he wouldn't have gone near the altar. Besides, fed by her own guilt, Joyce had allowed their two daughters to turn into blimpish cartoon characters. Thankfully, two damn fools had married them and taken them off his hands. Now, at least he didn't have to look at all three of them every day.

Wally got up and returned the yearbook to its place beside the others on the bookshelf. He was going to go out. He couldn't face walking into the living room right now and seeing Joyce, after just spending an hour looking at her the way she used to be. He was going out and have a little fun. He had to escape. He needed to get a few hours of relief from his problems. Which were piling up.

Today he had been unnerved by his call from the Cayman's. He'd have to go talk to Tony and see what was going on. He was sure the girl Lieutenant Martin was looking for was the one he had seen at the phone booth. He knew she had been up to something. He also knew there were things Tony wasn't telling him.

Now Jack Stone expected him to go up against LAPD, for God's sake. And Jack Stone could not be ignored. He was a powerful man, with influential connections. Wally knew he had to move very carefully. He could not aford to make an enemy of Jack Stone.

Susan and Flora were putting away the leftovers from their Chinese dinner, cartons of Hunan beef, oriental noodles, sweet and sour pork, Peking chicken, and egg rolls. Susan laughed. "I'm surprised we have any leftovers at all, the way we were going at it! What a meal! You'll have to come back for lunch tomorrow to help me finish it."

"That is, if we're not in jail tomorrow, having bread and water," Flora responded wryly.

"We're not going onto any private property, remember?"

"Yes, I remember real well," Flora retorted. "The problem is, you might not remember."

Susan laughed. "I think my fortune cookie made you nervous."

"Let's just say it made me more nervous."

Flora had opened her fortune cookie first, finding the favorable message: 'New opportunities are coming your way.' Then, when Susan opened hers, they had both been amused at the apt fortune inside: 'Do not be afraid to take a risk.'

At the start of their meal, Flora had asked Susan about the phone call she had received that morning, and Susan had animatedly told her all about Charlie. Then she had a little reluctantly related the story of what had happened when she got home. As much as she needed to talk about it to someone, she knew Flora would be terribly worried, and would want Susan to stay with her until the intruders were caught. But Susan had remained resolute that she would not be forced from her own home.

True to her word, Flora had dressed in fitting clothes for their nighttime outing. She was wearing a long-sleeved navy blue tee shirt with her jeans, under a black denim jacket. Susan had also put on a dark outfit, making it harder to be spotted. Flora had her flashlight, and Susan had her new night vision scope. They were both anxious to see how well it worked.

Now that darkness was approaching, they closed up the house, leaving on plenty of lights. They were planning to take Susan's car, leaving Flora's Buick in the driveway to give the appearance of a guest being present. After bestowing Fritz with some farewell rubs and kisses, they locked the door and were on their way.

The day had been cloudless, so they had their hopes up for a clear night. Susan's scope intensified existing light, so as they drove along, they were watching the sky for appearing stars. The waxing moon would provide enough light, but still, the more bright stars, the better. By the time they reached the Black Diamond turnoff, darkness had fallen, and they were both delighted that the moon was high and the sky was ablaze with stars.

As planned, Susan continued up Cedar Creek Road past the Black Diamond gate, then took the forest service road that ran in back of the ranch. She was nervous behind the wheel, afraid Tony might happen to be outside and notice car lights. At that late hour, if he recognized her Subaru, he'd be pretty sure she was up to something. Not only would their mission be thwarted, but a confrontation with Tony would make for an ugly scene.

BLACK DIAMOND

Having the same thoughts, Flora apprehensively looked over the moonlit grounds as they drove by. "I didn't see a soul," she said as they started up the mountainside. "So far, so good."

After they had driven about a half-mile, they came to a turnoff, and Susan pulled off the road and parked. They kept to the side of the road as they made their way back down the mountain, ready to duck into the woods at the sign of approaching headlights. About ten minutes later, they reached the bottom, crossed the road to the ranch, and began walking along the rail fence.

They talked in undertones as they went along. "This is the fence we're staying on this side of, right?" Flora said.

"Right," Susan answered with a smile, coming to a stop. "We should be able to see pretty well from right here."

"This does seem like a good vantage point," Flora agreed. She gestured toward a thick stand of spruce trees ahead. "Anyway, if we go much further, those trees will block our view."

Susan pulled her monocular out of the case and held it to her eye. She was delighted to find it gave her a clear picture of the grounds. Everything had a greenish cast, created by the infrared light. Although Susan couldn't see the front of the lodge, the driveway was in the field of vision, affording a picture of who came and went. "This is amazing!" she said excitedly, handing it to Flora. "Try it!"

Flora eagerly took it from her, and put it to her eye. "Wow! It *is* amazing!" After she looked at the main lodge, she scanned the property, taking in all the small cabins and out-buildings. "Big place," she commented. "And it's pretty isolated. A perfect spot for some illegal activity. Uh-oh!" she whispered suddenly. "Speaking of illegal activity..."

"What? Let me see!" Susan said eagerly, reaching for the scope.

"It's my turn," Flora said, pulling it away. "Yup! I think he's trying to break into that shed."

"Flora! Let me see!" Susan whispered hoarsely, taking hold of the scope.

"Go ahead," Flora answered, handing it over.

Susan peered through the lens, but couldn't see anybody. "Where is he?" she hissed.

"He was right there," Flora answered, pointing in the direction of the shed.

"I don't see him," Susan said in frustration. "Here, take it. See if you can still spot him."

Flora took the monocular and aimed it toward the shed. "Yup, there he is. And, you know, he's really a cute looking guy!"

"Flora!" Susan seethed. "Tell me where to look!"

"On top of the shed. On the roof."

"On the roof?" Susan said in whispered astonishment. "Let me see!"

As Susan peered through the scope at the bushy-tailed gray squirrel sitting in the eaves, she broke into a big smile, in spite of herself. "Flora Finney! I'll get even with you!" At that minute the squirrel disappeared into the shed.

Before long they saw headlights coming up Cedar Creek Road. They both stood motionless, watching. "Now we're getting some action," Flora said in an undertone. "The first comings and goings of the night."

BLACK DIAMOND

"And I'm betting not the last," Susan answered promptly, training the night vision scope on the car as it turned into the ranch. Even at a distance, she was able to make out a lone driver, and as it drew near she could clearly see it was a sheriff's car. As she watched it drive up to the lodge, she saw that the driver was Wally Woods, out of uniform. "It's the sheriff," she told Flora. "At this time of night, and not in uniform. I wonder what's up."

"Me, too," Flora answered. "We came out here to see bad guys, and a good guy shows up."

After a time, more headlights appeared, and a BMW came into view. Susan watched as it, too, pulled up to the lodge and parked. With the scope directed towards the driveway, not long afterwards she saw the sheriff come outside and drive off.

In a few minutes, Susan recognized Tony in jeans and a windbreaker as he came through the back door of the lodge. "There goes the head honcho," Susan told Flora.

They dropped to their knees as Tony began walking towards the biggest out-building. "Here, you can watch him," Susan said, handing Flora the scope. "I don't want to be selfish. But, for heaven's sake, don't let him out of your sight."

"The way I let the squirrel out of my sight?" Flora retorted.

"Sorry," Susan said. "It's my nerves."

Flora couldn't see the front of the building, but the time lag between when Tony approached it, and when the lights came on, suggested he had spent time unlocking the door. He was inside for about five minutes, then the lights went off, and he came back out. He walked briskly toward the lodge, appearing to be empty-handed, then once again vanished from sight as he opened the back door and went through.

"So he left that guy in the lodge while he went to do something," Susan pondered aloud. "I wonder what it was."

"Me, too. I thought he was going out there to get something," Flora responded, "but he didn't seem to."

There was no further trace of activity until the BMW left about ten minutes later. Susan and Flora stood at their post keeping watch, leaning on the fence from time to time as they passed the monocular back and forth. They both tried to get another glimpse of the squirrel while they were waiting, but he remained out of sight. They decided he must still be inside the shed, busy at something.

New headlights cut through the darkness on Cedar Creek Road. "Here comes somebody else," Flora whispered excitedly. She trained the night scope on the Black Diamond gate, waiting for the vehicle to drive through. "It's a pickup," she reported. "There's a guy and a girl inside, somewhere in their twenties. They're pulling up to the lodge. Now they're out of sight."

Flora handed the scope to Susan just as the back door of the lodge opened. Instead of Tony, this time a different man came out. He had about the same burly build as Tony, and was jacketless, wearing a long-sleeved polo shirt. He headed towards the out-building that Tony had gone to, taking long brisk steps. Just as before, the lights were turned on for about five minutes, and the man came out and strode back to the lodge. He was carrying a small package.

"So he went out there to get something," Susan said in a hushed voice.

BLACK DIAMOND

"Do you think that same size package would've fit in Tony's pocket?" Flora suggested. "Remember, he was wearing a jacket."

Susan smiled at her. "Now you're talking my language. I'll make an investigative reporter out of you yet."

In a few minutes, the pickup rumbled off. While they watched its taillights trail away onto Cedar Creek Road, a pair of headlights came into view as the two vehicles passed. Susan squeezed the monocular tensely, waiting to see who was coming. She soon observed a flatbed truck riving through the gate. "Two guys," she told Flora as the truck drew close to the lodge.

Without stopping, the truck proceeded past the front entrance, making the turn to drive around back. Susan could clearly see a tarp stretched over the contents of the flatbed. Expecting it would park beside the other vehicles by the rear door, they were surprised to see it slowly continue along towards the same out-building that had been visited that night. It rolled to a stop, then turned around and backed up. Shortly, Susan and Flora heard the truck doors opening and closing, and assumed the men were going inside the building. But Susan saw them walking away, and handed the scope to Flora. "Take a look. They left the truck, and they're headed back towards the lodge."

Not wanting to risk being seen, they stayed in a crouch as the two stocky men tramped off. "I wonder what's in that flatbed," Susan said as the pair disappeared through the back door. "I have the feeling it would tell us a lot."

"I agree," Flora answered. "But don't be getting any ideas. They'll be back any minute."

As time went on and no one appeared at the back door, Susan began shifting from foot to foot impatiently. "We could have easily been there and back," she said in frustration.

"You mean *you* could have easily been there and back," Flora retorted. "And I'm afraid you're starting to forget something you were supposed to remember."

"But I didn't know I was going to be faced with such temptation," Susan told her.

"Exactly what I was afraid would happen," Flora answered.

Minutes ticked by and nobody came. Burning with curiosity, Susan stared at the back door of the lodge, waiting. "I absolutely can't stand it," she said at last. "We're losing a golden opportunity."

"It'll be a golden opportunity for Tony to have us thrown in jail."

"He'll never see us. Those trees would provide perfect cover."

"What about that clearing where there aren't any trees? What do we do about that?"

"We'd stay low, and hope no one comes."

"Take a risk, you mean. A big risk," Flora protested. "Fortune cookies aren't meant to be taken seriously, you know."

"I'm going," Susan said. "I have to. But, please, you stay right here."

"If you're going, I'm going," Flora answered. "As you well know."

"Come on, then," Susan said. "Let's do it."

They quickly climbed over the fence and took to the cover of the trees. They kept in a low crouch as they threaded through the stand of spruce towards the flatbed truck. As they moved along, they watched closely for a sudden light that would signal the opening of the lodge door. As they neared the first shed, Flora was startled by a crackling sound in the underbrush, and let out a stifled shriek. "What was that?" she whispered in alarm.

"That was your friend, the squirrel," Susan whispered back in amusement. "You know, that cute-looking little guy you were so fond of. Don't tell me he scared you?"

"Susan Muir, I don't know how I ever got talked into this."

New headlights were coming up Cedar Creek Road, and Susan readied the monocular, waiting for a vehicle to drive through the gate. But the engine noise indicated it wasn't slowing down, and she watched in surprise as the car continued on and turned onto the forest service road, starting up the mountain.

Flora was following the headlights with her eyes. "Whoever that is will see our car."

"I know," Susan responded. "I wouldn't have expected anyone to be going up there this time of night."

The flatbed truck was now only about thirty feet away. As they left the trees and entered the clearing, they dropped to the ground and began crawling towards it. Tingling with anxiety, they kept their eyes glued to the back door of the lodge. Sharp pains shot through their hands and knees as they rapidly crawled along the rocky ground. At last they reached the truck, and stood up behind it, the view from the lodge blocked.

They quickly took hold of the tarp and pulled it back to peek under. Flora readied her flashlight, but in the light of the moon, they could make out the black lettering on the big bags. FERTILIZER. Susan had a sharp intake of breath. "Now let's see what else." Keeping an eye on the lodge, they crept to the side of the flatbed and again pulled back the tarp. ACETONE was printed on the fifty-five gallon drums. "I've seen enough," Susan said. "Let's get out of here."

As they crawled back to the cover of the trees, they kept checking over their shoulders for any sign of activity at the lodge. Headlights came sweeping up Cedar Creek Road. "Someone's coming," Flora whispered in a voice filled with panic. "They might drive right up here."

They began making their way faster and faster, frantically trying to reach the trees. Susan turned her head and held the scope to her eye for a moment as she went along. "It's a van," she whispered breathlessly. "And it's driving around the back. They'll see us. C'mon, we have to hurry." She desperately pulled on Flora's arm, trying to make her go faster. Panting from exertion, they fell to the ground in relief as they finally reached the dark grove of spruce trees.

Susan watched through her monocular as the van came to a stop, and two men opened the back door and went inside the lodge. Not daring to take any longer to catch their breath, Susan and Flora began winding their way back through the trees. When they got to the fence, instead of climbing over it, this time they slithered under.

As they began walking back, Susan took another look through the scope, just in time to see the two men come out and get in the van. Tony and the two stocky men who had arrived in the flatbed followed them through the door and piled into the back seat. The van slowly rolled to the out-building, then made a turn and backed in. When the lights came on inside the building, Susan and Flora hurried along their way, anxious to get to the car.

"Well, for once you were wrong," Flora said. "You put me through all that for nothing."

"What do you mean?"

"We risked going to jail to find some fertilizer and acetone. Two ordinary things. Naturally they'd need a lot of fertilizer, and they must plan on doing a lot of painting. Acetone is a paint thinner."

Susan laughed. "Why, Flora Finney! Didn't you know? Fertilizer and acetone are also two main ingredients used in making meth!"

Standing outside the building as the van pulled away, Tony suddenly noticed lights up on the hill. He froze as he saw a car making its way down the mountainside. He called to the men inside. "Get the hell out of there, and lock the place up!"

Johnny and Phil rushed outside, locking the door behind them. "What's up, Boss?"

"Here comes a car. We could be getting a visitor."

The three of them set off at a fast pace towards the lodge, looking over their shoulders at the car driving along behind the ranch. "I bet it's that fucking lieutenant," Tony said venomously. "He might've been up there spying on us."

As they reached the lodge, the car turned down Cedar Creek Road, and they stood outside watching it, surprised when it continued on past the gate. "Follow it!" Tony barked. "See who it is, and get the plate number!"

Johnny and Phil jumped in a pickup and went tearing away. Tony walked to the front porch and puffed nervously on a cigarette while he waited for them to get back. Just as he was lighting another one, the pickup came racing up the road, spitting gravel as it turned into the ranch. Johnny and Phil pulled up to the lodge and sprang out as they came to a stop.

"Not the lieutenant, Boss," Johnny said. "Two babes in a silver Subaru."

"A Subaru?" A flash of sudden understanding lit Tony's face. "A Legacy?"

"Right, Boss," Phil said.

"That nosy bitch!"

"Who is she, Boss?" Johnny ventured.

"Susan Muir, some writer that likes to nose around other people's business. Call Wally and get him to double-check the plate number. And tell him we want it yesterday."

As Johnny and Phil disappeared inside, Tony lit a new cigarette. As if he didn't have enough on his plate, now Susan Muir shows up. He probably made a mistake pissing her off the day she came by, but what was he supposed to do? She wanted to take a look around the place, for Christ's sake. She liked to see new settings for her books, or some shit like that.

Well, whatever she was up to now, she sure was interested in more than seeing a new setting. He had the uneasy feeling she and her friend had left the car up on the hill while she took the look around the Black Diamond Ranch that she wanted so bad. One way or the other, she had to be scared off. He was short-handed right now, but there was someone around who could do it. He went inside and punched in Bruce Fione's cell phone number.

CHAPTER 13

DOMINICK Garcia sat at the bar next to the Sunset Motel, drinking Jack Daniels over ice. Goddamnit, it wasn't even one o'clock yet, and here came the lousy bartender announcing last call. He'd love to punch him out. No matter that there were only three people left in the place. One other guy at the bar, and some crazy-ass idiot over there playing pinball. Ding, ding, ding, ding. He'd love to punch him out, too. It would be fun watching his eyes roll around in his head like fucking pinballs. Then maybe he could have some peace.

The whiskey hadn't done a thing for him. He was still in a rage. Susan Muir had ruined all his plans. His big Saturday night action plans. When he saw her car parked on the mountain, he should have stopped and pushed it over the edge. But instead of taking the chance, he had kept right on driving until he looped back onto Cedar Creek Road. Then he had gotten the hell out of there. He sure didn't need to be seen by Ms. Investigative Reporter.

So she was onto the Black Diamond, and she had gotten in his way. Thanks to her, he had wasted the whole night. While she was having fun doing her little investigation at the ranch, he was sitting in this crappy bar listening to a stupid pinball machine. And without her on the scene, by now he would have found Heidi and had that problem all taken care of. It was too much to take. It was just a goddamn shame how she couldn't be happy unless she was poking around in somebody else's business. He had already hated her for what she did to him in LA. Now he loathed her with an undying passion. As soon as he took care of Heidi, he'd go out to Loon Lake and take care of her. And she'd be out of his life once and for all.

He had two doubles lined up in front of him from the last call. He threw his head back and tossed one down, then took a sip of the other. He grew calmer, and a smile began playing at his lips as he thought of the looming demise of Ms. Susan Muir. He would take his time so he could enjoy her nice slow death. He could hardly wait to watch her suffer. He would savor every moment. He would slip a plastic bag over her head so he could see her face while she struggled for air. Her hair would be disheveled, her eyes bulging, terrified, her mouth agape. He would hold her tight against him while she flailed around, slowly smothering to death.

Oh, yes. Now he had gotten hold of himself. Tonight had only been like a rain delay. Tomorrow night the action would begin again. And when the game was over, Heidi Townsend would be dead. Then would come the oh-so-sweet second game of the double-header.

He knew the She-Devil might come prowling around again out at the ranch tomorrow night, but at least this time she wouldn't be taking him by surprise. He could handle it. What he couldn't handle was waiting another day. This had already taken way too long. And now there was a new factor. If Tony and his guys were making meth out there, Susan Muir could have already found enough evidence to report to the sheriff. For all he knew, the place was about to be busted wide open. Then what would become of Little Miss Orderly? Or, just as bad, what if the sheriff called in the feds, and they put the place under surveillance, trying to catch bigger fish? How would he ever get near the place?

But chances were, nobody would make a move until Monday. So that gave him tomorrow. A day he was going to take advantage of. Nothing was going to stop him this time. One way or the other, he would find Heidi Townsend tomorrow night. Even if the game had to go into extra innings.

After dark tomorrow, he had to take care of one little thing before he went out to the ranch. A definite plan had been hatching in his mind for taking care of the bodies. He knew he had to put them where they couldn't possibly be discovered. Everything was taking so much longer than he had planned, it was making him edgy. Too many people had seen him, and they could ID him later if he became a suspect. And if Heidi Townsend's body was found, and she had called LAPD, he would definitely be a suspect. Especially when Ms. Susan Muir informed the police he had been in town. Then he'd be crucified with fucking DNA. But if there were no bodies, there would be no murder raps, and no murder investigations.

He had decided to take advantage of Loon Lake. He had learned it was almost two thousand feet deep. If he weighted down the bodies and dumped them out far enough, they'd never be found. His plan was to strangle Heidi. Like mother, like daughter. Except if he was lucky enough to find her in one of the out-buildings, this time it would have to be quicker, so she wouldn't have time to scream. Afterwards he'd throw her body into the Ford's trunk and head out to Loon Lake Road.

He was going to borrow Jack and Jocelyn Stone's boat, since they were off having fun at the Cayman's. He had seen the sleek blue runabout moored at their private dock, and was sure it would be easy enough to hot wire. It was so convenient, being as it was in the neighborhood. He could dump Susan's body right in front of her house. He'd leave Heidi's body down the shore, across from the camping spot on Loon Lake Road where he planned to park. Then he'd just have to start up the boat and make two quick stops to pick them up. Easy as pie.

Using the Stones' boat would be much better than renting one, too, because he wouldn't have to leave any kind of a paper trail behind him. Besides, there was less chance of being noticed down at the southern end of the lake. It was the only way to go. And so, on his way to the Black Diamond tomorrow night, he was going to give the hot wiring a try. He needed to plan things so he didn't have any last minute problems. He wanted everything to go smoothly when it was time to take the ladies for a ride.

Late Saturday night Heidi was lying in the corner of the shed crying. She was desolate. The rainbow she had imagined about her father had evaporated into thin air. She had nothing to hope for. She no longer even cared what day it was. After spending hour after hour alone in the dank, sour-smelling shed, time meant nothing to her. It had become endless. Except for the occasional birdsong she could hear through the wall, her only comfort was Jeremy, and she wished fervently the little squirrel would come and snuggle against her.

BLACK DIAMOND

She still had a few small pieces of bread saved for him. Late in the afternoon, she had finally received two more sandwiches. She had been miserably hungry, and had spent the day anxiously waiting for someone to bring her food. At last she had heard the sound of footsteps. Her terrible hunger overrode her fear, and her heart leaped. Butch opened the door and wordlessly tossed two foil-wrapped sandwiches on the floor, not even leaving any water.

She had eagerly gulped down half of one, then forced herself to save the rest. Before she put the sandwiches away, she broke off a piece of bread for Jeremy. The squirrel had come back twice that day, and she had used up her bits of bread, trying to coax him to her. Although he still hadn't come near, each time he had come closer and closer.

She tore off a little square of foil to wrap his bread in, so she could get it out without having to look at the sandwiches. It was becoming almost impossible to resist eating them all at once. Then she had sat down and anxiously waited for the squirrel to come. Hours passed before he appeared and scrambled down the wall. When he reached the floor, he made his usual little chattering sounds as he jerked his head back and forth, checking for signs of danger.

After long seconds, he scampered toward Heidi and found the bit of bread she tossed towards him. He hunkered down and eagerly ate it up. Then he sat staring at her while she talked to him in her low, soothing voice. She threw out another piece of bread, a little nearer to her. Jeremy blinked a few times, then scampered over to it. Heidi's heart surged with joy. Now he was only a few feet away. He was getting used to her. She yearned with all her heart to hold the little living creature, so warm and soft and loveable.

Her pulse racing, Heidi reached out and put a piece of bread at arm's length. She held her breath as the little squirrel sat looking at her warily. She began talking to him again in her warm, kind voice. He answered with a burst of chatter, moving his head from side to side as he thought it over. At last he shook his tail and blinked, then scurried away.

Heidi's heart fell. Although she was filled with disappointment, she told herself she had to be patient. She knew it would take time for her to earn the squirrel's trust. Then her heart lifted again as Jeremy began scampering around the shed, instead of climbing straight back up to his exit the way he usually did. Heidi watched him happily, delighted to have his company.

Right after Jeremy finally left, Heidi had gotten her hopes up that someone was coming to rescue her. She had heard muffled voices through the siding. When she pressed her ear to the wall, she made out the sound of two women, talking in undertones. Her heart had begun pumping fast. She felt sure they were looking for her. She tried and tried to make herself call to them through the wall to let them know she was there, but she kept losing her nerve.

That morning Heidi had been terrified. Tony had come to see her, mad as a charging bull, threatening her. He had stormed in and stood towering over her, shaking with fury. When he talked, spittle sprayed from his mouth. He knew she was a fucking liar. He knew she had called the police. If someone came nosing around looking for her, and she made a sound, she was dead. Her father had sent Tony to tell her they weren't playing games. And so Heidi had sadly realized how foolish she had been to ever let herself imagine her father cared about her at all.

Even though she thought the police must be looking for her, Heidi didn't have the feeling these women were connected with them. Nor did she have any idea who they could be. The only women she had ever noticed around the ranch were the ones that came to see Tony. They had brassy voices and fancy swept-up hairdos, and wore spike heels with their leather miniskirts. Heidi had seen enough women on Hollywood Boulevard to recognize them for what they were. And they would hardly be out at night walking around a ranch.

She heard one of the women outside the shed let out a little shriek. She was pretty sure Jeremy had startled her. If only Jeremy could talk to them! If only he could somehow tell them she was being held captive inside the shed! But he couldn't. Heidi had to help herself. She would knock on the wall and call to them. She determinedly clenched her hand and pulled it back to pound against the wall. But an image of Tony's dark furious face and the sound of his threatening words shot through her mind, and she remained silent and let her hand fall. She was too afraid.

Then she thought anew about how the women would free her. Tony wouldn't be able to hurt her. She'd be gone. Once more she pulled her hand back to pound on the wall, but then again slowly let it drop back to her side. She just couldn't do it. And then she had stood despondently listening to their voices trail away. She had lost her chance to get out.

For a long time, Heidi had kept her ear pressed to the wall, hoping the two women would come back. The more she had thought about it, the sorrier she had become that she hadn't called to them in some way. She was sure they were two good people who would have found a way to get her out. She should have acted on her instincts and taken the risk. She should never have let Tony get her so beaten down and scared. She was ashamed of herself.

Then she had fallen onto her blanket and begun sobbing. She was so miserable and lonely she thought she couldn't bear it. She was sure if she didn't get out of the shed, she was going to die. When her tears finally stopped, she resolutely made up her mind if she got another chance to escape, the next time she would have the courage to act.

On Sunday afternoon, Susan was in the kitchen humming to herself as she rolled her cheese mixture into balls. After deciding what to have for *hors d'oeuvres* when Charlie came by later for drinks, she had made a quick trip to the grocery for Roquefort cheese, avocados, fresh tomatoes, and scallions. While she had worked on *Blood Money* that morning, as hard as she had tried to keep her concentration, the evening that lay ahead kept creeping into her mind. By the time she closed down her computer, she had written six new pages and settled on making nut cheese balls and guacamole.

Other thoughts had also intervened with her writing. Vivid images of Flora and her scouting out the Black Diamond the night before kept running through her mind. She had decided to talk things over with Charlie that evening, and wait until Monday to contact the sheriff. Then too, she wondered if Charlie had made any progress at all towards finding Heidi.

BLACK DIAMOND

She had called his hotel at nine o'clock that morning with the intention of offering her help, but found he had already left.

As Susan began peeling the avocados, she smiled to herself, thinking that her late Friday night housecleaning had served a dual purpose. The house needed no attention at all, and that gave her time for a long walk along the lake with Fritz. She was looking forward to clearing her head with some leisurely exercise under blue sunny skies. When she returned, she would shower, put on her black sheath and a strand of pearls, set out the *hors d'oeuvres*, give Flora a call, and sit on the porch to eagerly await the arrival of Lieutenant Charlie Martin.

Three hours later, her heart leaped as she watched him turn off the road and pull into the driveway, parking next to her Subaru. She raced down the steps and welcomed him with a dazzling smile. "You're right on time," she said as he got out and gave Fritz a friendly pat. "You must be good at following directions."

"No, you're good at giving directions," he countered, his beaming smile matching hers. "Some place you have here," he added, as he picked up a stick and threw it for Fritz.

"Thank you. I do love it here," Susan answered. "I haven't missed the hustle and bustle of LA yet."

When they went inside, Charlie looked around admiringly, particularly noticing the grand piano. At Susan's urging, he sat down on the bench and played a short piece he had written. Susan sat listening with great pleasure, entranced with the harmonious chord transitions. She mentally compared his music to Richard's rock and roll songs he had pounded out on the same piano. While both kinds of music were entertaining,

Susan recognized that Charlie's piece had more depth.

As she watched Charlie with his back hunched over the keyboard in quiet concentration, she remembered the jerky movements of Richard's shoulders, his back in constant motion, the unruly red hair flying as he vigorously shook his head in time to the rhythm. While she sat looking at Charlie in his dress shirt, tie, and tweed jacket, she smiled to herself, thinking of the difference in Richard's flashy, sequined outfits. Susan began wondering how things were going for Richard in LA. She hoped they were going well.

Charlie declined an encore, offering instead to mix the drinks. He followed Susan into the kitchen and looked over the well-stocked bar. Susan agreed to join him in a martini, and he expertly mixed up a pitcherful, adding it to the tray she had assembled. Enthusiastically approving of Susan's suggestion, he carried the tray to the front deck as she opened the door and led the way. He poured them each a drink, and they seated themselves on the comfortable wicker chairs and looked out at the lake. Susan was amused at how Fritz curled up by Charlie's foot.

"Well, did you have any luck this weekend?" she began.

Charlie flashed her a boyish grin. "When I'm sitting here with a beautiful woman, overlooking a beautiful lake, on a beautiful evening, with a beautiful trayful of *hors d'oeuvres* in front of me, and a very dry martini in my hand, why would you ask me a crazy question like that?"

Susan grinned back. "I meant on other fronts."

"Well, I did find out that our Daniel Gallo probably rented a brown Ford Escort at Speedy Rentals on Thursday morning. But if it was him, he's now going by the name John

Grenco. It was the only car rental to someone with a California driver's license that day. Which I take to mean, Dominick Garcia, now alias John Grenco, is still prowling around Marble Point. But so far the patrolman hasn't been able to trace him any further. Garcia probably checked into a motel under another name, as though he didn't have a car."

Susan sat listening in interest. "Well, when you get his picture tomorrow, it will be very helpful. Any leads about Heidi?"

"Not really. But I got a lot of places eliminated. Heidi Townsend is not staying in a hotel, a motel, a boarding house, the YWCA, a trailer court, or a campground. No one recognized her picture at the gas stations, movie theater, pizza parlor, video arcade, drugstore, grocery store, or any other place that's open on the weekend."

"You must be beat," Susan responded.

"Beat, maybe, but not beaten down. These things always take time and patience," Charlie answered. "Speaking of patience," he added, "mine pretty much ran out yesterday with one of your local people. I wanted to clean his clock."

"Who's that?" Susan asked with interest.

"Tony Rizzo, out at the Black Diamond Ranch. Ever have the pleasure of meeting him?"

Susan sat straight up in the chair, her eyes widening. "You're kidding! You went out to the Black Diamond yesterday?"

"Why do you say it like that?" Charlie asked in a puzzled voice.

Susan's lips turned up in a smile. "Because that's where I was last night."

"Now you're kidding!" Charlie sputtered. "Okay, who tells who first?"

As Charlie kept their glasses full from the pitcher, they exchanged their stories about the ranch. Charlie knotted up his eyebrows in concern as Susan told him about their nighttime adventure. "You can't be putting yourself in that kind of danger!" he protested.

"You sound like my father," Susan answered with a laugh. "I've been glad lately that he's halfway across the world, so I wouldn't have to hear that!"

"But your father's right!" Charlie pressed on. "You could've been killed. Those guys don't play around. Promise me you won't go back."

"I can do that, at least for now," Susan said. "I think we got the evidence we needed to set things in motion."

"And I'm paying them another visit," Charlie told her. "I'm waiting to catch them off guard."

As they sat talking, Susan still refrained from mentioning the break-in on Friday night. Now she felt certain he would insist on staying with her. She smiled to herself, admitting that, although she prided herself on her independence, she found his concern endearing and comforting.

When it approached seven o'clock, they carried the tray inside and prepared to leave. Susan was glad to see the guacamole was nearly gone, and only one cheese ball remained. It seemed to be a testimonial that Charlie's enthusiastic compliments had been sincere.

After they bade Fritz farewell, Susan slipped into a short-cropped brocade jacket and they left for the Marble Point Inn. During the drive, they engaged in light conversation, and Susan remarked on points of interest along the way. Promptly at seven, they arrived at the inn's dining room and were ushered to their reserved table by the window overlooking Marble Lake. The softly lit room had the same cozy, yet elegant, ambience as the main lobby, with a large plate glass window extending the full length of the lakeside wall.

"What a view!" Charlie said as he peered out the window. He looked across the table at Susan and smiled. "But I guess a lake view isn't quite as special to you."

Susan laughed. "Oh, but it is. Anyway, although I do think Loon Lake is beautiful, Marble Lake definitely has a charm all its own."

Susan caught a fair-haired, pleasant faced man waving to her from a few tables away. "That's Casey Drews, the undersheriff," she told Charlie as she waved back. "A really nice guy. We were in the same class all through school. I wonder why he's eating alone," she added.

Without consulting the menus, they both ordered the Sunday night special. "Do you think we should have a bottle of wine for our reunion?" Charlie asked with a smile. "After our martinis?"

"Why not?" Susan answered, smiling back. "It's definitely a special occasion. And, in case you haven't found out yet, their house wine is wonderful."

Before long, a smiling waiter appeared at their table, presenting a fine bottle of aromatic red wine. Two warm plates of juicy pot roast served with roasted potatoes, carrots, and onions soon followed, along with a mixed green salad and fresh homemade rolls.

During the meal they steered their conversation away from serious subjects, touching upon their families and childhood. They listened to each other intently as they told interesting stories about their pasts, laughing together over humorous escapades. When their plates were cleared, and the dessert and coffee ordered, Charlie sat back in eager anticipation. "Here comes the moment I've been waiting for," he said with his usual grin.

Soon his slice of apple pie was before him and he picked up his fork with a flourish to take the first bite. "Are you joining me?" he asked Susan, holding his fork in midair.

"Not yet," she answered. "I want to devote my full attention to watching you. As a writer, I'm interested in human reactions."

Charlie put the first forkful in his mouth, chewing it slowly, savoring the tart apple flavor and flaky crust. He leaned back, closed his eyes, and sighed with pleasure. "A pie to kill for," he pronounced.

"That would make a good book title," Susan commented in amusement.

When the meal was over, Charlie decided against a second piece of pie and excused himself to go up to his room to make a quick phone call. Susan assured him she didn't mind at all, and settled back with a fresh cup of coffee. It was just then that Casey Drews got up to leave, and he walked over to Susan's table, seeing she was alone. "Susan, I've been wanting to tell you how sorry I was to get your call on Friday night. It's just terrible there was an intruder in your house."

"Intruders," Susan corrected.

Casey Drews looked taken aback. "Right," he said.

Susan saw the flicker of confusion in his eyes. "Casey, what aren't you telling me?"

"Please forgive me. I obviously spoke out of turn. I never should have brought the subject up." Casey nervously shifted on his feet.

Susan invited him to sit down and he slid into the chair next to hers. "Casey Drews," she said, "what's going on?"

"Susan, I'm sure Wally had every good reason to tell you it was the same two culprits that were involved in the other break-ins. The prints matched all right, but there was only one set of them. The sheriff must not have wanted you to worry. I guess somehow one person seems much more personal, so it might be a little scarier."

"Actually it is," Susan agreed, her mind spinning. "Where's Lorene tonight?" she asked, wanting to change the subject.

Casey smiled. "She bailed out on me at the last second, and I had my heart set on the Sunday night pot roast." His face took on a serious look as he got up to leave. "Susan, I know Wally is taking good care of you, but if there's any way I can help, please give me a call."

When he left, Susan's eyes took on a distant look as she stared out the window thinking. So her break-in was not the same as the others that had been plaguing Marble Point. There had been a lone person in her house, playing her CD's, drinking her beer, going through her drawers, using her bed. Very likely a man. Who would do such a depraved thing? Was it someone who knew her? Was it someone crazily attracted to her? Was it someone she even knew?

The questions triggered her memory of Bruce Fione's unwanted advances the night she and Flora went to the Blue Moon. She thought of the sexual way he had looked at her with his dark, long-lashed, mocking eyes, chilling her to the bone. She remembered his tiny pupils, likely drug induced. She had known then he could be dangerous. Susan's mind raced on. If it was him, why wasn't his partner with him on Friday night? A woman in all probability, since they had used a bed every time. But this time only one person had been in her bed. Why would that be? She gasped. If it had been Bruce Fione, maybe in his drug-crazed mind, Susan had been his fantasy partner.

Shaken at the thought, Susan knew she had to compose herself before Charlie returned, or he would realize she was upset. She wasn't going to let anything spoil the evening. Here he came now! Susan's heart melted at the sight of him, and a natural smile returned to her lips. She watched him cross the dining room in long, sure strides, with a confident set to his shoulders. As he neared their table, he grinned at her and quickened his step. Oh, how she had fallen for this man!

CHAPTER 14

DOMINICK Garcia stepped out of the shower at the Sunset Motel on Sunday evening and toweled off in disgust. The goddamn towel felt like sandpaper, and it wasn't even big enough for a fucking pygmy. At least he had washed away the effects of another wasted day. He had woken up that morning with a killer hangover and an aching back from the crap-piece mattress. He had finally pulled himself out of bed and moved unsteadily into the bathroom to swallow a few aspirins.

His lousy room didn't have a coffeepot, so he had to suffer through making a trip to the lobby to get some. Averting his head to avoid eye contact with his fellow human beings, he passed through the hallway to the coffee bar, filled a couple of Styrofoam cups, and carried them back to his room. While he drank them down, he sat staring at the TV, flipping channels. Nothing but shit. Fifty-two channels of fucking shit. He punched the power off and threw the remote at the wall.

He knew he should get going, but damnit, he needed more time to recover. Pocketing his room key again, he headed back to the lobby for more of their crap coffee.

This time he walked over to buy a newspaper. For God's sake, now the newspaper dispenser was empty. Everything about this place was shit. He looked around and found an abandoned copy of the *Marble Point News* on a table, and took it with him.

When he got back to his room, he sat down with the coffee and started leafing through the small local paper. Oh, how quaint. In two weeks the Sportsmen's Association was sponsoring their annual regatta on Marble Lake...sailboat races...fishing contests for the kids...band in the lakeside pavilion for dancing...special fireworks display... oh, so fun. Especially the fireworks. Too bad he wasn't going to be here. He'd be happy to put on a special fireworks display for them. But not the kind they were expecting. He'd blow up the whole goddamn town and wipe it off the map.

Oh, the quaintness just wouldn't quit. Now there was an ad for the Marble Point Inn's local favorite, Sunday night pot roast. Accompanied by their famous homemade apple pie. Damnit, if that didn't sound good. He hadn't had a decent meal since he got here. Always grabbing crap food on the run. Burgers, tacos, pizza, greasy chicken and jo-jos. Now that he thought about it, no wonder he felt lousy. He couldn't eat a bite of anything yet, but by tonight he'd be ready. And a good hot meal would give him extra stamina for his long-awaited, oh-so-sweet action night. Somewhat cheered by the idea, in the late morning Garcia had pulled on his clothes, stuffed a bottle in his pocket, and headed up to his spot on the mountain.

Not much had happened. The usual pattern, except he hadn't seen any of the teenagers. Maybe they had the weekend off. No sign of Heidi again, but his instincts still told him she was there. By now he was burning to take a look in that building they were forever going in and out of. He knew something illegal was going on.

Even if Garcia found Heidi on his own, the more he thought about it, Tony Rizzo was going to pay for the way he had treated him. Instead of making it easy by turning Heidi over, he had forced Garcia to camp out day after day on that goddamn mountain. And it had all been for nothing. He couldn't wait to get even. That would be his last item of business before he left town.

Now it was almost six-thirty in the evening, dinnertime. Then action time. Garcia dropped the towel on the floor and pulled on his clothes, strapping on a leg holster under his loose fitting black chinos. As he buttoned his dark polo shirt, he began making a mental inventory of what he needed to take with him. The two plastic bags were already in the trunk of the car. He had his burglary tools, an extra clip for his Beretta, a small flashlight, and a Swiss army knife.

In case he had trouble with Ms. Muir's door locks, he also had a glasscutter and a suction cup, so he could easily get through a window. He was prepared for whatever might come up during the evening ahead. Right now he was going to eat. He had gotten hungry, and he couldn't wait to sit down to a pot roast dinner and a slice of apple pie.

Garcia's adrenaline was pumping as he left the motel by the back door and climbed into his Ford Escort. At last he was setting out to get the job done. Before the night was over, there would be two bodies at the bottom of Loon Lake. Then he could finally have some peace. He could hardly wait to get going. As he drove towards downtown Marble Point, he checked the time on his dashboard clock. 6:48. Oh, so perfect. By the time he had dinner, it would be dark, and the action would begin.

Just before seven, Garcia spotted someone vacating a parking spot in front of the Marble Point Inn. He sped along the busy block to claim it, smiling to himself. What were the odds of someone pulling out of this prime spot the same second he wanted to pull in? Luck was with him tonight. While he was maneuvering in, a white Chevy Caprice drove past and turned into the hotel's parking lot for registered guests. Just as he got the car parked, a couple alighted from the Caprice and started across the parking lot.

Garcia's jaw dropped open in shock. Susan Muir and Lieutenant Charlie Martin from LAPD Internal Affairs were walking arm in arm toward the entrance of the hotel. Charlie Martin, the son of a bitch do-gooder all the cops hated. The knight in shining armor out to save the world. Mr. Clean, always nosing around looking for dirt. He'd love to shove his nose right into a pile of shit, and let him smother to death in it. Now the two of them were laughing together as they went through the door. It couldn't be. This wasn't happening. Garcia began hyperventilating.

As he pulled back out of the spot and drove away, his mind was spinning wildly. What was going on? How had those two teamed up? Little Miss Orderly must have called LAPD, but why the hell was IA in on it? He had always known he could count on Hollywood Homicide to try to keep the whole thing under wraps no matter what happened, but now, sure as shit, that little party was over.

Maybe Martin had already gotten a statement from the little bitch. But Garcia knew that, without her live testimony at the trial, a good lawyer could make mincemeat out of it. His mind started spinning faster and faster. How did Martin know where she was? Maybe Heidi had told the cops, but Garcia didn't think so. She'd still be too afraid he'd find her. But LAPD didn't have caller ID, except on their 911, and she couldn't use that number from Idaho.

His spinning mind sparked with an idea. Maybe Heidi had phoned in without giving her whereabouts. Then Ms. Bitch Investigative Reporter had called her chums at IA to report that Garcia was in Marble Point. It would be easy for them to put two and two together and come up with the answer that he was there to get Heidi. Garcia stiffened. And maybe Susan Muir hadn't been snooping around the Black Diamond looking for drugs like he thought. Maybe somehow she knew Heidi was there, and was trying to find her. Damnit to hell. Well, there was no use wasting time thinking about it.

Garcia yanked out his bottle and took a long swallow, then worked it back into his pocket. He couldn't get drunk. Not now. He couldn't fail tonight. It was more important than ever to get the job done. There was a good chance Martin hadn't found Heidi yet, and he could beat him to it. It was beginning to look like Tony had her hidden away out there pretty well for some reason, probably because he didn't want involved with the cops.

And, as far as his other problem, if Susan Muir was at the bottom of the lake, she could never testify in court that she had seen Dominick Garcia in Marble Point. If they tried to bring anything else into the trial about her seeing him in town, it would be secondhand evidence, and a good lawyer would rip it to shreds. Oh, he'd get out of this. He just had to hurry.

So he had been lucky getting that parking spot after all. Now he knew Ms. Muir wasn't home, so he could pay a call. He'd get things set up for tonight. It would make it much easier when the time came. When he finished up there, it would be getting dark and he could try out the hot wiring of her neighbor's boat. He'd just grab one final crap hamburger to eat on the way. While that bitch was sitting in the plush Marble Point Inn dining room with her chum Martin, forking down a juicy pot roast dinner. Damnit, it was hard to take. He pulled his bottle back out and took another swig. It was all right. Let her have her fucking pot roast. She was entitled to have a last meal of her choice.

On Sunday night someone else was also waiting for darkness to fall. Bruce Fione was finally getting the big break he had been waiting for. Tony had told him if he got a certain matter taken care of, and didn't fuck up, he'd put him on full time. And it would be a piece of cake. All he had to do was scare off Susan Muir, and make sure she didn't go snooping around the ranch anymore. It was a shame to scare the pretty lady, but it had to be done.

And in a way, he was doing it for both of them. Working for Tony full time would mean having the money to buy her nice things when they started seeing each other. Flowers and candy and good wine. The kind of things a classy woman like her expected. Of course he hated to upset her. But that would work out good, too. Since he already knew she'd be upset by his telephone message, he could drop by and comfort her. And he didn't have to worry at all that she'd recognize his voice on the phone. He had used his small electronic device that disguised voices many times before.

 He'd go back to her house that night on his cycle and tell her he just happened to be taking a ride around the lake, and stopped to see her. He was sure she'd welcome his company then. She would tell him all about her tires being slashed, and how the phone call scared her. Her eyes would fill with tears, and her voice would tremble. He would take her in his arms and hold her close to him. His strong muscular body would make her feel safe. His breathing became heavy as he imagined what would follow.

 He jumped out of his chair. All that would come later. First he had to take care of business. He went to the cracker tin in his kitchen cupboard and got his packet of meth. Damn, he was almost out, and he was afraid Laura's supply might be temporarily shut down. She had called him last night from Sand Cove, a town about twenty miles away. Tony had put her up in a motel, with orders to stay away from the Black Diamond till further notice. Two others were with her, and none of them knew what was going on.

 Bruce could tell right away that something was wrong when he went out to the ranch the night before. Tony had lost his cool, and was totally strung out. Of course he was really set off about Susan Muir nosing around the place, but Bruce had the idea it was a lot more than that. He wondered if the cops were there looking for Heidi. He knew something was up, the way they were keeping her locked in the tool shed. But Tony would handle it. He always did.

He carried some meth into the living room and sprinkled it on his glass table, lining it up with a playing card. He fished a twenty out of his wallet, rolled it up, and took a snort. Sweet Jesus, it felt good. Tomorrow night he'd be able to smoke a whole pipeful. He had a special adventure lined up, and Laura had assured him she'd be handing over her usual ticket.

Last week when he was out on the North Fork servicing the Jensens' spa, they were all excited when two tickets for the Monday night Spokane Indians game arrived in the mail. A surprise present from their son. A nice present for Mom and Dad, but even a nicer present for Bruce and Laura. Game time was seven-thirty, and Spokane was almost an hour's drive, so he and Laura would be safe till eleven. They'd have a blast.

The Jensens' place was utterly fantastic. It was no wonder it was featured every year in the annual Marble Point springtime open-house gala. And their deluxe outdoor hot tub was set in lush surroundings, overlooking the waterfall at the bend of Stony River. It would be an incredible night. And while they were there, they could help themselves to Mr. Jensen's rare gold coin collection he'd read about in the paper. It would be worth a fortune.

Bruce flattened out the twenty and returned it to his wallet. Now he was ready to go. He ran his hand over the bulge in his jeans pocket, checking to see if his jack-

BLACK DIAMOND

knife was there. It was there all right, and it felt good. The little tool that would get him into the big time. He hoped slashing Susan's tires would be enough to scare her off. He didn't want to be too hard on her, when he cared for her so much. But if it became necessary, he had plenty of other plans.

As he turned onto Loon Lake Road, Garcia took the last bite of his hamburger, then crumpled up the wrapper and tossed it out the car window. His excitement about the night ahead was building. He gave the engine more gas and sped along the eastern shore toward the camping spot where he planned to park. Great little place, never anyone around. He knew in the summer, it would be a different story.

When he reached the southern shore, Garcia took a drive past the Stones' to make sure no one was home. No lights, no sign of activity. Reassured, he doubled back to the camping spot and parked. As he made his way toward Susan's, he mostly stayed low and kept to the trees and shrubbery that lined the road, staying on guard for a random vehicle or an evening jogger. In time he reached Susan's fence and went through the gate, going around to the front of the house where there was less chance of being seen.

Thinking he'd start by checking out the lock on the front door, Garcia climbed up the steps. Oh no. A goddamn dog started barking inside. Right by the door. Son of a bitch. He had never seen a dog out in her yard. Garcia abandoned the front door and tiptoed around the deck. Damnit to hell, now the dog was barking by the side door. The little bastard.

But maybe he wasn't so little. Maybe he was big and vicious.

Garcia clenched his teeth in anger. Why couldn't something go right? Why was he having all these problems? Garcia moved away from the side door and crept around back, hoping the dog would think he had left. Then he'd shut up his goddamn barking. It was driving him crazy. This time the dog beat him to it, and was already barking by the back door when Garcia got there.

Garcia automatically felt for the bottle of whiskey in his pocket. No, he couldn't drink yet. He didn't want any problems later on. He had to figure out what to do about the damn dog. If he started barking like that tonight, Susan Bitch Muir would have the cops called before he ever got through the door. He had to find another way to get in.

Garcia went down the steps and began circling the house. After a few yards, he stopped in his tracks and smiled. The basement window was the answer. And there was hardly any chance at all it would be noticed from the inside. He walked over and stooped down to examine it, framing his eyes with his hands as he peered through. Beautiful. Easy drop to the floor, and over near the wall were the steps that led upstairs. And, best of all, the fucking dog had stopped barking. Tonight he'd be able to take him by surprise, and get him good with his pepper spray. Then he'd kick him in the head, right behind his ears. That would take care of him.

Garcia pulled out his whiskey and took a long swallow. Now he deserved a drink for solving his little problem. He returned the bottle to his pocket and looked up at the sky. The light was already fading, and it would be dark in fifteen minutes or so. Instead of getting the glass-cutter from his car now, he'd bring it with him tonight. That would be better anyway. Then there would be no chance at all the broken window would be noticed. It would only take him a few minutes to do. He just had to attach the suction cup to the window pane, cut a little square, and pull out the section of glass. And then reach in and unlock it. Easy as pie.

He could start over to the Stones' dock right now to check out the hot wiring. He didn't have to really worry about being seen. This end of the lake was always deserted anyway. He walked down to the water and started along the shoreline. The cool, moist air coming off the lake was invigorating, and he picked up his step. In five minutes he was at the Stones' dock, ready to go. The night was so quiet and still, he noticed the sound of his own breathing as he stood looking over the boat.

He reached under the dash and took hold of two wires leading to the ignition. He yanked them and shorted them out to engage the engine, feeding it some gas. Vroom, vroom, vroom, vroom. Beautiful sound. He shut the engine off again. No problem here. He deserved another drink. He pulled out the whiskey bottle, tipped back his head, and took a long drink. Vroom, vroom, vroom. What was that? He stuffed the bottle in his pocket, and listened hard. Vroom, vroom, vroom. Louder now. But it wasn't the boat engine.

Garcia snapped to attention as a single light cut through the darkness. A motorcycle was coming down Loon Lake Road. He hunkered down low and remained stock still, his eyes following the headlight on the roaring motorcycle as it continued on down the road. When the cycle reached the western side of the lake, it stopped, and its lights went out. What the hell? Why would anyone stop there?

Garcia jumped up, remembering the thick patch of bushes at the corner of the road. A good place to hide a cycle. Then his mind tumbled to the motorcycle driver who had pulled up to the Black Diamond a couple of days ago. And Ms. Investigative Reporter had been nosing around out there last night. Maybe Garcia wasn't the only one paying her a call.

He sprang up and started back along the beach. There wasn't any cover, so he played the part of someone out for a nightly jog. He was panting heavily when he neared Susan's yard. Seeing no signs of anyone, he kept up his jogging pace as he rounded the house. The loud sound of hissing air fell upon his ears as he reached the driveway.

A shadowy figure was crouched down, making his way around the back of Susan's Subaru. Garcia saw the gleam of a knife. Now the figure was thrusting the knife into the rear tire. More hissing air. Garcia watched him move cat-like to the front of the car. The vandal pulled his arm back and struck hard, slashing through the tire. Garcia sprang at him from behind, encircling his throat with his arm. "Who the fuck are you?"

"Bruce." It came out like a gurgle.

"Bruce Who, fuckhead?"

"Bruce Fione." He was close to strangling.

"Drop the knife."

The jackknife fell to the driveway with a tinny thud. Garcia stretched down to pick it up, then snapped it shut and dropped it in his pocket. "Now I'm going to let up on you just enough for you to tell me exactly what's going on." Garcia's voice was edged with steel. "Turn around and look at me, and if you make one move, you're dead. This is a Beretta .25 you feel on your head. Got it?"

"Yeeesss."

As Bruce turned around and faced him, Garcia recognized the driver of the motorcycle he had seen at the Black Diamond. So he had been right. "What are you up to, fuckhead? You know you could get jail time for this?"

Bruce's eyes widened. "Are you a cop?"

"Yeah, I'm a cop. How did you ever guess?"

"I was just following orders from my boss. He told me to scare her off."

"Does your boss happen to be named Tony?"

Bruce's eyes popped wide open. "How did you know?"

"I know a lot of things. For instance, I know Susan Muir was nosing around the Black Diamond last night. That's why you're here, and that's why I'm here."

Bruce's mind was racing. He couldn't keep up. He never should've had any meth before he came. He knew it screwed up his head.

"Now I'm going to ask you a few questions, so let's get something straight. I'm not playing games. And I'm not a nice cop. You don't want to piss me off."

Now Bruce's body was jerking in nervous spasms. "Tony will kill me."

"I think you should remember there's a Beretta pressed to your head at this moment in time." Garcia jammed the gun with more force. "Is there a big meth operation going on at the Black Diamond?"

"Yeah."

"Is the meth distributed across state lines?"

"Yeah."

"Tell me more."

Bruce's words came flooding out. "I don't know nothing else. I'm not in the inner circle. I'm just a part-timer. You gotta believe me."

"You better hope I believe you," Garcia said in his steely voice. "One more thing. Where's Heidi Townsend?"

As Bruce hesitated, he felt intense pressure from the gun, then heard the safety click.

"Locked in the tool shed."

"Now we're talking business," Garcia said. "We need to go somewhere. Do you know the bar out on the strip, Joe's Place?"

"Yeah. I've been there a few times."

Garcia patted him down for a gun. "Okay. Get your ass on that cycle and take off. No stops along the way. I'll be following you."

"Whatever you say," Bruce said in relief as Garcia shoved the Beretta back into its holster.

"If you try to pull anything, you know I'll have to let Tony know right away what a bad boy you were telling on him."

"Yeah, I know," Bruce answered. "Don't worry, I'll stay with you."

"That would be a smart move on your part for a couple of reasons. Short term, I don't think Tony will be real happy with you. Long term, he's going to get busted wide open on a federal rap. If you work with me, when it comes down, I'll cut you a deal."

Bruce's eyes were darting around in his head as he tried to figure out what was happening. "Are you with the feds?"

"That's right, fuckhead. Now are you ready to cooperate?"

"I'll do whatever you say."

A half-hour later the two were seated in a booth in the back of the dark bar. A country western singer was droning out a sad story about lost love on the jukebox. Garcia had two double Johnny Walkers in front of him, and Bruce had a bottle of beer. "Now let's talk about how we're getting Heidi out of there tonight," Garcia said in a hard voice. "I need to talk to her."

"Tonight's out."

"What the fuck do you mean, tonight's out?" Garcia shot back.

"The place will be crawling with people," Bruce told him. "Four pick-ups scheduled, and the guys are going to be out there all night making meth. That's why they sent me to take care of Susan Muir."

"Fuck that. There's got to be a way."

"It'll never work. The tool shed's not far from the meth lab. Tomorrow will be quiet. All the guys are making out-of state deliveries. Tony's shorthanded right now."

"Why?"

"He sent all the kids somewhere. I guess he knows the heat's on."

Garcia's mind was turning fast. So that's what happened to the teenagers. This guy was telling it straight. "Do you have a key to the shed?"

"No way. I told you, I'm not in the inner circle."

"What kind of a lock's on it?"

"A padlock."

"Beautiful. You can use a bolt cutter. Got one?"

"Yeah."

"Can you get the girl to go with you?"

"Yeah. She knows me. But if she tells Tony I let her out, I'm a dead man."

"She won't be telling Tony anything," Garcia answered. "She won't be going back."

"So what do you want me to do?"

"She knows her father's car, so tell her he got her message and sent a friend to pick her up."

"Okay. But what if she hears me cutting the lock?"

"That's easy. Say that Tony's gone somewhere with the keys, and the guy's in a hurry. She won't question it. She'll jump at the chance to get out of there."

"Sounds good. Then what?"

Dominick took a long, thoughtful swallow. "When you come out of the shed, start walking towards the road. Don't give her a chance to think it through. Remind her the guy's in a hurry. When you get to my car, just open the door and make sure she gets in. Then shut it fast and stand back. I'll take over from there."

"Sounds like a plan," Bruce said, gulping his beer.

Dominick stared at him hard across the table. "But it fucking has to be tomorrow night. I won't wait any longer. I'll be by the back gate at ten o'clock."

Thoughts of his big adventure at the Jensens' flashed through Bruce's mind. Now he needed the gold coin collection more than ever. "Eleven would be better. Less chance of Tony out walking around."

"Okay. Make it fucking eleven. But if you don't show up with the girl at eleven sharp, you'll seriously regret it. And don't make the mistake of thinking I won't find you."

"You can count on me," Bruce assured him, getting up from the booth. "I'll get the job done. I'm working with you now."

Garcia tossed off the rest of his drink as Bruce walked out of the bar. At last he had had some real luck, meeting up with this stupid fucker. Now things were going his way. He liked this plan. It seemed to be foolproof. He just had to wait one more night. He'd stay here now and have a couple more drinks. He'd take care of both of them tomorrow night. Then he could dump them in the lake together, just the way he had it all planned.

CHAPTER 15

THE night was starlit when Susan and Charlie drove home from the Marble Point Inn. Susan's mind was filled with romantic thoughts, and she didn't want the evening to end. As they neared her house, she turned to Charlie, tall and broad-shouldered behind the wheel. "Would you like to come in for a nightcap?"

"I was hoping you'd ask," he answered buoyantly as he pulled into the driveway next to her Subaru. "Uh-oh," he said with a sudden change of voice. "I think you had a visitor."

"What do you mean?" Susan asked in alarm.

"Let me check," Charlie said, jumping out of the car.

Susan hurried out after him as he inspected the Subaru's tires. Under the light from the gas lamps, they could plainly see the tires were flat and they had all been slashed.

Charlie saw that Susan was shaken. "Come on inside," he suggested. "I'll fix you a drink."

After being eagerly greeted by Fritz, they went into the kitchen. Susan noticed the light on her answering machine was blinking. "Do you mind if I check my messages?" she asked Charlie. "It could be my parents. They haven't had e-mail access the past four days. They took an excursion on the Yangtze River in a Chinese sampan."

"Go right ahead," Charlie answered.

Susan went over and pressed the Play button while Charlie poured them each a snifter of brandy. "This message is for Susan Muir," came the husky, masculine voice. "Take a good look at your tires, because that's what's going to happen to your throat if you keep nosing around."

The two of them stood listening in shock. "A messenger from the Black Diamond," Charlie said.

"Right," Susan agreed. "It looks like whoever followed us down Cedar Creek Road Friday night got my license plate number."

"Do you recognize the voice at all?" Charlie asked.

"No. I'll play it again."

Susan's face registered surprise and anger as once more the words rang through the still kitchen. "What a shameful, nasty thing for someone to do," she declared.

"They sure don't know you very well," Charlie commented with a little smile.

"What do you mean?"

"After this, I'm sure you're more determined than ever to nail them, right?"

"Right."

"I'm glad you already promised me you wouldn't go out to the Black Diamond again," Charlie told her. "You do remember, don't you?"

Susan smiled. "Yes, I remember. But anyway, now there's no doubt the sheriff will have enough evidence to get a warrant. I'm glad I decided to wait until Monday morning to tell him about finding the meth materials, and all the suspicious activity out there. I'm sure when Wally comes here tomorrow and sees my tires and hears the message, it will have a real impact. He'll have to act."

They had moved into the living room with their brandies, and Charlie walked over to the hearth. "Would you like a fire?"

"I'd love it," Susan said. "I'll go get a fire starter and some matches."

Using kindling from the hearth basket and four pieces of Tamarack from the built-in wood boxes, Charlie quickly built a fire, then closed the screen and settled onto the couch. Susan was seated in an easy chair across from him. In no time the fire was crackling, and the pleasant smell of wood smoke was drifting into the room. They sat and watched the fire thoughtfully, sipping their brandies.

"Marble Point might not match LA," Susan said. "But you've got to admit, it's an action-packed little town."

"And you've got to admit it wouldn't be fair for you not to let me stay tonight. I'll sleep right here on this comfy couch. Please, be reasonable. Don't make me leave you here alone."

"You mean, you'd really be nice enough to stay?" Susan answered with a smile. "I'd really appreciate it."

"You mean you'll let me?" Charlie sputtered. "I thought you'd throw me out for even suggesting it. I know how independent you are."

"Maybe sometimes. But tonight I'd love to have a strong shoulder to lean on."

Charlie grinned. "Show me."

Susan walked over to the couch and sat down next to him, her head resting against his shoulder. "That feels good," Charlie said. "Just right."

She looked up and smiled into his eyes. "To me, too."

After a time, Susan sat straight up. "I'm going to come clean with you. Someone broke into my house on Friday night." She told him how she had arrived home from the country club to find an intruder inside, relating all the surrounding events of her break-in and all the others. Then she recounted how the sheriff had reported finding the same fingerprints left at the other houses, but that evening by chance Casey Drews had revealed that only one set of those prints had been found in her house.

"That's absolutely terrible," Charlie said, his face set in a deep frown. "You should have told me all this."

"I didn't want to worry you."

"You mean you didn't want me butting in."

"Well, in a way I didn't. But in another way, I did."

"I do understand," Charlie said. "Independence dies hard. But it's a good thing you already agreed I could stay. There's no way you'd get rid of me now. You could be in real danger."

"I'm beginning to have the same feeling," Susan responded. "I'll feel much better with you here. I'll make up the sleeper in the den. It's more comfortable than the couch."

"It's closer to the road, too," Charlie observed.

At that moment, they both sat up in alertness at the sound of a roaring engine. "I'm going to take a look," Charlie said, springing up and heading towards the back of the house.

Susan went along and together they rushed into the unlit den, both kneeling underneath the window to peer out. "It's a motorcycle," Susan commented, as they watched the solitary headlight approaching. As it neared the house, the motorcycle slowed, and the changing direction of the headlight gave the impression it was turning into the driveway. Its dark red color gleamed in the radiance of the gaslights. Then the motorcycle veered back and continued on its westward course down the road.

"Did you get the same idea I did, that he was going to turn into the driveway?" Susan asked.

"Absolutely," Charlie answered. "Until he saw my car. I'm glad the den's in the back of the house. I'll sleep with one ear open."

"Just so you don't sleep with one eye open," Susan said playfully. "You'd look pretty funny. And speaking of sleep, we should probably get some. I know you want to get an early start in the morning."

Turning on the lamps, she removed the cushions from the hide-a-bed and pulled out the mattress, then got bedding from the den closet. Charlie helped put on the sheets and blankets, then piled up several pillows against the back. "Do you mind if I browse through your bookcase?" he asked. "I usually read myself to sleep."

"Please do," Susan told him. "Make yourself completely at home. There are plenty of towels and a spare toothbrush and razor in the bathroom next door. If there's anything else you need, please help yourself, and if you can't find something, call me."

Fritz followed Susan upstairs and settled down in his usual spot outside her door. When she was ready for bed, Susan began to put on the same pajamas she had slept in the night before. Suddenly changing her mind, she pulled on a cotton nightgown patterned with small pink flowers, then opened the window and snuggled under the comforter.

But sleep wouldn't come. Thoughts of Charlie downstairs in the hide-a-bed kept floating through her mind. Did he find a good book? Was he comfortable? Was he awake or asleep? Was he thinking about her? Thoughts of the helmeted motorcycle driver also kept creeping into her mind. She hadn't been able to tell what he looked like. Who was he? Was he the same one who slashed her tires? The same one who did the break-in? Would he come back?

Remembrance of a dark red motorcycle flashed through her head. She had seen a red motorcycle somewhere in the past few days. Where had it been? A shiny red Harley Sportster had caught her eye in a parking lot. She concentrated hard, trying to think back. It had been dark outside. The Blue Moon! She had seen a red motorcycle in the parking lot the night she and Flora went for pizza. She hadn't seen it when they went in, but she noticed it parked by the door when they came out. And Bruce Fione had arrived and left after them. The first thing tomorrow morning, she would find out if he owned a red Harley Sportster.

She wanted to talk to Charlie about it, but she hadn't mentioned her suspicions to him about Bruce, so there was no reason now to tell him about her new revelation. But she wanted to be with him. Maybe she should go down and suggest they have another nightcap. She knew Charlie was too much the gentleman to ever take advantage of the situation that had been created, with him staying over to protect her. She would have to be the one to make a move if anything were to happen. Should she?

She knew the evening might have gone differently if they had arrived home under normal circumstances. She had wanted things between them to proceed naturally, but here he was downstairs, and her up. How natural was that? It actually seemed kind of crazy. They had already lost their opportunity in Los Angeles. Now, miraculously, they were getting a second chance. And it was possible that Charlie would get everything wrapped up in Marble Point in the next day or two, and then he'd be leaving. What should she do? Maybe she'd at least go down and make sure he was comfortable.

She stepped out of bed and shrugged into the pink flannel robe she knew was so becoming to her, with her long auburn hair. When she opened the bedroom door, she was surprised to see that Fritz wasn't outside. He had deserted her for Charlie! She smiled to herself, thinking of the saying: 'Love me, love my dog.' Susan and Charlie had certainly passed that hurdle. Susan had already noticed how Charlie and Fritz displayed great affection for each other.

She went downstairs and entered the den on soft slippered feet. Fritz was curled up on the floor next to the hideaway bed. Charlie, in a white tee shirt, was propped on his pillows, an open book in hand. "So you stole my dog?" she began.

"He felt sorry for me, being all alone," Charlie countered, realizing Susan was giving him an opening.

"And who feels sorry for me being all alone?" Susan responded, putting on a little pretend pout.

'I kind of do," Charlie answered.

"What does that mean?" Susan asked, taken aback.

"It means that I do feel sorry for you, but now it's too late for me to do anything about it."

Susan's face fell, settling into a look of surprise and disappointment. "Well, good night," she said. "I just wanted to make sure you were comfortable."

"Good night," Charlie answered. "I'm sorry you didn't come to get me sooner. But the problem is, I got started on this book, and now I just can't put it down."

"Well, I'm sorry I bothered you," Susan said, walking from the room in embarrassment. As she went through the doorway, she stopped in her tracks and turned, a look of dawning spreading across her face. "What book?"

"*A Time For Murder.*" Charlie flashed her his boyish grin. "It's really good. If you haven't read it yet, you should."

"You monster!" Susan shrieked. "You absolute monster!" She threw herself laughingly on the bed, wrapping her arms around his neck.

In a moment she drew back and looked deep into his eyes. "Since you like the book so much, how would you like to sleep with the author?"

"I would like it very much," Charlie said, taking her in his arms.

The next morning, Susan was humming and Charlie was whistling as they moved about the kitchen preparing breakfast. Wrapped in her pink robe, Susan started a pot of coffee, while Charlie fried some pepper bacon and scrambled eggs with onion, green pepper, and cheese. Susan poured orange juice, and toasted rye sourdough bread with caraway seeds. Fritz was underfoot, attracted by all the cheerful activity and the tantalizing smell of sizzling bacon.

When the coffee was ready, Susan handed Charlie a steaming mug where he was standing by the stove. "Thanks for taking good care of me last night," she said, her face glowing. "I'm already looking forward to tonight."

Charlie grinned. "Me too."

Over breakfast they laid their plans for the day. As soon as Charlie left, Susan was going to put in her call to the sheriff. After he came out, she'd phone the insurance company and the tire shop to get her car taken care of. Charlie was going back to the Marble Point Inn the first thing, to shower and change clothes. He rather apologetically told Susan that although tonight he'd be wearing a different shirt and tie, she could expect to see him in the same tweed jacket, since he hadn't brought another one along. She told him he looked so handsome in it, she was glad it was the only one he had with him.

Charlie was going to get his partner to e-mail a picture of Garcia to his laptop. LAPD didn't have the necessary scanning equipment, but Sergeant Julia Richards, a friend of his in IA, had her own personal scanner in her office, and he was sure she'd lend the use of it for something so important. Then Charlie would take Garcia's picture along when he paid his courtesy call to the sheriff later in the day. Hopefully, the sheriff would be willing to assign a patrolman to show the picture around motels and other establishments Garcia might be frequenting. That would leave Charlie free to concentrate on finding Heidi. He was anxious to cover all the new ground he could. He also planned to pay another call to the Black Diamond.

If Susan needed anything at all, she could reach him on his cell phone. If he had any big break, he would give her a call. Since she would be without a car part of the day, he would bring back two New York strips, makings for a salad, a loaf of French bread, and a bottle of wine. Susan would make them lattes to drink on the front deck, and Charlie would marinate the steaks and barbecue them on the gas grill.

After breakfast Charlie helped Susan clear the table, then she insisted on finishing up. He had more important things to do. When he left, she stood in the doorway watching him pull away, then went inside and called the sheriff's office. Learning that the sheriff would be there in a halfhour, Susan quickly showered and dressed in faded Levis and an emerald green sweater that complemented her light olive skin and lit up her face.

From her bedroom window, she viewed the sheriff's car pulling in, and hurried downstairs. When she opened the back door, she saw the sheriff closely inspecting her tires. "I'm so sorry this happened, Susan," he said, looking up as Fritz ran out the door. "Such a terrible act of vandalism."

"Come on in, Wally," Susan said. "I want you to hear the message on my machine."

"You look wonderful, as usual, Susan," the sheriff said as he reached the door.

"Thank you," Susan answered, closing the door behind him. "We can listen to my machine in the kitchen. Would you like some coffee?"

"You never fail to be thoughtful," the sheriff responded.

"Yes, I certainly would."

Susan poured out two mugs of coffee, and the sheriff sat down at the kitchen table. She went over to her machine and hit the Play button, then joined him at the table to listen. They sat silently looking at each other as the message rang out in the room. Susan watched his face fill with dismay. "Terrible, terrible," he muttered. "Who would do such a dreadful thing?"

"Someone from the Black Diamond Ranch, I'm sure," Susan answered. "That's where I was nosing around, as he put it." She went on to tell him about her surveillance with Flora on Friday night, including the exposure of large quantities of fertilizer and acetone.

"My, my," the sheriff said as they ended their discussion. "You put yourself in such danger, Susan. Why didn't you just report your suspicions to me?"

Susan chuckled. "I must have an undying calling to be an investigative reporter."

"But Susan, you've retired, after all," the sheriff reminded her.

"I guess I was only semi-retired," she answered with a little smile. "Reporter's instinct runs thick in my blood, I think. Originally I went to the ranch to look into it for a friend of mine. I was under the impression it was a guest ranch. Then something about that Tony Rizzo really set me off."

"I know exactly what you mean," the sheriff agreed. "I've been going out there fairly often, keeping an eye on the place. There's been some rumors going around." He leaned back in the chair and gave her a penetrating look. "Now that I think about it, if you were out there Friday night, you probably saw my car coming and going."

"Actually we did," Susan replied. "And we saw another guy show up while you were still there. Then, as soon as you left, Tony made a trip out to what we now know is the meth lab, and the guy left a few minutes later."

"Really?" the sheriff said, stiffening in his chair. "Tony made his apologies to me for cutting my visit short, saying the two of them had a pool game scheduled." He gave Susan a little smile. "He knows I don't play pool, so it looks like it was a convenient excuse to get me out of the way so he could sell some meth. That guy's as cool as a cucumber. It's no wonder I've never been able to catch him at anything."

"So now do you have enough for a search warrant?" Susan asked.

"I'm sure I do, thanks to you. As a member of law enforcement, I couldn't go looking around for evidence. But as a private citizen, you can get away with it. As long as I don't arrest you for trespassing!" he added with a short laugh.

"So you'll move right away on the warrant?" Susan pressed.

"As soon as I get back to the office. When I present this information to Judge Walker, I know he'll cooperate. Evidence found by a citizen is quite valid." He smiled at her. "Of course, even more valid coming from a person as highly esteemed as yourself."

"Well, that's good," Susan said. " The faster everything happens, the better."

"Well now, you do realize it will take time to get the hazardous materials team assembled. And I certainly want the criminalist from the state crime lab to be present during the raid. I want this covered from every angle so it will hold up in court."

Susan saw the logic. "Will you keep me posted on the timetable?"

"Of course. I'll be in contact with you the second the raid is scheduled."

As Susan warmed their coffee, she deliberated about confronting the sheriff with her knowledge that he had found only one set of criminal fingerprints in her house, but finally refrained, reluctant to cast Casey Drews in a bad light. "Any headway on the break-ins?" she asked instead.

"Not yet, I'm sorry to say," the sheriff answered with a serious look. "But we're thoroughly investigating every lead we get, and I'm very sure one will pay off soon. And again, I thank you for your cooperation in the matter."

He gave her a charming smile as he rose to leave. "As I said before, Susan, your commitment to civic duty is admirable. You've been very helpful indeed. I'll be in touch with you soon."

After Susan made arrangements with the tire shop, she turned her attention to the plan she guiltily had withheld from Charlie. She knew he would have insisted on being present, and she didn't want to take away from his time. She knew finding Heidi was his top priority, and she could handle things on her own. She had thought of a way to get Bruce Fione's fingerprints. Then she could stop wondering. She would know once and for all if he had been the intruder in her house.

Putting her plan into motion, she picked up the phone and hit the number for Oasis Spa. She was glad she hadn't called Gus Woodbridge yet to ask him not to send Bruce to her house again for the spa servicing. It made her request easier. She guiltily told Gus a friend of hers had brought her children over for a picnic lunch on the deck, and the youngest one had accidentally spilled a can of pop in the hot tub. Susan would be ever so grateful if he could send Bruce out to service it.

When Gus told her Bruce would be there right after lunch, Susan hung up with an enormous feeling of satisfaction. And the timing was good. The tire shop had promised to have her car done that morning. She wouldn't have relished the idea of Bruce being there when they were changing the tires, because it would be natural for him to comment on it. Which would be odd if he had been the one who slashed them.

Next she put in a call to the Department of Motor Vehicles. Since she was acting only as a private individual, she didn't know if they would tell her whether or not Bruce Fione had a Harley Sportster registered in his name, but she thought she'd give it a try. Twenty minutes later, after punching options, being re-routed, put on hold, and reaching only voice mail, she hung up, seething in frustration. Sensing that Wally had been chiding her about her investigating, she called the undersheriff, Casey Drews, who had offered to help any way he could. She thought if ever she needed help, it was now. If she was put through to someone's voice mail one more time, she was afraid she'd track them down and murder them!

Casey answered the phone, assuring her he would be more than happy to get the information she wanted. He called back within ten minutes to report that indeed a 1993 red Harley Sportster was registered to a Bruce Albert Fione who lived in Marble Point. Susan thanked him and hung up with a feeling of elation and an even greater sense of mission. He had been the one driving past the house last night, no doubt about it. She shuddered at the thought, thankful that Charlie had been with her.

She went purposefully out to the deck and poured a can of pop into the hot tub, smiling to herself as she watched the water cloud up. Then she returned to the kitchen and made a pitcher of lemonade. What the heck? she decided, and threw together a batch of chocolate chip cookies she knew Bruce would find irresistible. And when he picked up the glass of lemonade to wash them down, he would leave his fingerprints on the glass. The same fingerprints he had left all over her house on Friday night.

When Bruce left, she would wrap the glass in a silk scarf and take it to the sheriff for print identification. Her heart skipped a beat. Bruce Fione's fingerprints were going to match the ones found at all the break-ins! Wally would be very happy. She'd let him take full credit for ending the crime wave. She could imagine him on television with his chin-strap hat proudly making the announcement.

At mid-morning, the truck from the tire shop arrived. "A terrible thing to happen," the driver remarked as he slid the hydraulic jack under the car. "But don't worry, we'll get it back in ship-shape for you in no time."

Deciding to go for a walk while he took her wheels to the tire shop, Susan locked up and set off down the road, with Fritz happily accompanying her. When she passed the McCullys' she smiled to herself, betting she would have big news to tell them before long. She could imagine the three of them gathered around their kitchen table talking it over. And they would be getting their silver back! When Wally found out where Bruce had sold it, he'd be able to track it down. Susan smiled. Every bone in her body told her she was right. Bruce Fione's fingerprints on the lemonade glass would be a perfect match with the ones the sheriff had on file from all the break-ins.

When she got home, she freshened her appearance and smiled into the mirror, feeling sure Bruce Fione would find her attractive in her flattering green sweater, and would eagerly comply with all her suggestions. She went downstairs, checked to see if the hot tub was still cloudy, and paid the tire serviceman as he was finishing up. Then she fixed herself a sandwich and took it to the side deck so she could watch for Bruce's arrival, wanting to see if he had a reaction to her new tires.

It wasn't long before Fritz barked at the Oasis Spa truck pulling in, and she hurried to the back of the house and peered around the corner. Bruce got out and quieted Fritz, glancing at her car as he walked past. Then he stopped and took a closer look before he went up the steps. "Hello!" Susan called to him as she walked onto the back porch.

"Hello, Ms. Muir," Bruce said, eyeing her closely. "You look pretty cheerful today. You don't seem upset, or nothing."

"Why would I be upset?" Susan responded.

Bruce's eyes darted, and he ran his tongue over his lips. "I mean, I thought you might be upset the way that kid messed up your hot tub."

"No, no, not at all," Susan said with a chuckle. "Kids

will be kids." She put on a bright smile. "Thank you for coming on such short notice."

"My pleasure, Ms. Muir," Bruce answered. "I'm glad I can help out. I'll have that hot tub fixed up as good as new in no time."

"Well, I'm very grateful," Susan told him. "After you pump the water out and you're waiting for it to refill, come on in the kitchen, so I can show you my appreciation. I bet you'd enjoy a fresh homemade chocolate chip cookie."

Bruce's smile stretched from ear to ear. He couldn't believe this stroke of luck. "That would be great! I'll get things started and be there in a jiffy."

Before long Bruce entered through the kitchen door, leaving Fritz outside. "This is mighty nice of you, Ms. Muir. Especially for a busy lady like yourself."

"Well, I'm just glad to do it. I enjoy my hot tub very much, and I'm thankful I have Oasis Spa to take care of it for me."

"I'm always at your service," Bruce said enthusiastically. "Day or night. I'll be glad to come out any time."

Susan motioned him to a chair at the table, putting the plate of cookies in front of him, next to the empty glass she had carefully placed there. "Help yourself," she said. "I made a pitcher of lemonade, too."

"Oh, wow! You shouldn't have gone to all that trouble."

"It was my pleasure," Susan said, smiling as she poured the lemonade into his glass.

"You look radiant today, Ms. Muir," Bruce ventured as he chomped on a cookie. "Even prettier than usual."

BLACK DIAMOND

"Why, thank you," Susan said, not liking the personal nature of the compliment.

"You look really good in green," Bruce went on. "It goes great with your hair. Your hair is really beautiful," he added, his voice a little hoarse. "I bet it's really soft."

"Wouldn't you like a drink of your lemonade?" Susan asked.

"Oh, I will, Ms. Muir. I love lemonade, and I really appreciate you making it. But first I just want to enjoy the taste of these great cookies. Did you really make them all by yourself?"

Susan nodded mutely, apprehensive about the way things were going. He was giving her the same languorous looks she remembered so well from the last time he was there. His long-lashed eyes were following her every movement, as he leaned back in his chair and chewed on one cookie after another. How could someone eat so many cookies without needing a drink? She never should have put them out. He would have drunk the lemonade and gone back to work. And the fingerprints would have been on the glass waiting for her.

Bruce reached for the plate again. "Did you honestly make these just for me?"

"Yes, and the lemonade too. But you don't seem to like the lemonade."

"Now don't go getting a silly idea like that in your head," Bruce drawled. "I'm just not ready to wash away the good taste of these chocolate chips yet."

He leaned across the table. "Just let me touch your hair."

"No," Susan said sharply, drawing back. "I think it's time for you to get back to work." She stood up from the table.

"Now that's not very nice," Bruce said, standing up with her. "You've been so nice to me today, you must like me. Why won't you let me touch your hair?" He stepped closer, reaching out.

Susan moved back. "Because you're a serviceman, here to do a job."

"But I'm your friendly serviceman," Bruce said, his voice hoarse. "I always like to lend a personal touch."

"I'm not interested in the personal touch," Susan answered, growing more nervous by the second, thinking her idea had been foolhardy. "I just want the job done."

"Don't worry your pretty head," Bruce told her. "The job will be done to your complete satisfaction." He advanced towards her again. "I just want to see if your hair's as soft as it looks. What's the harm in that?" He began lightly panting, his breath hot against her face as he stepped close to her.

"The harm in that is, you're a serviceman here to do a job, and you're not acting like it," Susan said in a rush of stinging words, backing towards the door to let Fritz in. "Especially after I made the cookies and lemonade to show my appreciation. Now why don't you sit down and drink your lemonade?"

"Now, now," Bruce said, following up with a little clucking sound. "I didn't mean to upset you. I was only trying to be friendly."

"Well, you could be friendly by drinking the lemonade I made especially for you," Susan answered, trying hard to turn up her lips in a smile.

"Well, well. You're right about that," Bruce said, pushing back his curly locks. "Will you sit down and join me?"

"Of course," Susan answered, her heart leaping. She

poured herself a glass of lemonade and sat down again at the table. "Cheers!" she said, holding up her glass.

"Cheers!" Bruce repeated, picking up his glass to tap against hers in a toast. He took a long drink. "That is mighty tasty," he declared with enthusiasm.

"Good. And now I have work to do," Susan said, standing up dismissively. "I must bid you good-day. Thank you again for coming. The shed where the chemicals are kept is already unlocked."

As Bruce went out on the deck, Susan double locked the door behind him. After that she went to both other doors and checked the locks. She gingerly picked up the lemonade glass with a cloth and dumped out the ice cubes, then wrapped it in a scarf and slid it into a manila envelope. When she was through, she sat down in the den and waited for Bruce to leave.

CHAPTER 16

IN downtown Marble Point, Charlie was walking into the sheriff's office, a white concrete building across the street from the courthouse. When he went inside, he was greeted by the day desk sergeant. "Lieutenant Charlie Martin, LAPD, here to see Sheriff Woods," he said, showing his badge.

"One moment, Lieutenant," the sergeant said, picking up the phone.

Charlie looked around the lobby while he waited for him to make the call. Through a big plate glass window, he could see the radio control room manned by uniformed dispatchers, and hear the squad car chatter as the police talked back and forth.

"Sheriff Woods will see you right away, Lieutenant," the sergeant told him. He gestured toward the hallway. "Second door on the right."

As Charlie started down the hall, he was met by the sheriff coming through the doorway, with his vigorous, springy step. The sheriff smiled cordially and reached out to shake hands. "Come right in, Lieutenant Martin. I was expecting you. Sergeant Mercereaux told me you were dropping by today." The sheriff led him to a chair and sat down across from him, behind his large desk.

"Sergeant Mercereaux was very helpful to me on Saturday," Charlie began. "I really appreciated the department's cooperation. And the patrolman he assigned did a fine job." He pulled Garcia's picture out of his briefcase. "This is the man we're looking for. Dominick Garcia, a detective sergeant with LAPD, currently under suspension. I only found out he was in town after I arrived Friday evening, and had his picture sent today."

Sheriff Woods stared at the picture, then leaned back in his swivel chair and gave Charlie a broad smile. "I must ask. If you found out Garcia was here only after you arrived, what brought you to our fair town?"

"I came to Marble Point to track down a potential witness in a murder case." Again Charlie reached in his briefcase, this time pulling out Heidi's photo and handing it to him. "A seventeen-year-old by the name of Heidi Townsend. Do you know of her whereabouts by any chance?"

The sheriff's eyes flashed as he looked at the photo. "No, I can't help you there." He continued to study Heidi's picture. "A nice looking girl," he finally commented. "What is she doing in Marble Point?"

"That's still anybody's guess. We traced her call to the phone booth at the Gas 'N Go north of town." Charlie smiled ruefully. "But I must admit, I still haven't made any progress beyond that."

"And you say she's a potential witness in a murder case?" the sheriff probed.

"Yes. She claimed she saw the man who murdered her mother." Charlie held up Garcia's picture again. "This scumbag. And since I've found out he's in town too, I'm afraid she could be in real danger."

"So I see," the sheriff said thoughtfully. "Of course I'll be glad to help any way I can."

"I would be very grateful," Charlie answered. "On Friday night I learned that, under the name of Daniel Gallo, Garcia had checked out of the Wayside Inn Thursday morning. He also turned in his Lincoln Town Car to Avis on the same day. I have every reason to believe he thought he'd been ID'd, so he changed identities and motels. On Saturday your patrolman learned that a brown Ford Escort had been rented to someone with a California driver's license on Thursday morning, a John Grenco. The patrolman checked out all the motels in the area, and had no luck. I presume if Garcia's still in town, as I strongly suspect, he's registered at a place that doesn't require ID, or under another name, with no vehicle of record. If you could assign someone to show his picture around, it would be very helpful."

"Of course I will," the sheriff said heartily. He let out a chuckle. "Everything you see in the movies about small town cops not wanting to cooperate with the big boys from the city is stuff for fiction." He flashed Charlie a charming smile. "At least I can personally guarantee they wouldn't get material for a movie like that in Marble Point, Idaho!"

Leaving Garcia's photo, Charlie rose and the sheriff walked around his desk to shake hands in parting. "It's been a real pleasure meeting you, Lieutenant. I'll have a man assigned to your case right away. We have your phone number, and I promise we'll call immediately about any development."

Charlie smiled. "Thank you very much, Sheriff Woods.

You have been most cooperative."

"If there's anything further I can do to assure your stay in Marble Point is a profitable and pleasant one, please let me know. I'm at your service."

As Charlie was going out the door, the sheriff stopped him with a question. "Lieutenant, forgive me, but my curiosity has gotten the better of me. How did you find out Garcia was in Marble Point?"

"I ran into an old friend of mine from LA who knew him," Charlie answered. "The two of us put it together."

The sheriff smiled. "A lucky break."

"Yes," Charlie said, smiling back. "It turned out to be very lucky."

Charlie walked back to his car with a disquieting feeling. The sheriff was a charmer, no doubt about that. And he had offered his full cooperation. So what was bothering him? The sheriff's comparison with the movies had been apt and colorful, but had he gone overboard to express his spirit of cooperation? In truth, Charlie often ran into attitude problems with small police forces in other jurisdictions, but this guy had come on as the champion of teamwork. Almost a saint. Was his charm only a veneer? Was he, in fact, hiding something? Had there been a flash of recognition in his eyes when he saw Heidi's picture? Had he held onto it a little longer than necessary, making a show of giving it careful enough scrutiny? Did he know more than he was telling?

At Susan's house, in the mid-afternoon, Bruce had finished cleaning the hot tub and was putting on the cover.

Susan had remained downstairs to keep an eye on him. She was keenly aware that he had found a way to get into the house, if he had been Friday night's intruder, as she suspected. Peeping through the den window, she breathed a great sigh of relief as she watched him climb back into the Oasis Spa truck and drive off.

She phoned ahead and was told the sheriff would be back momentarily, and was expected to be in the rest of the day. She hurried out to her car, carefully handling the envelope that held the lemonade glass, and pulled out of the driveway. Before too long she was maneuvering into a parking spot in front of the sheriff's office, in eager anticipation of her meeting. She got out of the car, fed a coin into the meter, and went inside, walking up to the desk sergeant. "I'm Susan Muir, here to see Sheriff Woods," she announced.

"The sheriff just went out on an emergency call," the sergeant answered. "Can someone else help you?"

Susan hesitated, filled with disappointment. She had expected to finally have her proof within the next five or ten minutes. Now she would have to wait. Besides, she had wanted to be present at the triumphant moment. She had imagined examining the two sets of prints with the sheriff as he made the comparison, and sharing in his excitement.

"Is Undersheriff Drews in?" she finally asked.

"No, ma'am." He smiled apologetically. "We're having a busy day."

"Well, perhaps then I'll leave this here with you," Susan said, holding up the envelope. "Would you please give it to Sheriff Woods the moment he comes in?"

BLACK DIAMOND

"Of course, Ms. Muir."

"I'll just enclose a note," Susan told him, reaching in her purse for a notepad and pen.

She quickly wrote out a message asking the sheriff to compare the fingerprints on the glass with those he found when he investigated her break-in, and to report the results to her as soon as possible. After opening the envelope and slipping the note inside, she handed it over to the sergeant, explaining it needed to be handled with care.

"I'll see that he gets it right away," he said, placing the envelope in his desk drawer.

Susan thanked him and took her leave, driving home thoughtfully. Traveling along the western side of Loon Lake Road, as she approached the McCullys' house, she found she was so anxious to tell them about her plan in progress, she wanted to stop in. But realizing it would be premature before she heard back from the sheriff, she continued on.

When she reached home, she let Fritz out and put on a pot of coffee. It was 4:15 on the kitchen clock. Hopefully the sheriff would call any minute. She paced through the downstairs restlessly, willing the phone to ring. She plumped the couch pillows, rearranged magazines, and replaced the water in her vase of roses. Now it was 4:30. In another half-hour, the sheriff would probably be leaving for the day. Or the desk sergeant could go off duty before the sheriff returned to the office. Maybe she should call. The phone rang, and she dashed to the kitchen.

"Hello. This is Susan."

"Susan, this is Sheriff Woods. I am so sorry I wasn't here when you paid your call. If I had only known you were coming, I would have made myself available."

"I understand, Sheriff," Susan said. "But I see you got my message."

"Yes I did, and I made the print comparison for you. I imagine you anticipated they would be the same as the others, so I'm sorry to report they don't match."

"They don't?"

"No, they absolutely don't. I'm sorry, Susan, but as I told you this morning, you should leave the investigating to me."

"So my intuition was wrong," Susan said, trying to regain her equilibrium. "Well, I'm sorry I put you to trouble for nothing, Wally. But at least you've allayed my suspicions."

"Can you tell me who you suspected, Susan? It might end up being helpful."

"I'm sorry, Wally," Susan said. "I don't feel right about doing that, now that my notion has proved to be unfounded. Did you get the search warrant for the Black Diamond?" she asked, quickly changing the subject.

"Yes, indeed," the sheriff said. "Judge Walker was quite responsive to the information you provided. All the paperwork is done, and we're ready to go. The judge gave me a little latitude on the time because there is still some uncertainty revolving around the availability of the state criminalist. But I expect to have him pinned down the first thing tomorrow morning. Then I'll be in touch with you."

"Well, thank you, Sheriff," Susan said in closing. "I'll look forward to hearing from you tomorrow."

She took a cup of coffee into the living room and sank into a chair. How could she have been so wrong? She felt so foolish. She didn't even want to tell Charlie about it. What could he feel for her, except ridicule? Maybe he would even be critical of her for wasting the valuable time of a police official. No one knew any better than Charlie how busy they were. Doing important things. They weren't sworn into office to take fingerprints off a lemonade glass on someone's hunch. She was so embarrassed. She went outside and walked around listlessly. No, she wouldn't even mention it to Charlie. It might change his feelings for her. But now she was being foolish again. Of course it wouldn't change his feelings. She could imagine him grinning at her, saying, "You can't win them all."

Now she couldn't wait to see him, and receive his comfort as she licked her wounds. It would be another twenty-five minutes before he got there. She'd go in and check her e-mail. Her mother and father should be back in Shanghai by now. She went up to her study and logged on to the Internet, delighted to see that, yes, she had mail from her father.

She opened it up, scrolling through on the screen, anxious to see how they were doing, and whether he had responded to the question she had asked in her last e-mail, if he had heard any rumors about the Black Diamond. Her mother and father were both well, their excursion on the Yangtze River had been wonderful. They would both write tomorrow. They were spending the day resting up, and her mother sent her love.

Yes, there it was at the end. "So my little girl hasn't retired, after all! I do understand. I still find my own ancient blood roiling at the thought of uncovering villainous mystery and intrigue. In answer to your question, yes, last year, when I was about ready to retire, I began hearing rumors about illegal activity going on at the Black Diamond Ranch, probably drug trafficking. It was after Tony Rizzo came in from California and bought the place. There were also a few rumors in my world that he had the police in his pocket. Sad to say, I don't see how something like that could go on for so long without the support of the sheriff. And I don't really want to think that Wally Woods isn't all that we believed he was. I still like to think of him as a hero. I'll write more tomorrow. Lots of love to my little girl. Good luck, and please take good care of yourself. Dad."

Susan turned misty-eyed as she read and re-read her father's words. Could it be? Was it possible Wally Woods was no longer the hero of Marble Point? Had the voters been fooled? Had she been fooled? Had he lied to her about finding one set of fingerprints so she wouldn't worry, or for his own purposes? Was he concerned about her investigating because she was putting herself in danger, or because she might uncover something? The Black Diamond was under county jurisdiction, and some locals had gone to him about their suspicions. Was he making so many trips out there to keep an eye on the place, or because he was in cahoots with Tony? Was he having a hard time scheduling the state criminalist for the raid, or was he giving Tony time to clean up? Did the fingerprints on the lemonade glass match the ones in the file?

Susan picked up her phone to ring the sheriff's office, and was put through immediately.

"Susan, what a delightful surprise, hearing from you again so soon!" the sheriff said in an ebullient tone. "What can I do for you?"

"Wally, I'd like to have the set of fingerprints I

dropped off. If you'll leave them out front, I'll come by and pick them up."

"Oh, Susan, I'm so sorry," the sheriff answered, his voice full of apology. "I had no idea you'd be wanting them, and they're already destroyed."

"How about the glass?"

"All washed, ready to return."

"Oh, I see," Susan responded. "Well, thank you. I'll speak with you tomorrow. Have a good evening."

As she thought over the new turn of events, she scrolled through her father's e-mail once more on the screen, printing it out to save. Then she checked her watch again and closed down the computer. She'd e-mail back in the morning. It was almost time for Charlie to come home. Come home! That sounded so nice. She walked into her bedroom and looked out the window. There he was now, getting out of the car! So handsome in his tweed jacket! She ran downstairs and out the door, relieving him of a bag of groceries. "Boy, am I glad to see you!" she said happily. "And after you tell me all your news, wait till you hear mine!"

When Sheriff Woods hung up the phone after Susan's call, his shoulders slumped, and his head fell slowly to his desk. She suspected. No, he might as well face it. She knew. And her revelation was coming on the heels of his visit from Lieutenant Martin. He had dug himself in so deep, he had been forced to lie to a fellow police officer. Unpardonable. And from what the lieutenant had told him, Heidi Townsend could be in real danger. He'd wait until tomorrow when the search warrant was executed. If Heidi didn't surface, he would have to get in touch with Lieutenant Martin. After Jack Stone's phone call from the Cayman's, Wally had no doubt they were keeping her hidden out there.

How had it all gone so wrong? Everything was caving in on him. Why had he done it? The voters had entrusted him with the safety and welfare of their county, and he had failed them. He was a disgrace. He who had once walked so proudly on the sidewalks of Marble Point.

He thought back to the day three years ago when he had stood in his crisp new sheriff's uniform, cameras whirring as he was sworn in and presented with his badge. He thought his heart would burst with pride. Wally Woods, hometown boy, had won the election by a landslide. The voters loved him. They trusted him. His glory days were legendary. People were looking forward to the old high school captain being a member of the top team of county government, guiding it with the same sure hands the crowds had counted on to carry the football over the goal line. Marble Point would be a better place to live with their new sheriff, their hometown boy made good.

Tears welled up in Wally's eyes. He pulled his head up and ashamedly brushed them away. He wasn't a schoolboy. He was a grown man who took full responsibility for his actions. Even if he didn't get found out, his sense of honor demanded that he resign. New tears sprang to his eyes. No. He brushed at them furiously. Let him at least go out with dignity. He would resign for personal reasons, with his sincere regrets for letting the voters down by not completing his term. He would make his last television appearance in full uniform, taking his badge off before the cameras, showing his shame.

If only he had resisted temptation. Standing up and looking out the window, the sheriff thought back to how it had all begun. Over a year ago, he had gotten a phone call from Jack Stone, asking him to come by his Loon Lake home that evening. It was highly unusual to be called to a private home without any explanation, and Wally wondered right away what was up. He knew Jack Stone was a big player who had his finger in a lot of pies.

At eight o'clock that night, Wally pulled into Jack Stone's driveway in his personal car, a black Ford Mustang. He was apprehensive as he sprang up the steps of the large gabled house, knowing Stone was the kind of guy who got sheriffs elected. Whatever he wanted, he had to be treated just right. Before he reached the front door, it was opened by his smiling host, informally dressed in a short-sleeved Hawaiian print shirt. Stone cordially invited him in, making it known that Jocelyn was out for the evening.

"It's good to see you, Wally. Nice of you to come out."

"It's always a pleasure to see you, Jack."

As they talked, Stone led the way down the hallway towards his office. When they walked in, Stone went over to the built-in bar, stocked with bottles, ice, and assorted glasses. "Pick your poison!" he said with his thin-lipped smile.

"Bourbon on the rocks," Wally responded, wondering more than ever what was up. He didn't believe for a second it was a social occasion.

After he mixed their drinks, Stone smiled again. "If you don't mind, I feel most comfortable at my desk," he said, offering Wally a chair across from it. "Especially when

I'm presenting a business proposition."

Stone took a few sips of his Scotch and soda, then set the glass down on one of the cocktail napkins he had carried over. "To get right to the point, I set a friend of mine up at the Black Diamond. Tony Rizzo. The ranch came up for sale, and it seemed like a good place to do a little business."

"Are you keeping it as a guest ranch?"

"Actually, no. Not in the usual sense. But the cabins do afford the opportunity for Tony to put up his friends who fly in from California. Tony's a bit of a pool shark," he went on, interspersing his thin smile. "He plays in professional circles, and draws some top players. And you know how that goes. The stakes can get pretty high."

Wally was beginning to get the idea. He was supposed to look the other way when gambling started up at the Black Diamond. But had he been called out here only about pool games?

"Tony's friends like to play cards, too," Stone continued, in answer to the unasked question. "Mostly poker. A little gin rummy." His mustache spread with his wide smile. "These people love to gamble. I think they're born with it in their blood." Another mustachey smile. "Tony was thinking about putting in a few machines, so they wouldn't have to drive over to Montana."

A few moments of silence passed between them. "I understand, Jack," Wally finally responded. "Not a casino. Just a few machines for his friends' pleasure."

"Exactly." The smile again. "Even though it won't be much of an operation, a little money will be changing hands, and we want to show you our appreciation."

BLACK DIAMOND

Stone pulled out his wallet and started counting out hundred-dollar bills, smacking them down on his desk. When he had ten in a stack, he stood up and held them out to Wally. "Every week you'll get the same amount, but from now on, you'll deal only with Tony."

Wally was incredulous. A thousand dollars a week to look away from gambling? Impossible. Something was wrong here. "That's not necessary," he said. "I don't want any money."

A final thin mustached smile. "Oh, but I insist. I won't have it any other way."

"I promise you, Jack," Wally said. "I'll stay away from a little gambling. I don't need paid to do that."

"You don't seem to understand," Stone responded, the smile gone, his voice cool. "I absolutely insist on it. There's some money to be made, and we want you to have your share. And as an added sweetener, I'll put your money in a special Cayman's account. High returns, no taxes. Take out what you need for monthly expenses, and you still have a sweet retirement fund. You deserve it. We all know public officials don't get paid enough."

Wally picked up his glass and took several long swallows. His wheels were spinning. Sure, he had taken the occasional five- or ten-dollar bill when he was a beat patrolman, just making ends meet. And now there were Christmas presents, front row tickets to ball games, a few things like that. But this was different. This would put him in the big time. He wouldn't need to plan for his retirement. He wouldn't have to worry about being reelected time after time. He and Joyce would be able to keep up with their old friends. They could join the country club, have dinner at Emille's. Wally would tell people he got lucky on the stock market. They'd be happy for him. And the old gang would be glad to have him and Joyce back.

"You've made it pretty tempting," he said at last. "I'll think it over."

Of course, in the end, he couldn't turn it down. He told Joyce he had made a couple of good decisions on the market, and they suddenly had enough money for all the things they wanted. She was ecstatic, and with starry-eyed visions of again traveling in the inner circles, vowed she would do whatever it took to get back into her size eight clothes. Wally good-humoredly told her she could buy all new tens or twelves. After all, she'd had two kids since she was a size eight. He bought a set of golf clubs. He was a natural athlete, and he'd pick the game up in no time. And he had. Before long he was enjoying Saturday rounds of golf and beer in the clubhouse with the gang.

Oh, what a fool he had been. He had known in his heart that all that money had been a payoff for more than just gambling. By the time he learned they were making and distributing meth, it was too late. Jack Stone owned him, with copies of his illegal Cayman bank account with its regular large deposits. Wally couldn't do anything to close down the Black Diamond without putting himself in jail. He convinced himself the users that didn't make their own meth were going to buy it somewhere. So it might as well be from Tony Rizzo.

Then, as if that wasn't bad enough, he caught Bruce Fione in a break-in, and Fione mouthed off about how he worked for Tony, and Tony wouldn't be happy with the sheriff if he arrested him. Bruce wasn't anxious for Tony to know what he was up to, either, so he'd make a deal. He had a good thing going at Eddy's Pawn Shop, and if the sheriff worked with him, he'd make sure he got his cut. Getting greedy, Wally told him the cut would have to be big enough to make it worth his while. Fione agreed. And so, while Joyce was working to get thinner, Wally Woods was working to make his pockets fatter.

Now it was all over. There wouldn't be any more big money coming in. As luck would have it, today Tony had gone to Montana. Wally had tried calling him over and over again, but he was out of cell phone range. He was due back at nine o'clock that night, and Wally would be waiting to tell him he had until morning to get the place cleaned up. He couldn't do any better than that, not with Susan Muir breathing down his neck. The search warrant would have to be executed the first thing tomorrow. Then in all likelihood he would have to arrest Fione and his girlfriend. Once Susan Muir got her teeth into something, she'd never let go. Before it was over, she'd prove Fione's fingerprints had been on the glass she had taken him, and were the same ones on file from all the break-ins. And Wally would be charged with obstruction of justice and at least five counts of burglary.

Maybe he could convince Susan he had made an honest mistake, but he knew when Fione was arrested, he'd plea bargain and sing like a birdie about the sheriff's involvement. Wally wouldn't even be allowed to resign. He would go to jail. Then Joyce would never again be able to hold her head up in public. They would have to leave their beloved Marble Point. As he thought it all over, Wally decided what he would do. Referring to his personal directory, he pressed in Bruce Fione's telephone number. No answer. No machine. He would go out and look for him. He'd check at the Black Diamond first, then try the Blue Moon, and go from there. When he found him, he'd tell him what was going down. Then Fione and his girlfriend could get out of town before they were arrested.

It might work. Wally's eyes filled with pain, and he sadly lowered his head. Even if he didn't go to jail, he was still about to lose the position he had valued so much. He loved being the sheriff. If only he had it to do all over again.

CHAPTER 17

OVER their lattes, Susan and Charlie discussed the day's events. Charlie told Susan he had received a preliminary report on Jack Stone, and it didn't look as if he'd be winning any ideal neighbor awards. He had been cited for suspicious activity, and had association with known underworld figures. Since Stone had been operating in LA before he moved to Marble Point, there was a good chance he and Garcia had been hooked up.

Charlie had made no headway in finding Heidi and, in fact, had wasted almost two hours following a false lead. As it turned out, he was surprised to find a Heidi Townsend look-alike who lived in Marble Point. His visit to the Black Diamond had also proved fruitless. The place had been deserted, except for Butch Rivera, the same one who had been present the last time Charlie was there. Butch had told him the part-timers had a few days off, and the others were due back that evening.

As Susan related her account of Bruce's spa visit, Charlie listened in a state of anxiety. "If you don't stop putting yourself in such danger, you'll be the death of me!" he pronounced.

Susan laughingly told him not to worry, that as much as she wanted to get a new set of fingerprints to send to the state crime lab, she wouldn't take that kind of risk again. It had worked fine once, but she wasn't going to push her luck.

Susan went inside to refill their lattes, and Charlie sat absently patting Fritz's head in thought. When she returned, he gave her a cheerful look. "Get ready to say, 'Why didn't I think of that?'"

Susan smiled. "Okay. I'm ready."

"Since you want those fingerprints so bad, and I don't trust you not to change your mind and do it your way again, I thought of a different way to get them."

Susan's face lit up instantly. "How?"

"Did Bruce put chemicals in your hot tub after he filled it?"

"Yes, I'm sure. He always does."

"Did he hold the cans of chemicals in his hand?"

Susan's eyes widened. "Now why didn't I think of that?"

"I'm a detective, remember? That's why you're keeping me around."

"Just one of the reasons," Susan answered with a laugh.

"I'll get hold of a fingerprint kit in the morning," Charlie said. "Not Wally's. It would be pretty rude to ask him to lend me his own fingerprint kit to incriminate him with."

Susan smiled. "There will be other prints on the cans, like Gus Woodbridge's for instance. But they can be separated out, can't they?"

"Easily," Charlie said. "I'll send the prints to the crime lab tomorrow. If they don't have a copy of the fingerprints from the break-ins, they'll request them from the sheriff's office. And, if you're right, Sheriff Wally Woods will be exposed."

Susan smiled wistfully. "I must admit, I don't feel very happy about it."

"Why not?"

"I've always been fond of Wally," Susan answered slowly. "It makes me sad to think he would do this." She went on to tell him about how the people in Marble Point had always looked up to him, and remembered him as a hero.

Charlie looked out at the placid evening lake as she talked, listening quietly. "It's a shame how people in law enforcement can end up breaking the law themselves," he remarked as she grew silent.

"Yes," Susan responded. "I always thought Wally was as honest as they come."

"He probably did start out that way," Charlie answered. "But the temptation out there can be pretty strong." He grinned at her, trying to lighten her mood. "Like the temptation of those New York strips marinating inside."

Susan smiled. "Get ready to say, 'I hate you.'"

"That's pretty strong language," Charlie answered with another grin. "What's up?"

"I can't stop wondering if the sheriff warned Tony about the raid, and he's out there cleaning the place up."

"And we should go out there and see, instead of sitting down to our juicy, delectable New York strips?"

"Right. Do you hate me?"

"How could I hate you, when I was thinking the same thing myself?"

Susan gave him a radiant smile. "I'm glad you don't hate me, because at this moment, I definitely love you."

Charlie grinned again. "We'll have to talk about that

some more when we get back. Right now, let's get going. The lucky thing is, I have a good reason to make a visit, since no one was around today to look at Heidi's picture. I already told them I'd be back. And there's no law against taking along a beautiful woman."

Susan smiled at him. "And while you keep them busy inside, I can stroll around the grounds, and take in the fresh country air."

"Exactly. But you have to promise me you'll stay near the lodge. You'll be able to get an idea of what's going on. Lights, voices, guys carrying stuff, loading trucks, things like that. And when I come back out to the car, you'll tell me if you saw any suspicious activity, and we'll go from there. Together. And I'm absolutely not taking you unless you promise you won't do anything rash."

"That's an easy promise. When I'm lucky enough to be in the company of a detective lieutenant, somehow my good sense tells me to let him lead the show."

"You're not getting out of it with a fancy answer," Charlie said firmly. "Promise me."

"I promise."

Charlie went to strap on his shoulder holster, and Susan got her cell phone, knowing she might need to call the sheriff. Leaving Fritz inside, they climbed into Charlie's Caprice and drove off. "Would you call this going out on a date?" Susan asked in amusement as they started down the western lake road.

"Sure," Charlie responded. "You might even get a new book title out of it, like '*A Date With Death*'."

Susan laughed. "Well, if this is a date, you might say

we're having a strange courtship."

"Didn't you ever hear the saying, 'Rules for courtships are as ever-changing as the tides'?"

Susan arched her eyebrows. "Who said that?"

"Charlie Martin."

They laughed together as they rode along, making lighthearted conversation. A little before eight, they reached the Black Diamond turnoff, and they grew serious as they drove up Cedar Creek Road in the gathering dusk. "Here we go," Charlie said as he pulled through the gate and drove towards the lodge.

"It looks as dead as a doornail," Susan remarked, looking around as he pulled into the driveway. All the outbuildings appeared to be dark, and there was no sign of activity on the grounds. From what they could see, a single light burned in the lodge.

"It does appear that way," Charlie agreed. "But there might be more going on than meets the eye."

According to their plan, when they got out of the car, Susan disappeared around the lodge while Charlie went up to the front door. His knock was answered by Butch Rivera.

"Lieutenant!" Butch said in greeting. "Nobody's here again. Just me. I'm sorry you wasted your time driving out."

"It's the nature of the game," Charlie answered, pulling himself up to his full six-foot-one and standing his ground. "Since I did drive the whole way out, do you mind if I come in and sit down for a minute?"

"Come right in," Butch said, pulling the door open wide. "We can sit right over here." He moved toward two worn easy chairs near the fireplace.

"Have you made any headway, Lieutenant?" Butch asked as they got seated.

"Can't say as I have," Charlie answered. "But I will."

"I'm sure you will, Lieutenant. Just takes time, I guess."

"Too much time," Charlie shot back. "I want to know exactly when the other three will be back."

Closely watching Butch's reaction, Charlie saw he was beginning to squirm around in his chair, and was nervously pushing at his oily black hair. "Tony told me he'd be back at nine o'clock, Lieutenant. So it should be some time around then. Johnny and Phil thought they'd be back by ten or eleven."

"Where did they go?"

"Over to Washington."

"Buying ranch supplies?" Charlie pressed.

Butch squirmed more visibly. "I'm not real sure what they were doing, Lieutenant."

Charlie thought Susan had had plenty of time by now to take her look around, so he stood up to leave. "Well, I'll be back," he said. "You can count on it."

Butch followed him across the room and ushered him out. Charlie closed the door behind him as he stepped onto the porch. Seeing to his relief that Susan was already in the car, he bounced down the steps and climbed into the driver's seat. "Anything going on?"

"Nothing I could see."

"Nothing doing in there, either. Tony's supposed to be back at nine, and the other two sometime after that, maybe ten or eleven." His face took on a happy look. "The way I see it, that gives us plenty of time to attend to our New York strips!"

"It sure does!" Susan agreed enthusiastically. "Look!

BLACK DIAMOND

He's watching through the windoiw to make sure we leave."
Charlie smiled. "And wondering when we'll be back."

Inside the tool shed, Heidi's heart sank as she heard the car pull out. Her ears had become attuned to every little sound, and her hopes had soared when she heard the car pull in. She thought maybe it was one of the regulars returning, and she'd get something to eat. She was faint with hunger. That morning Tony had tossed her a peanut butter sandwich, and said that's all she was going to get, so not to be expecting anything else. He had cursed at her horribly, and told her she had caused so much trouble, she was lucky to get anything at all. She had begged him for some water, but he just laughed at her, saying he hoped she died of thirst. Nothing would make him happier.

Her stomach hurt all the time now. Cramps overtook her so badly, she doubled up in pain. Then she lay on the horse blanket with her knees bent, trying to find a position that would alleviate the painful spasms. Not only was she starving, but she was dehydrated. She hadn't had water since early the day before. Her lips were cracked, her mouth and throat parched. She felt achy and feverish, and longed for her mother to put a damp towel on her forehead, the way she used to do. She missed her mother so desperately, she thought her heart would break. She was trying to have courage, but it was getting harder and harder. She was losing hope. She didn't think she could survive much longer.

When she had gotten the sandwich that morning, she had broken a few pieces of bread off for Jeremy. But, although the little squirrel had come up close to her several times during the day looking for crumbs, she hadn't given them to him. She felt terrible about it, but she was afraid she was going to die. The squirrel was now coming within two feet of her, and she yearned to touch him with all her heart. She wanted to use the bread crumbs to lure him close, but she knew she shouldn't. To him they were just a treat. To her they could mean survival. And so she had sadly withheld them.

Heidi went and got a bit of bread and put it in her mouth. She rolled it round and round, savoring the taste, the texture, the idea. At last she swallowed it and reached for another one. No, she had to save it. There were only two more little bites. She reluctantly put them back. Then she lay on the blanket with closed eyes, trying not to think about food. She thought about the policeman who might be looking for her, and the two women who might come back. If only someone would find her in time.

Bruce finished strapping a new leather saddlebag onto his Harley and stood looking at it through starry eyes, envisioning how it would soon be filled with the rare gold coins. A fortune! At last he was getting the big score he had been hoping for, and he could take off. He wouldn't have minded working for Tony full time for awhile to add to his savings, but it wasn't in the cards.

Even if the Black Diamond's operation wasn't closed down, Tony might not have put him on full time anyway. It looked like Susan Muir wouldn't be as easy to scare off as he had thought. He smiled to himself. It was really lucky he had run into the federal cop. Sure, he'd help him out tonight. No use making an enemy of a powerful guy like that. But then he was out of here.

He had only one regret. He had wanted so much to get together with the pretty lady. He had come so close today, it hurt to think about it. It had taken all his self control to stop. But he couldn't take any chances that she'd be upset enough to call the police and turn him in. It would've ruined all his big plans for tonight. As bad as he wanted her, of course he wanted the coin collection more. Especially now. He needed the money to get out of there before the Black Diamond got busted. He was glad he at least had her panties to take along as a keepsake.

His Firebird was all packed up. When he and Laura left the Jensens', he'd drop her at the motel, come back here with the coins, load them into the Firebird, and drive it to the Black Diamond. The bolt cutter he'd use on the lock was under the front seat. After he handed Heidi over to the cop, he was gone. This time he wasn't dealing with any two-bit pawnshop like Eddy's. And there wouldn't be any cuts for Sheriff Wally Woods. He was heading out east where he knew there were places to buy what he had to sell. And he sure as hell wasn't trusting some screwed-up airline not to lose his baggage. No, he would pilot his own vehicle the whole way. Then, after he got the big cash, he'd buy his plane ticket to some exotic far-away place. He'd pick up some travel brochures along the way, and figure it all out.

He zipped up his leather jacket, strapped on his helmet and backpack, and set off for Sand Cove to pick up Laura for their last adventure together. They had made a good couple, no doubt about that. Especially since they had started using the .357 Magnum as a bedtime toy. It was too bad he had to cut loose. But he knew there were plenty more where she came from.

The twenty-mile ride invigorated him. The two-lane highway was smooth under his tires, and the traffic was light. He kept one eye on the speedometer, not taking a chance of getting pulled over and wasting time. He wanted to have plenty of time at the Jensens' house, so after they packed up the coins they could smoke a pipe and enjoy the fantastic hot tub overlooking Stony River. He didn't want to pass that up.

When he pulled into the parking lot of the Sleep Inn Motel, Laura was outside her door waiting for him. She was wearing jeans and her matching brown leather jacket, with her backpack hanging from her shoulders. She ran towards the cycle and climbed onto the seat behind him. "I've missed you, Angel," she said throatily, throwing her arms around him.

"Same here, Babe. Got your ticket for the ride?"

"Just like always," she answered, reaching into her pocket and handing him the package of meth.

Bruce took it and peeled out, heading for the Jensens', the gold coins, and his future. Laura hung on tight as they rode toward their destination. In a half-hour they started up the North Fork on the lightly traveled road along the bubbling Stony River. Five minutes later they turned into the Jensens' drive and rode around to the front of the house facing the river.

They stood looking in awe at the dramatic one-story home. It stood in the middle of thirty beautifully landscaped acres, thick with fir and pine trees. The entire front of the house was plate glass, broken only by solid cedar support beams. Three chimneys rose from the pitched shingled roof.

BLACK DIAMOND

"Wow!" Laura breathed admiringly. "This is something else. How much time do we have?"

"They won't be back until after eleven, but we'll have to leave around ten. I gotta meet a guy about some business."

"Oh, my dearest Angel," Laura said softly. "I wish we could stay here forever."

"Some day we'll have a place like this," Bruce told her. "That's what we're working for, remember? And now we better get started. Business first tonight. No fun and games till the coins are loaded up."

While Laura stood looking at the foamy waterfall at the bend of the river, Bruce went to work with his bronze passkey. Ten minutes later he was still struggling. Laura had grown edgy, hearing him curse. Finally she went up to his side. "Having trouble, Angel?"

"I'll get it," Bruce said curtly. "Just leave me alone."

Laura went back down to her spot, watching him over her shoulder anxiously. After a time, she went back to where he was working. "You could try a different door, Angel," she suggested nervously.

"You are so damn dumb, I don't know why I put up with you!" Bruce answered hotly. "Did it ever occur to you that the other doors can be seen from the road? And there are cars on the road, in case you haven't noticed. If you'd shut your mouth for one damn minute, you might hear them."

Laura crept away and went back to watching the river. At least fifteen more minutes went by. She was convinced his passkey was not going to work, and he was just wasting time. Finally she got up her nerve to go back and try again.

"You've broken windows before," Laura reminded him.

"Not when the whole fucking front of the house was plate glass, I didn't."

"I mean around in the back. I could stand by the road and watch for cars."

Bruce looked up from the lock and pushed at his curly locks. "Why didn't you suggest that before?"

"I'm sorry, Angel," Laura said in relief.

Bruce found a good-sized rock, and with Laura standing guard, broke the kitchen window with one blow, reached in and turned the lock, opened it, and climbed through. Laura ran to the front of the house, arriving just as he opened the door.

"Oh, my lover!" she breathed. "What a paradise!"

The room gave the feeling of being outdoors. The floor to ceiling glass wall afforded a magnificent view of the river, with the frothy, tumbling waterfall at the bend. The full branches of white pine trees showed through a grand, extra-large skylight. The ceiling was supported by thick beams of rough-cut larch that had a warm reddish cast. One whole wall was stone veneered with sparkling Idaho mica, and contained a huge wood-burning fireplace. In the center of the room, a raised sitting area with patterned carpeting had a wide step on two sides that led to additional sitting areas with matching green carpet.

Bruce and Laura walked through the doorway into the den and stood transfixed at the sight of the coin collection. One wall was covered with various sized gold coins mounted in glass-covered frames backed with royal purple velvet. The magnificence of the display was breathtaking, and the cozy room provided a marvelous setting. The adjoining wall held a large sliding glass door that opened onto a deck set in a forest of trees. A reddish-orange Swedish fireplace stood in one corner.

Bruce walked over to the coins to get a better look. "Wow!" he said in awe. "These are absolutely incredible."

Laura went over and stood by his side. "They'll be worth a whole lot, won't they, Angel?"

Bruce smiled. "A whole, whole lot."

He took the packet of meth from his pocket and sprinkled some on the coffee table. "We'll have a little snort before we start, Babe," he told her, lining it up with his knife. "We have a lot of work ahead of us."

"Good idea, Angel," Laura said softly, as she leaned to sniff through the rolled-up twenty he gave her.

When the powder was gone, Bruce picked up a paperweight off the desk and walked over and smashed the first frame. He yanked it off the wall, slamming it against a table to release the shards of glass. He quickly flipped his penknife open and began prying out the coins. In a few moments, he was staring unbelievingly at the first handful of rich, glittery coins. Then he greedily stuffed them into his pocket.

"Go find a stepladder," he said to Laura. "You can get down all the ones I can't reach."

"Sure, Baby," Laura answered. "You're the boss."

"And bring back a knife or something. After you get the things off the wall, you can help me pry the coins out." He bestowed her with a confident smile. "This job will be a piece of cake."

Sheriff Woods steered his Mustang into the parking lot of the Blue Moon and circled the building, taking one last look for Bruce Fione's Harley Sportster. To his dismay, he saw it still wasn't there. It had been two hours since he had first gone to the Blue Moon looking for Fione, and he was hoping by now he might have showed up. He knew he was out somewhere on his Harley, because his Firebird was parked in his driveway. But damnit, where?

The sheriff had driven to every conceivable place he could think of. He pretty much knew where Fione hung out. It was like he had vanished from the face of the earth. And now time had run out. He had to be at the Black Diamond at nine o'clock when Tony came back. He'd have to look for Fione later, after he delivered the news about the search warrant. Which he was not looking forward to.

This was all so nerve-wracking, his stomach was in knots. When he had gone home to park the cruiser, Joyce had been disappointed when he turned down the dinner she had made, meatloaf with mashed potatoes and gravy, one of his favorite meals. Then she had insisted on fixing him a ham sandwich to take along. There it sat in its plastic wrap on the front seat, untouched. Food was definitely the last thing he wanted.

He pulled back onto the frontage road and started for the ranch. After he warned Tony, if he still couldn't find Fione, he'd camp out at his place all night till he came home. He had to get him out of town tonight. Tomorrow could be too late. As he turned onto Cedar Creek Road, he grew so apprehensive, his stomach began churning. This was not going to be a pleasant scene.

When he reached the Black Diamond, he drove around back and parked, seeing that Tony's pickup was there. He walked around to the front of the lodge and went up the steps, his heart racing. Taking a moment to compose himself, he knocked on the door. Butch opened it.

"I see Tony's back," the sheriff said.

"Yeah, he's back," Butch answered, not offering to admit him inside.

"I need to talk to him."

"I'll see if he wants to see you." Butch shut the door, leaving the sheriff to stand outside.

He waited nervously until Butch returned in a few minutes and let him in. He steered him toward Tony's desk, then disappeared down the hallway.

"This better be important," Tony began, without inviting him to sit down. His face was lined with fatigue, and there was a slump to his shoulders. "I've had a long day."

"I'm afraid it's going to get longer," the sheriff answered.

"What the hell's that supposed to mean?"

"I did my best, but Judge Walker issued a search warrant for the place. I stalled today, but Susan Muir's breathing down my neck, and I'll have to move on it in the morning."

Tony's face turned white. "What the fuck are you talking about? What do you think we're paying you for?"

The sheriff's cell phone rang, and he automatically reached for it.

"Forget it!" Tony thundered. "Turn the goddamn thing off!"

"I'm really sorry, Tony," the sheriff said, putting the phone back. "There was no way I could stop it. Susan Muir saw your meth supplies when she was nosing around Friday night."

"Holy shit. I don't believe this. We pay you a grand a week to protect us, and you're standing there telling me that tomorrow morning you're coming out here with a search warrant?

Are you out of your mind? Jack will give the judge a call."

"He already did. I got in touch with him at the Cayman's. Judge Walker wouldn't help him. It's a done deal. It's set up for tomorrow morning. I bought you some time. That's all I can do."

"I don't believe you," Tony said, his eyes bulging with fear in his chalky white face. He picked up the phone and hit Jack Stone's number in the Cayman's, gripping the phone like a lifeline. At the first ring, he lit a cigarette and waited for the familiar voice. The phone rang a second time, then a third. Tony broke into a cold sweat, and his hands began shaking. His pulse throbbed in his neck. A haze of smoke surrounded him as he puffed furiously on his cigarette. The phone rang and rang and rang through the vast trans-oceanic line. There was no answer.

CHAPTER 18

BRUCE and Laura sat side by side in the Jensens' den, intent on prying out coins. As they accumulated small handfuls, they dropped them into the bag that sat between them. Every time they filled a sack, Bruce carried it to his motorcycle and added the coins to the saddlebag. By now it was almost full, but Bruce was getting edgy, and kept consulting his watch. It had taken them much longer than he had thought it would. There were still quite a few frames stacked in front of them, and they only had another hour. They had long since given up on having time for fun and games. They only hoped they had all the coins loaded up by ten o'clock. Bruce wouldn't be satisfied until he had every last coin in the collection.

"Ouch! Damnit!" he exploded.

"What's wrong, Angel?" Laura asked solicitously.

"I cut myself with the damn knife."

"Oh, my poor Angel," Laura said in an upset voice. "That's too bad. Let me trade you. You take my screwdriver, and I'll use the knife."

"That's not the problem," Bruce said irritably. "It's getting so damn dark in here, you can't see what the hell you're doing. We'll never get done."

"Do you think it would be okay to turn on one lamp,

Angel? I don't think anyone could ever see it, with all the trees outside the window."

"Go ahead," Bruce snapped. "There won't be many people going up the road this time of night anyway. Just hurry up."

Laura jumped up and turned on the closest lamp, and a soft glow cut through the gloom. Then she hurried back to Bruce's side and began working again. "Is that better, Angel?" she asked in concern.

"Yes. Now quit talking and get something done."

They began to work faster with some light, and the bag was soon filled. Bruce stood up. "I'm taking these coins out to put in the saddlebag, and then I'm closing it up. Start filling your backpack. And don't waste a second."

At nine o'clock, Margaret and Jim Carlson were returning home from their trip to Cy's, a small local convenience store near the foot of the North Fork. The amiable, silver-haired couple had been at home working together on the Sunday *New York Times* crossword puzzle, when Margaret had been overcome with a craving for mocha fudge ice cream. Doing the puzzle together had been their forty-five year Sunday ritual. This week they were running a day behind because they had hosted a family get-together on Sunday in their beautiful North Fork home.

Jim had agreeably told her it sounded good to him, too, and a little break would sharpen their minds for the attack on all the hardest words they had left for last. They had smilingly set down their pencils, locked up the house, and climbed into the car. When they arrived at Cy's, they had looked through the shelves companionably and decided to go all out, buying chocolate sauce, whipped cream, and a can of peanuts. Now, on their way back, they were looking forward to their treat, and enjoying the view of the moonlit Stony River.

"Oh, Jim! Look at the waterfall tonight!" Margaret exclaimed, craning her neck to take a lingering look. "Oh no! There's a light on in the Jensens'!"

Jim smiled and raised an eyebrow. "What's so unusual about that?"

"They aren't home, and there was no light on when we came down the road."

Jim looked over his shoulder at the sprawling one-story house, seeing a glow of light through the trees by the side deck. "There's a lamp lit in their den, alright," he said. "Are you sure it wasn't on before?"

"I could be mistaken, of course," Margaret replied. "But I remembered Patsy and John were at the baseball game tonight, and I particularly looked to see if the house was dark."

"Let's give them a call," Jim said. "Maybe they got home early and parked in the garage."

"Maybe," Margaret agreed. "But something tells me they didn't. It doesn't seem as if they would only have on one lamp in the whole house if they just arrived home."

"So you think it's a break-in?" Jim said, his face creased in concern.

"Well, we've been worried about it happening on the North Fork, haven't we?" Margaret responded. "And someone could have known they wouldn't be home tonight."

Jim fed the car more gas. "That does sound logical."

"And if there are burglars in there, if we call, it could scare them off."

"You're right," Jim said, picking up speed. "We'll call NO CRIME."

Undersheriff Casey Drews was on shift until eleven o'clock. He had his paperwork cleared up by nine, and decided to call home and tell his boys good night. When they went off to bed, his wife got on the phone, and they were chatting together when the NO CRIME call came in. "Gotta go!" Casey said, quickly hanging up.

"NO CRIME. Undersheriff Drews."

"Casey, it's Jim Carlson. I'm calling to report suspicious activity. The Jensens are in Spokane tonight, and there's a light on in their den. Margaret is fairly certain it wasn't on a half-hour ago when we drove down the road. Could mean a break-in."

"Sheriff Woods will be there immediately. Thank you very much for calling."

According to standing orders, Drews called Sheriff Woods on his cell phone. The undersheriff's face took on a puzzled look as the number rang time after time, with no answer. The sheriff had given an explicit directive that he personally wanted to handle the NO CRIME calls, and could be reached on his cell phone twenty-four hours a day.

Well, he had tried. While he looked up the Jensens' address, he punched the sheriff's speed dial one more time. After the fifth ring, he hung up and put out an emergency call to the police cruisers. "Attention, all cars. There's a report of a possible burglary in progress at the Jensen residence at 150

BLACK DIAMOND

North Fork Road."

Deputy Nick Raines was driving through the north side of town, drinking coffee and chomping on powdered doughnuts. It had been a quiet night, and he snapped to attention when the alert crackled through his radio.

"Number 137 responding from Center Valley Road," Raines said in a loud, clear voice. "Will proceed at once."

About ten miles away, Corporal Murphy began speeding toward the North Fork. "Number 204 responding for backup," he barked into his radio. "I'm on East Tellee Road, and I'm on my way."

The two cruisers made radio contact with each other, and met up where the river road branched onto the North Fork. They turned off their siren and lights and began their approach. Five minutes later, both cars pulled into the Jensens' driveway. They got out with drawn guns, cautiously making their way around the dark, shadowy house. When they reached the front, a sudden loud roar startled them, and a red motorcycle streaked past. "Stop, or I'll shoot!" Deputy Raines bellowed.

His words were met by a deafening roar as the helmeted driver crazily zigzagged off at top speed. Deputy Raines shot at his tires, but missed the moving targets in the darkness. Bullets ricocheted off the driveway, as Corporal Murphy also fired off six rounds. The motorcyclist escaped, and turned down the North Fork Road. "I'll go after him!" Corporal Murphy snapped. "You check inside the house."

Murphy jumped in his police car and took off after the cycle, siren blaring and lights flashing. He saw the motorcycle's taillight ahead of him in the distance, and stepped hard on the gas pedal. The speedometer inched higher and higher, but the cycle kept its lead.

When it got to the foot of the North Fork and started down the two-lane highway, the motorcycle built up even more speed. Holding the steering wheel in a white-knuckled grip, Corporal Murphy floored the police cruiser, hoping it wouldn't go out of control. He glanced at the speedometer, horrified to see he was going 125 miles per hour. He couldn't believe the motorcyclist was driving so recklessly. But he wasn't going to get away. This lowlife was going to be locked up where he belonged.

A mile ahead where the road curved, he saw the cycle lose control, skidding and teetering before it finally careened off the road. Corporal Murphy raced to the spot and jumped out of his car. The smashed cycle lay on its side by the tree line, its driver sprawled beside it. He saw immediately that he was unconscious, and called in for a medical team. He turned off the cycle key, threw a blanket over the driver, then pulled out his flashlight and shined it around the scene. Bright gold coins were scattered all over the ground, glittering in the flashlight's beam.

At the Jensen house, Deputy Raines walked through the unlocked front door. He made his way slowly toward the den, his gun out in front of him. When he stepped into the room, he was dumbstruck at the sight of the girl sitting on the floor, still prying out coins. He watched as she dropped them into a backpack.

The room was in a state of total disarray, with broken frames and pieces of glass everywhere. The deputy returned his gun to its holster and approached the girl quietly. She looked up at him with vacant eyes, then went back to work, her long stringy hair falling across her face as she bent over the frames.

"What's your name, miss?"

"Laura."

"Laura who?" he asked, writing in his notebook.

"Laura Finley."

"Was there a guy doing this job with you?"

She nodded her head.

"What's his name?"

"Angel. He'll be right back."

Dominick Garcia was losing it. He never should've let Fione set the time for eleven. His nerves wouldn't take anymore. Here he was, stuck in this lousy motel room for another hour. He took a nip from his bottle, and paced around restlessly. The room was worse than a jail cell. A jail cell didn't have beat-up furniture, stinking drapes falling off rods, threadbare carpet, and a godawful picture of flowers hanging on the wall.

In fact, he had absolutely had it with that goddamn picture. Talk about shining shit. Why would anyone in their right mind hang a picture in this shithole? Suddenly taking action, he climbed up on the bed and yanked it off the wall. He slammed it down on the floor, then got down and jumped on it, crushing it to pieces. He kicked it under the bed, sure the lousy maids wouldn't find it for years.

With some of his frustration vented, he sank into a chair, leaned back, and closed his eyes. He just had to be patient. He had waited this long. Now it would all be over very soon. He smiled with pleasure at the thought of getting his hands around Little Miss Orderly's throat. He'd make her pay for all the trouble she had caused him. He would take hold and squeeze tighter and tighter, listening to her strangled gurgle. His smile widened at the thought of watching Ms. Susan Muir suffocate to death in the plastic bag, her eyes bulging in terror. Yes, it would all be worth it for those two sweet moments.

Oh, so sweet. And only one more hour. It would be all right now to go over to the bar and wait. He would just have one or two. Then he would head out to the Black Diamond Ranch to meet up with Bruce Fione. That was one date he wasn't going to be late for.

It was after ten by the time Sheriff Woods got away from the Black Diamond. He had been browbeaten and blackmailed, and had finally been coerced into stalling the raid until the next afternoon. He didn't know how he was going to pull it off, but he'd have to figure something out. He had no choice. Tony had absolutely demanded more time, and wouldn't take no for an answer. When Johnny and Phil got back, they'd all start cleaning the place out as soon as they could. But they had to wait until the lieutenant had made his appearance.

As he drove down Cedar Creek Road, the sheriff checked the Caller ID on his cell phone to see what incoming call he had missed. The number for headquarters lit on the screen. He punched it in, wondering what was up.

"Sheriff's office. Undersheriff Drews."

"Casey, it's Wally. Did you try to reach me? My phone didn't ring through."

BLACK DIAMOND

"I sure did. A call came in on NO CRIME, and I followed your orders and tried to turn it over to you. When you didn't answer, I dispatched two cruisers."

Sheriff Woods began sweating. His heart was fluttering, and he suddenly had difficulty breathing. He pulled over to the side of the road. "So what happened?"

"A burglary out on the North Fork, at the Jensens'. Guy and a gal. We nailed them red-handed. They were in the process of stealing a very valuable gold coin collection. Looks like it was the break we've been waiting for. I'm betting it's the same two we've been after."

The sheriff's heart was skipping wildly. His voice turned hoarse with nervousness. "What are their names?"

"Bruce Fione and Laura Finley."

"Well, I'll be damned. Good work, Casey."

"Thank you, Sheriff. I only wish you could've been in on the bust, after all the work you've put into NO CRIME."

"That doesn't matter at all. Just so the culprits are caught." The sheriff took a deep breath to calm his pounding heart. "Have they made a statement yet?"

"No. Fione's in the hospital unconscious. He crashed his motorcycle at high speed. If he hadn't been wearing a helmet, he never would've survived. He has broken bones, multiple cuts and abrasions, and severe concussion. He's not in very good shape at the moment, but the docs say he'll recover."

"Is he under guard?"

"Yes. There's an officer on duty twenty-four hours a day."

"What about the girl?"

"She's being held in a padded cell, under close watch. The jail nurse is keeping her heavily sedated. When

Deputy Raines brought her in, they passed the crash sight, and she became hysterical. True love, I guess, because the bastard had taken off and left her alone inside the house. Nick says when she saw the wrecked motorcycle, she begged him to stop and let her out. She told him she could see he was hurt, and he needed her. When Nick wouldn't stop, she started crying and screaming, throwing herself against the car door. She's pretty bruised up from it."

Wally drew in his breath. "So no statement from her, either?"

"Not yet. We have to wait till the jail doctor gives the okay."

"Well, good job, Casey. I always knew I could count on you."

"Thank you, Sheriff."

The sheriff pulled back on the road and began driving. Driving where? It was over. What was he going to do? Where was he going to go? He could make a getaway to the Cayman's. He still had time, and his bank account was there waiting for him. Maybe Joyce would forgive him and join him there. With investments, they'd have plenty of money. She could come back and visit her family whenever she wanted. He'd miss it here so much. Tears welled in his eyes at the thought of leaving his beloved home. He always fondly referred to his town as 'Marble Point, Idahome.'

Tears rolled from his eyes. But he didn't want to live in disgrace. He didn't want to go to jail. He couldn't bear the pain of giving up his uniform for a shameful orange suit. They could have a nice home in the Cayman's, and the beaches were beautiful. They could buy a boat. They would make new friends. The kids could come and visit. He came to a stop at the frontage road, deciding which way to turn. He was tempted to go down to the Blue Moon and have a few drinks to escape reality.

But then he turned toward home. Home to Joyce. He would confess everything. He could already feel the heavy burden lifting. He had felt so guilty lying to her. He loved her. He always had, he always would. And she loved him. Since their carefree school days, they had been through a lot together, and had forged the close bonds that can come only with time. He hoped she could find it in her heart to forgive him. He needed her so much.

At the end of their meal, Susan and Charlie leaned back in their chairs and sighed with pleasure. They had eaten at the table in the kitchen alcove that looked out over the side deck. Susan had set it with a blue cotton tablecloth and napkins, using her brightly colored dishes. By silent agreement, they had kept the conversation off the problems at hand, making the meal a relaxing interlude.

"Well, I have to say, that was the best steak I've ever had!" Susan said.

Charlie gave her his usual grin. "Wait till you taste my barbecued chicken!"

Susan smiled. "Well, do you want to see if you find my chocolate chip cookies as irresistible as Bruce Fione did?"

Charlie glanced at his watch. "It's 10:45. Maybe I should wait until we get back." His deep blue eyes lit up. "Anyway, by that time, I'll have room for more."

As they began clearing the table, Charlie's cell phone rang. His expression turned serious as he pulled it out of his pocket. "Lieutenant Martin."

"Lieutenant, it's Undersheriff Drews. Patrolman Jeffries just called in. The clerk at the Sunset Hotel out on Highway 95 ID'd Garcia's picture. He's been registered there since Thursday under the name of John Grenco. Jeffries went around back and found a brown Ford Escort, with a license plate number that matched the one the rental agency gave us."

"Very good," Charlie said.

"There's more. Garcia came walking out of the bar next door, got in the Escort, and pulled out. Patrolman Jeffries went back to his cruiser and followed him, thinking maybe he'd get him on a DUI. He stayed with him for eight miles. He's sure Garcia knew he had a tail, because when he exited Highway 95, he pulled a few fancy moves and lost him."

"What exit did he take?"

"Exit 15. Patrolman Jeffries thinks he was probably headed for the north frontage road."

"Interesting," Charlie responded. "I'm headed out that way myself. I'll keep a lookout. Thank you very much, Undersheriff Drews. Excellent work."

"You're certainly welcome, Lieutenant. I'm glad we could help you out."

Charlie gave Susan the news, and went into the den to put his shoulder holster back on. Susan got her jacket and went in the den to wait for him. "Do you always wear your gun on dates?" she asked him.

"Only when I'm going out with dangerous women," Charlie retorted.

He started packing up his briefcase to take with him.

BLACK DIAMOND

He had brought it back inside to get out an e-mail address. Some of its contents were still spread out on the small coffee table by his laptop. As Susan watched him return the items to his briefcase, she let out a gasp and her mouth dropped open in shock.

Charlie gave her a questioning look. "What's the matter?"

"Let me see that again!" Susan said, her eyes wide.

"What?"

"That picture."

Charlie pulled the glossy eight-by-ten back out and held it up for her. Susan stared at it in disbelief. "Is that Heidi Townsend?"

"Yes. Why?"

"She's staying at the Black Diamond."

Charlie looked at her in astonishment. "You saw her there?"

"Definitely. The first time I went out. And she looked so woebegone, I couldn't get her off my mind."

"Unbelievable!" Charlie exclaimed. His eyes sparked. "The patrolman tailing Garcia lost him near the frontage road. He could be going after Heidi!"

"You're right!" Susan cried. "Especially at this time of night. We might not be the only ones who suddenly found out where she is."

Charlie hit his cell phone for the sheriff's office. "Undersheriff Drews, this is Lieutenant Martin again. Susan Muir just positively identified Heidi Townsend's picture, and has seen her at the Black Diamond Ranch. The people I questioned out there claimed they never saw her before. And I'm afraid there's a good chance Garcia found out where she is, and he's on his way. Heidi could be in real danger. Can you send out a couple of cars?"

"As soon as possible, Lieutenant. And I'll head out there myself."

Eleven o'clock. Where was that fucker? Dominick Garcia sat in his Ford Escort, parked near the end of the forest service road behind the Black Diamond. The Escort was facing Cedar Creek Road, so when Bruce Fione handed Heidi over, he could hit the power door locks and take off. But Bruce Fione wasn't here. He wasn't going to show up. The lousy bastard wasn't coming. Garcia had waited till eleven o'clock for nothing. And picked up a tail in the process. The cop saw him coming out of the bar and thought he'd get him for drunken driving. The stupid ass. Losing him was as easy as taking candy from a fucking baby.

Now Fione had made a fool out of him, and he was going to pay for it with his life. But he'd have to take care of that later. Right now he had to deal with the business at hand. The little girl. He would get inside that tool shed one way or the other. He had been crazy not to come prepared to cut the padlock. Goddamnit, he wasn't thinking clearly anymore. He had his burglary tools with him, but if he started working on the lock, Little Miss Orderly would hear him, and know something was wrong. And she would scream. And the screams would carry to the lodge.

Garcia got out his bottle and took a few thoughtful sips. A smile began spreading over his face. He'd shoot the fucking lock off. He'd wrap his Beretta in his jacket to muffle the noise. Then he would put it against the lock, pull the trigger, and blow it apart. Nobody would hear the shot except the little girl, and she'd never have a chance to scream. He

BLACK DIAMOND

would burst through the door and take her by surprise. He'd have his hands around her throat in an instant. Afterwards he'd carry her body to the car and throw it in the trunk.

Yes. It would work. He stepped out of the car and closed the door quietly. Walking across the road, he climbed over the fence, and took to the cover of the trees. When he came to the clearing, he stopped to establish the direction he would take. He would make a dash to the back of the smallest building. There was a good chance it was the tool shed. But it would take only short minutes to find out. He would keep close to the side of the building as he made his way around front. If the door was held shut by a padlock, he would know his search was over.

What the hell? Here came a vehicle up Cedar Creek Road. It might turn into the ranch. He'd have to wait and see. He didn't dare risk being spotted. 11:10. Maybe Fione was showing up after all. Garcia tensely followed the headlights to see if they would continue up the road. No. He watched as a pickup turned into the ranch and drove through the gate. Now it was coming around back. Garcia observed two men get out and walk toward the back door of the lodge. He couldn't make out their faces in the darkness, but from their size and gait, they appeared to be two of the regulars he had seen around.

They opened the door, and went through. Now he could make his move. He began running towards the tool shed.

CHAPTER 19

HEIDI heard pounding footsteps behind the shed. She sat straight up, listening hard. Now they were gone. Maybe she had just heard a strange noise, and the pounding was from her own heart. She ran over and pressed her ear to the wall. She could hear the squirrel moving around in the eaves. Now he was skittering to the ground. With her ear flattened against the board wall, she heard a man let out a low angry curse. Someone was sneaking up on her, and Jeremy had startled him. Who was it? A policeman wouldn't be sneaking up. Dominick Garcia had found her.

She was done for. No one had come for her in time. Her heart began pounding so hard, she put her hand on it, as if to steady it. He was going to break the lock and burst through the door. The shovel. She'd stand behind the door and catch him off guard. She'd hit him with the shovel and stun him, then run out the door and hide in the trees. She would have to turn the light out, so he wouldn't see her. And in case she didn't make it out the door, she would break the string so he couldn't turn the light back on. Then she could at least try to hide from him in the dark shed. She ran over to the bare bulb and took hold of the string, yanking it hard. The string broke as the light went out, and the shed was plunged into total darkness.

  Heidi made her way to the door and planted her feet firmly in place, holding the shovel behind her shoulder to get a full swing. Already weak from hunger, and numb with fright, she felt as if her legs were going to fold under her. Courage. She had to have courage. She heard a sharp stifled sound outside, and the next instant the door burst open. In the moonlight filtering in from outside, she saw the dark shadowy form of Dominick Garcia framed in the doorway. With her heart beating chaotically, Heidi drew the shovel back and swung it at his head with full force. Stunned, he slumped over, and Heidi started running out the door.

  "Oh no you don't, you little bitch," Garcia said in a menacing tone. He slammed the door closed with one hand, and grabbed her leg with the other. Still holding the shovel, Heidi slammed it down on his head and broke free. Garcia cursed as he grabbed the shovel and wrenched it from her grasp, throwing it to the floor.

  As he fumbled on the wall for a light switch, Heidi crept to the other side of the door. When he moved off looking for her, she would make her escape. But no. Panic swept over her. She couldn't run out the door. She couldn't see where the shovel was, and without a weapon to give him a stunning blow, she knew he'd be right behind her. The hammer. If she could only get to the hammer. She began making her way noiselessly through the pitch dark shed. The hammer was in the far corner, under the horse blanket, where she kept it at night. She tried to quiet her breathing, sure that Garcia would hear her and follow.

"Don't think you're getting away, little girl," came the low, eerie voice through the darkness. "I'm going to strangle you just the way I strangled your mother. What's good for a whore is good for a whore's daughter."

Heidi's skin crawled with fear and loathing. A clatter sounded in the murky gloom, followed by loud curses. Heidi realized Garcia had bumped into one of the buckets. "It stinks in here, little girl. What happened? Have you turned into a stinky little girl?"

Heidi was quivering with fear. She had to get to the hammer. She inched across the shed through the darkness.

"Are you having fun playing hide and seek, little girl?" came the eerie voice. "This is a special game. You don't even have to take a turn being 'it'." He let out a sinister laugh. "The only problem is, I'm getting tired of playing."

A crashing sound broke the ensuing silence, and Heidi could tell he had knocked over a chair in her sitting area. He was getting closer. If she didn't hurry, she'd never make it to the corner in time. With adrenaline surging through her, she darted to the blanket and picked up the hammer. Then, holding it in a tight grip, she backed into the corner to wait.

"I heard you, little girl. The game's over. Here I come, ready or not."

Heidi was shaking all over. She strained to see in the darkness, watching for her attacker. As hard as she tried, she couldn't make out his form. But she knew he couldn't be far away. She picked up a loose stone from the floor and hurled it across the shed, hoping the sound of it landing would divert him.

"Are you trying to fool me, little girl?" came the voice. "It won't work. I've got you now."

Heidi could smell Garcia's whiskey breath. Through the enveloping darkness, she heard the sound of his breathing as he drew near. She tightened her grip on the hammer. She saw his looming figure as he reached for her throat. Heidi swung the hammer as hard as she could, landing a glancing blow on the side of his head. Then she ran for the door.

Susan and Charlie sped in silence toward the Black Diamond. They were both immersed in their own thoughts, wondering how the night would unfold. When they finally pulled into the ranch, Charlie slowed down as their eyes began searching the grounds. "It still looks quiet," Susan said in relief as they rolled to a stop in front of the lodge.

"The police should be here any minute," Charlie responded. "I'll go inside and see what's going on. Maybe the other two are back, and I can make them talk." He reached into the back seat for his briefcase. "If they have faulty memories, too, at least I'll have the pleasure of nailing all four of them for obstruction of justice."

Susan smiled. "That would be a nice little preview for the main event tomorrow when all the meth charges come down."

Charlie grinned. "And it would effectively eliminate their chance of a clean-up tonight."

They got out of the car, and Charlie paused. "If anything happens out here, give a quick holler."

"And a loud one," Susan added with a little laugh.

As Charlie started up the steps to the lodge, Susan made her way to the back. She stood looking around in the quiet, peaceful night. There was no sign of any motion. Even the pine and fir trees were still, with no breeze to stir their branches. The buildings were dark. Only the far-off hooting of an owl broke the silence. The sky was clear and bright. As she stood there keeping watch, Susan couldn't shake off the odd feeling it was the calm before the storm.

At the fringes of the grounds, a shed door burst open, and a girl with long blonde hair came running out, heading for the nearby stand of trees. It had to be Heidi. Why had she come bursting out the door? Was Garcia after her? Was he still inside the shed? She had to get Charlie. Her pulse racing, Susan moved toward the back door of the lodge. When she reached it and turned the knob, her heart fell as she realized it was locked.

The sound of blaring sirens suddenly filled the night. The police were coming! Susan glanced over at the whirling dome lights as the cars turned off their sirens and rolled through the gate. Looking back at the shed, she saw a dark figure of a burly man come charging through the door. Garcia! Susan's heart stopped as he turned his head in her direction. Could he see her? She felt completely exposed, standing by the back door under the outside light.

Yes, he saw her! Here he came, running towards her. He wasn't firing his gun because the noise would attract attention inside the lodge. And he wasn't going to leave a live witness behind. He was going to kill her with his bare hands, before he chased down Heidi. Susan began pounding on the lodge door. No one heard her from upstairs. Now she didn't have a chance. Garcia was gaining ground.

Like a deer trapped by headlights, Garcia stopped and froze, his full attention centering on the police cars' bright flashing lights. Suddenly he turned and raced toward the back fence. As Susan stood watching on shaking legs, she heard an engine start up behind the ranch. A car squealed off and turned north onto Cedar Creek Road.

Susan ran to the front of the lodge to get Charlie, just as two policemen were charging up the steps. "Charlie!" she yelled as the police flung the lodge door open. "Charlie!"

"Arrest all four of them!" Charlie yelled over his shoulder as he ran across the porch. "What happened?" he asked Susan, his face etched with worry.

"Garcia was after Heidi, but she got away. She's hiding in the trees. When the police came, Garcia took off up Cedar Creek Road."

"Are you alright?" Charlie asked in concern, putting his arm around her.

"I'm fine," Susan told him. "It's Heidi I'm worried about. That girl must be scared to death."

Sirens began wailing up Cedar Creek Road. "That's probably Undersheriff Drews," Charlie said. "I'll give him the information about Garcia so he can get out an APB."

Charlie ran to the undersheriff's car as it raced towards the lodge. Casey Drews came to a screeching stop and rolled down the window. His eyes burned into Charlie's as he listened intently. "I'll call Fayetteville and have them set up a roadblock. There's no escape route before that. In case he decides to turn around, I'll cover this end of the road myself till I can get a few cars out here." The undersheriff barked orders into his radio as he peeled out.

Charlie rejoined Susan, and they dashed out back. With Susan pointing the way, they began running toward the trees, calling Heidi's name. "We're friends!" Susan shouted. "We came to help you."

Before their eyes, a blonde girl emerged from the trees and began running towards them. As they drew close to her, Susan held out her arms as she ran, ready to enfold the frightened girl. Heidi streaked toward her, her long hair flying in the moonlight. They met in a crushing embrace. Heidi collapsed into Susan's arms, panting and sobbing. Tears came to Susan's eyes. "You're safe now. We won't let anything happen to you."

The two stood locked together, hugging each other tightly. Suddenly Susan felt another, stronger arm around her. She looked up and saw that Charlie had his arms wrapped around both of them. "Nobody will hurt you anymore," he said to Heidi softly. "You've been a very brave girl."

The next morning, Heidi sat in the kitchen alcove in her freshly washed clothes with a stack of French toast in front of her. Susan was pouring her a big glass of milk, and Charlie was at the stove frying country sausage. Its tantalizing smell rose in steamy clouds from the skillet, and Fritz stood looking on hopefully. Sun was streaming through the curtained window, highlighting Heidi's shining blonde hair.

The night before, after a soothing soak in the bathtub, Heidi had stepped into the shower and stood blissfully under a forceful spray of hot water to shampoo her hair, restoring it to its natural luster. Then, cozily dressed in a pair of Susan's pajamas, she had joined Susan and Charlie, and they had sat around the kitchen table eating chocolate chip cookies, until Heidi had finally had her fill. On the way home, they had stopped at a drive-through, and Heidi had gotten two double cheeseburgers, fries, and an extra-large Coke.

At night's end, Susan had turned back the comforter in the bedroom next to hers, and Heidi had gratefully crawled under it. Fritz jumped up on the bed and began licking her face. Susan had laughingly allowed him to stay, and Heidi had drifted off to sleep with her arm around the affectionate little dog, dreaming that Jeremy had snuggled up to her at last.

Charlie had slept downstairs in the den, and awoken early. He had called the sheriff's office immediately to find out whether or not Garcia had been apprehended. The night before, Charlie was told that somehow Garcia had avoided the two roadblocks and gotten away. This morning he learned that Garcia had escaped by turning off Cedar Creek Road onto a graveled forest service road that branched off it. After a few miles he had abandoned the Escort on an old logging road. Then, evidently he had made his way by foot to the Blue Moon and hot wired the bartender's old Toyota that was parked out back. The state police had put out an APB, and as soon as the Toyota was found, Charlie would be informed.

After his call, Charlie had made a quick trip to town to borrow a fingerprint kit from the Marble Point Police. He had dusted the chemical can for Bruce Fione's prints and used Susan's fax machine to send them to the state crime lab for comparison. Now he was waiting for the results. He had learned that Sheriff Woods had done all the fingerprinting himself in the Marble Point area burglary cases, and the crime lab did not have copies. They had put in a request to the sheriff's department for them to be sent by fax, and as soon as they arrived, the lab would notify Charlie of the findings.

During breakfast, they had talked over their plans for the day. Susan was taking Heidi shopping in the afternoon. Although they had picked up Heidi's belongings at the ranch the night before, Susan insisted on buying her a few new clothes. Susan said it would be fun, and she had her heart set on taking her shopping before she left for LA. Charlie had booked a flight for the following evening. He wanted Heidi to have time for complete rest and relaxation after her ordeal, but felt he should be back in the office on Thursday morning. Reluctant to leave, he was glad the only tickets available were for the late flight.

With Garcia still at large, he planned to keep Heidi with him in LA until he had made satisfactory arrangements for her to stay at a safe house. He would take her to her home to get the things she needed, and make a trip to her mother's grave. Heidi could finish the school year and graduate with her class. Susan was going to fly to LA in a week or so to help sort through whatever financial arrangements Heidi's mother had made. After that she would help Heidi with her college applications.

Susan felt a great affection for the abandoned girl, and had already begun bonding. She realized that not only would she miss Charlie terribly when they left, but she would miss Heidi, as well. That night, Flora and Brad were coming for dinner so everyone could meet. Charlie was doing the barbecued chicken on the outdoor grill, and Susan and Heidi were making potato salad, baked beans, and coleslaw. When they went downtown, they were going to pick up the makings for banana splits to top off the festive occasion.

When breakfast was over, Heidi took Fritz down to the lake, and Susan and Charlie settled in to read the local paper that Charlie had picked up. While he took the sports section, Susan began reading the front page.

"Oh, my goodness!" she exclaimed, continuing to read.

"Oh, my goodness, what?" Charlie asked, looking up at her.

"Bruce Fione and Laura Finley were caught last night in a burglary at the Jensens' out on the North Fork. Bruce crashed on his motorcycle trying to get away, and is in Bonham County Hospital. Laura Finley is being held in jail. The sheriff's office is expected to make a statement after the arraignment."

"Wow!" Charlie said. "So the culprits are caught. Pretty big doings last night."

"So it looks as if you went to all that trouble sending in the fingerprints for nothing," Susan remarked.

"We'll see," Charlie responded. "The way fingerprints are disappearing, who knows?"

Charlie's cell phone rang. He picked it up. "Lieutenant Martin, this is Sergeant Mike Mercereaux. I have an update for you on Dominick Garcia."

Charlie's facial muscles tightened. "Shoot."

"Due to a stroke of luck this morning, the state police found the stolen Toyota on a side street in Coeur d'Alene, not far from the Greyhound Terminal. The police found that a lone Caucasian male had boarded the 12:35 bus. The terminal was closed, and he gave the driver fifty dollars for a ticket to Seattle. The next stop on the route was Spokane, Washington, and the driver went into the station with him while he bought a ticket."

"Too bad Greyhound doesn't require ID," Charlie interjected.

"Right," Sergeant Mercereaux agreed. "But we still know he's our man. The Toyota wasn't found until nine, and the bus arrived in Seattle at seven-thirty, so he was long gone. But his photo was faxed to the bus driver, and he made a positive ID."

"Excellent police work," Charlie commented. "So we know he made it to Seattle, an international hub that could take him anywhere by just about any means of transportation."

"Exactly," Mercereaux answered. "I hate to say it, but I'm afraid he's given us the slip."

"He's one slippery bastard," Charlie replied. "But don't worry about it. You did your best."

Charlie was grim-faced as he hung up the phone. He knew Mercereaux was right. It would be next to impossible to track Garcia down. He might as well face it. Police Sergeant Dominick Garcia had gotten away. Damn, it was hard to take. It left him with a bitter taste. This time he hadn't even gotten a bite of the pie.

CHAPTER 20

SHERIFF Woods, wearing a tan cashmere sports coat and dark pants, sat in his window seat on a Boeing 737 cruising to Miami. Tomorrow morning he would board his flight to the Cayman's. He gazed out at the clouds as his mind ranged over the course of events that had led to his final decision. He had called the county hospital early that morning and learned that Bruce Fione was still unconscious. With time left to make up his mind, he had decided to go into the office as usual.

Upon his arrival, he was updated on the arrests at the Black Diamond the night before, and Heidi's close escape. He had been flooded with remorse, knowing that he, a trusted official, had allowed the girl to remain in a grave state of danger. He would carry the burden of guilt to his grave. He no longer deserved to be in office. The Black Diamond raid had gone off at nine o'clock as scheduled. In addition to the obstruction of justice and unlawful restraint charges already filed, enough solid evidence of meth manufacturing and distribution had been found to keep Tony and his workers out of circulation for many years to come.

When he had called Susan Muir with a report, although

she had sounded pleased, he had noticed the reserve in her voice. She no longer trusted him. He would never be able to convince her he had made an honest mistake with the fingerprints. Then, when he was going through his messages, he found a request from the state lab that he FAX them the prints on file from the burglaries. What was that all about? With trembling hands, in his last official act as sheriff, he had honored the request, then had called Joyce to tell her he had made up his mind. There was no way he could face losing his job and going to jail. Claiming a family emergency to the undersheriff, he had left the office and driven straight home.

Joyce had already called the airline to confirm his reservation, and packed two suitcases and an overnight bag. She would join him in the Cayman's when she had settled their affairs. The two of them had talked into the wee hours the night before. Wally had told her everything, admitting his shame. Joyce had declared that, even though he had done immoral things, she still loved him, and would stand by him whatever he decided to do. It was good he realized he had done wrong, and had learned from it. She knew he was truly sorry.

They had finally gotten into bed with their arms entwined around each other, feeling closer than they ever had before. After Joyce went to sleep, Wally slipped out of bed and paced around the house restlessly, weighing the consequences of the two choices he had. When Joyce awoke in the morning, he told her he was still thinking things over and was going into work.

When he had finally reached a decision and returned home, before they left for the airport, he had walked sadly through all the rooms of the memory-packed house for the last time. When he went into the den, his eyes roved over the familiar spines in the bookcase, resting on the Marble Point High School Annuals. Overcome with nostalgia, he walked over and pulled them off the shelf to take along with him. They would lend a touch of home during the lonely days ahead in the Cayman's.

Now, sitting on the 737, while he musingly watched the clouds sail past his window as he left Marble Point behind, Wally's mind drifted back to his high school glory days. As he thought of the yearbooks inside his suitcase, he began imagining the snapshots between their covers as clearly as if they were before his eyes. His proud expression, his proud stance. A sense of pride had emanated from him like a polar force. Now he had none. He had lost all his self-respect. How had he ever allowed the proud boy in the yearbook to grow up to be a shameful man?

On Wednesday evening, Heidi walked into the living room where Susan and Charlie were sitting side by side on the sofa before a crackling fire. Heidi was becomingly dressed in an outfit Susan had bought for her, a long-sleeved chambray shirt tied at the waist, worn with a pair of khaki capri's. A turquoise bead necklace highlighted her blue eyes. As she took a chair across from them, Fritz sat down beside her, laying his head on her lap.

"What is Fritz going to do without you when you leave?" Susan said laughingly. "He's going to be heartbroken."

"I'm going to miss him a lot, too."

As the three of them sat watching the dancing flames,

they cast occasional glances at the mantel clock, knowing the time for parting was drawing near. The air of gaiety that had filled the house the night before was absent. Last evening's dinner party had been a big success. For the special occasion, Flora had brought along a gift for Heidi, a piece of jewelry the girl had greatly admired when Susan had taken her by the shop that afternoon. When Heidi opened the box, tears sprang to her eyes when she saw the little rainbow pin nestled inside.

Susan and Flora told Heidi all about their Friday night mission to the Black Diamond, remarking on how they had gone right past the tool shed where she was locked up. In turn, Heidi revealed how sorry she had been about not getting up the nerve to call to them. When she told them about Jeremy, Susan and Flora smiled at each other in wry amusement. While they talked over events at the ranch, Charlie and Brad found common ground in the subjects of hunting and fishing. As a city dweller, Charlie admitted, he was envious of Brad having opportunities for both sports practically in his own back yard.

Towards the end of the evening, while the four adults sat conversing, Heidi went into the kitchen to make the banana splits. When she carried the tray into the living room, she was flushed with excitement. Now as the three of them sat quietly watching the fire, Susan studied Heidi closely. Though the girl no longer bore the same woebegone look as when Susan first saw her, her face still reflected deep sorrow and pain. Susan knew it would take time for Heidi's wounds to heal, and that she would be haunted by hurtful memories for many years to come.

BLACK DIAMOND

Besides all her own problems, Heidi had been greatly upset by the newspaper account of Laura's arrest. But her spirits had lifted again when Susan and Charlie assured her Laura would be put into drug rehab and have the opportunity to straighten out her life.

As Susan sat thoughtfully looking at her, she was pleasantly aware of how Heidi's face had taken on a sunnier look. She had a little color in her cheeks and her eyes had brightened. Still, tonight she seemed dispirited.

"Is anything wrong?" Susan finally asked.

"No. Not at all," Heidi answered quickly.

"Tell me the truth," Susan pressed, sensing something was troubling her.

"Well, I'm really anxious to see my friends and finish school," Heidi answered hesitantly. "But I guess I'm a little sad about leaving. You two have been so nice to me. It's been kind of like having a family."

Susan felt a stirring in her heart. She thought about how on their walk yesterday morning Heidi had gazed longingly at her father's house. Susan had been shocked when Heidi told her Jack Stone was her father, and she would like to see where he lived. Though all the facts weren't in yet, Susan was sure Jack Stone was involved in the drug trafficking at the Black Diamond, and would either remain in the Cayman's or go to jail.

Now Susan gave her an understanding smile. "I've been thinking, how would you like to come back when school's out, and meet some more of your new family?"

Heidi's face lit up instantly. "What do you mean?"

"My mother and father will be back from their trip,

and my sister Lillian and her family are coming on vacation. They would all love to meet you."

Heidi leaned forward in excitement. "You mean, those two kids in the picture on your desk are coming?"

"Yes," Susan answered with a big smile. "The ones I told you all about."

"Oh, I would love to meet them!" Heidi exclaimed. "And I could baby-sit if you all wanted to go out."

Susan laughed. "I have to warn you, they're not as innocent as they look in that picture."

Heidi laughed with her. "I can handle it. It'll be so much fun."

"I promised them I'd buy a boat before they got here," Susan said. "Do you like to take boat rides?"

"Oh, I love boats!" Heidi exclaimed, her smile spreading from ear to ear. Suddenly she jumped up and ran over to Susan, hugging her tight. "You're so nice!"

Charlie moved over on the couch, making room, and Heidi sat down between them. Charlie leaned forward to look at Susan, raising a quizzical eyebrow. "Am I invited to meet the family, too?"

"Of course. You wouldn't let Heidi travel by herself, would you?"

"Exactly what I was thinking," Charlie said. He rearranged his face into a frown. "Actually, I'm kind of sad about something, myself."

"What's that?" Susan asked sitting up in concern.

"Brad told me the Marble Lake regatta is a lot of fun, and Heidi and I are going to miss it."

Susan's heart raced. "Are you really thinking of

coming back next weekend for the regatta?"

"If anyone invites me."

Susan burst out laughing. "You're invited, you funny man!"

Heidi sat looking back and forth between them. "Do you mean it? Are we really coming?" she asked Charlie.

Charlie chuckled and wagged his finger at her. "If you behave yourself, and get all your homework done."

Heidi laughed. "You're so funny!" Then she threw her arms around his neck and gave him a hug. "You're really nice, too!"

Susan turned to Charlie. "Will you be coming in on Friday night?"

"That's what I was thinking."

"I have a dinner to attend that night," she said. "Wait a minute. I'll be right back."

In a few minutes, she returned and handed him a key. "Take this in case I'm not home yet when you get here."

Charlie grinned. "The night I arrived in Marble Point, I had a feeling good things were going to happen, but I never expected to be getting a key from a beautiful woman."

Susan smiled into his eyes. "Just don't lose it."

"Not a chance," Charlie said, slipping it onto his key ring.

Dominick Garcia sat at the bar in the Loon Lake Lounge in a state of murderous rage, waiting for darkness to fall. Susan Muir had ruined everything. She had ruined his whole life. And now he was going to get his revenge. When his scheme to get Heidi had been aborted, he had spent a sleepless night on the Greyhound bus, turning everything over endlessly in his mind. He knew he could never go back to LA. Now that the state had Heidi Townsend as a live witness, he didn't dare face going to trial. And, unfortunately, he didn't have enough money stashed away to leave the country.

His plan had become clear to him an hour outside of Seattle. To be on the safe side, he'd change his looks a little, so he wouldn't have to worry about being recognized. He'd grow a mustache, maybe a goatee, wear a different hairstyle. And keep the dark glasses. Then he would go to Chicago, make some mobster connections, and get into some big time vice. He had learned a lot during his years on the vice squad, especially about the big bucks to be made working outside the law. After taking penny-ante payoffs for so long, it would feel good to get into the real action.

But before he went anywhere, he was attending to unfinished business. He was going to make Bruce Fione very, very sorry he hadn't shown up for his eleven o'clock appointment. Payback time was going to be oh-so-sweet. But first he was taking care of Susan Muir. She thought she had won the game, but she was going to find out it wasn't over yet. Now they were going to play sudden death. And she was going to be the loser.

He would take the next bus back to Coeur d'Alene, then rent a car for his drive to Marble Point. He didn't have any more ID's, but the police would never guess to look for him in the place he had run away from. He'd left all his stuff in the Escort, so he'd have to pick up a few things. Like another glass cutter to get in her basement. He still had the plastic bag. It had been folded up in his pocket. Oh, he couldn't wait to watch the bitch suffocate to death. He would keep giving her just a little air while she struggled to breathe, to prolong her sweet suffering. Afterwards he'd follow through on his original idea and dump her body in the lake. It would be easier for him to disappear if the police weren't hot on his trail.

Last night the game had been postponed. When he had scouted out her house, he saw the lieutenant's Chevy Caprice in her driveway. When he drove past again, a little after midnight, all the lights were turned out, and he realized the lieutenant had something going with her and had temporarily moved in. Which meant the girl was there too. The lieutenant would be sure to keep his star witness with him. How nice it would be to go in there and take out all three of them. But he wasn't going to risk going up against a trained policeman. No, it was Susan Muir he wanted, and he wanted her to be alone.

But now his plans had changed. Visions of her and the lieutenant in bed together swam in his head. Vivid pictures of them doing things to each other played and replayed in his mind. Before she died, she was going to find out what it was like to be fucked by a real man's dick. She was going to feel it, get the taste of it, take it up her fucking tight ass.

Now the sweet moment was drawing near. That morning, with the help of his buddy on LAPD, he had learned that Lieutenant Charles Martin and Miss Heidi Townsend were booked on the red-eye to LA that night. Which meant his waiting game would soon be over. He had passed the rest of the day catching up on his sleep in his latest fleabag motel. Then, overcome with impatience to get started, he had set off for the

Loon Lake Lounge, the cozy-looking little place he had noticed at the northern end of the lake. He'd be nice and close to Ms. Susan Muir's house. And he could have a drink at the bar while he waited for it to get dark.

Every nerve in his body tingled as he got up and looked out the window into the gathering dusk. Oh yes. Fog was rolling in off the lake. Too perfect. It would make it so much easier to sneak up on her. He checked his watch. The lieutenant would be gone by now. And she'd be all alone. Just the way he wanted it. He smiled and returned to his barstool. One more drink, and it would be time to go.

Susan stood at her open living room window watching the thick fog roll off the lake, drifting around her house. She jumped as a loon let out a loud wail near the shoreline. She quickly closed the window and locked it. What was the matter with her? Why were her nerves so on edge? Why would she be startled by the cry of a loon? Had she gotten so used to Charlie's comforting presence, she was afraid to be alone? Well, she'd have to get over it.

Resolutely fixing herself a cup of tea, she carried it back into the living room, and added another log to the fire. While Fritz stretched out on the hearth rug, she sat down in an easy chair with one leg tucked under her. As she sipped the hot tea and listened to the crackling fire, she tried to assure herself there was nothing to worry about.

The state crime lab had reported to Charlie that Bruce Fione's fingerprints matched the ones from the burglaries, so she knew he was the one who had broken into her house. And he was in the hospital under twenty-four hour guard. Of course the sheriff's deception about the fingerprints was unsettling, and Susan planned to meet with him when he returned from the family emergency that had taken him out of town. Heidi was safe, and in good hands with Charlie. She had left with a smile on her face, eagerly anticipating coming back for the regatta. The Black Diamond was closed down and Tony and his gang were locked up in jail. Judge Walker had considered them at high risk to run and had set bail impossibly high. Dominick Garcia was still on the loose, but at least he had fled the state, and was several hundred miles away.

She suddenly realized her cup of tea was empty, and the fire was dying down. She would let Fritz out for a few minutes, then crawl into bed with a good book. That would get everything off her mind. After she opened the back door for Fritz, she went upstairs and changed into her favorite nightgown and robe. There, she felt better already. Much cozier. She should have changed clothes long before.

She went back downstairs and stepped onto the back porch to call Fritz. The cool, damp air blew against her face. A pair of loons made strange yodeling calls back and forth through the fog. Headlights glowing dimly through the darkness on the western side of the lake caught her eye. A car was coming! Now she could hear the muffled purr of its engine.

With growing apprehension, Susan watched it turn the corner and proceed towards her house. As it passed by her gate, in the halo of light from the gas lamps, she thought she distinguished a lone male driver. He seemed to turn his head to look at her, then quickly turn away. She felt a stab of anxiety, thinking the driver knew she was alone and vulnerable. Who was he? Why would he be taking a drive around the lake on such a foggy night? Was he coming after her?

Charlie and Heidi pulled into the Marble Point Inn on their way to the airport. In the hotel's longstanding tradition of warm hospitality, it had extended a late checkout to Charlie, convenient for his scheduled red-eye flight. When they went into the lobby, they stopped at the front desk, then went to Charlie's room to pick up his belongings. Before zipping the bags, Heidi insisted on making a final check to make sure nothing was being left behind.

Charlie stepped onto the balcony to take a farewell look at the town he had grown to love in the short time he had been there. He leaned on the railing, looking out at Marble Lake, picture-postcard-perfect under the darkening sky. But instead of having the same good feeling that had overtaken him the night he arrived, he was nagged by uneasiness. Why would he be uneasy? Things were good. Not only had he met up with the woman of his dreams, but he had found Heidi and was taking her back to LA.

Of course it had been hard leaving Susan. Leaving her all alone. That was it. He was worried about Susan. But why? He never would have left her alone if Bruce Fione hadn't been caught. He glanced at his watch. He and Heidi needed to get going to catch their plane. But first he'd give Susan a quick call. It would make him feel better to hear her voice. He pulled out his cell phone and hit her number.

"Hello. This is Susan."

BLACK DIAMOND

At the sound of her voice, Charlie felt a jolt of alarm. He could tell something was wrong. "Hi. It's Charlie. Is everything okay?"

"Charlie!" Susan exclaimed. "Where are you?"

"Just leaving the Marble Point Inn. I just called to say goodbye, but now that I hear your voice, I detect a note of anxiety. Am I right?"

"I'm fine," Susan answered. "Go catch your flight."

"Tell me the truth, Susan."

Susan had a sharp intake of breath. "Okay, I'm scared to death."

Charlie's body grew rigid. "What happened?"

"Nothing really. There's a heavy fog tonight, and a car just went past. It looked like a man driving, all by himself. But I know it can't be Bruce, so I don't know why I'm so edgy."

"With everything you've gone through lately, you have plenty of reason to be edgy," Charlie responded. "What kind of a car was it?"

"I'm not sure. A Dodge maybe. It was a dark green four-door."

Every muscle in Charlie's body tightened. Last night, sometime past midnight, he had seen a dark green Dodge Neon drive past. Was it the same car? Had it kept going last night because he had been there? "I'm coming back," he said evenly. "And don't bother arguing."

He stepped inside where Heidi was waiting. "I'm sorry," he told her. "Change of plans. I'm keeping the room and leaving you here. Double lock the door behind me, and don't answer it for anybody. Not for anybody." He tried his best to give her a reassuring grin. "Except me, of course. I'll be back for you as soon as I can."

Heidi's eyes grew wide with fright. "Is Dominick Garcia back?"

Waves of panic swept over Charlie. Was it possible?

CHAPTER 21

DOMINICK Garcia's head pounded in turmoil as he drove along Loon Lake Road through the dense fog, straining to see as he neared Susan's house. Oh yes, the driveway was empty, just the way he knew it would be. There she was all alone, out on the porch getting some air. His mouth twisted into a sardonic smile. A woman condemned to death by suffocation was entitled to take her last deep breaths of air. But now the time had come for her to die. He stepped on the gas pedal, speeding along to the campground. He parked well off the road, and took the footpath down to the lake. Then he started down the shoreline, his advancing figure hidden by the billowing fog.

Inside the house, Susan was in her bedroom waiting for Charlie. Unable to concentrate on her book, she was standing by the window, watching for a sign of headlights. She hoped fervently if headlights appeared, they would be Charlie's. He should be here soon. She knew he'd be driving at top speed. He had sounded so worried on the phone. Obviously he was worried. He had canceled his flight to come back. And what if he had canceled it for nothing? She didn't know why she had gotten so scared simply because a car had driven past her house. It's not as if it had stopped.

But yet Susan couldn't push the thought from her mind. What if the car came back? Or even worse, what if the driver had parked down the road so he could creep up on her? Susan shivered. If he were going to sneak up, he'd probably stay off the road, and make his way through the thick bank of fog along the lake. She'd go look out a front bedroom window and see if she saw anyone. She reluctantly left the coziness of her room and hurried down the hallway. Fritz got up and followed along after her.

Entering a spare bedroom with a clear view of the lake, she peered through the window into the enveloping darkness. Way down the shoreline, she thought she saw something moving. Now it had disappeared into the shroud of fog. Maybe it had been a loon taking flight. She needed her night vision scope. If only she hadn't left it in the car. In her state of nerves, she didn't want to go down to the basement and into the garage.

Another movement. She was sure of it. And it wasn't a loon. Her heart began thudding. Then, in the ever-shifting fog, she glimpsed a dark shadow moving along the shore. But she couldn't be certain. She had to go downstairs and get her night scope. Taking a last look out the window, she turned and left the room, hurrying down the hallway.

Filled with determination, she descended the stairs to the first floor, then went into the kitchen and opened the basement door, flipping on the light switch. A loud pop made her jump in alarm. Oh no! The basement light that operated from the wall switch had burned out. Of all times. Well, she didn't have time to go get a flashlight. She didn't

BLACK DIAMOND

have a minute to spare.

Summoning all her nerve, she made her way down the stairs in the dim light from the kitchen. When she reached the bottom, without taking time to turn on another light, she sped straight through the dark, gloomy basement into the garage, flinging the car door open. The dome light flashed on, and her heart fell as she remembered the scope was in the locked glove compartment, and her keys were upstairs. She hastily pulled the latch on the glove compartment, thinking maybe it had been left open. No, it was locked.

She'd have to go back upstairs. Her heart in her mouth, she re-crossed the shadowy basement. She mounted the stairs to the kitchen and looked for her keys on the counter top where she usually left them. They weren't there. She looked around in total frustration. This was taking way too long. Maybe she had left the keys in her jacket pocket. She hurried into the hallway and rummaged through the closet, finally finding the jacket she had worn earlier that day. Yes, there they were. She fished them out and ran back down to the garage. Opening the glove compartment, she got her night vision scope, slammed the car door shut, and rushed back through the basement.

What was that? A grinding sound at the basement window. Fritz had run over, and was barking frantically. Was it a tool cutting through the glass next to the lock? She put the scope to her eye and, through the unfocused lens, detected a blurry face outside the window. She made a mad dash for the stairs, her throat constricted with fear. She called to Fritz again and again as she raced up to the second floor. Suddenly she heard the dog give a loud yelp, and his barking stopped.

When she reached the top of the stairway, Susan ran into her bedroom and slammed the door shut, locking it. With trembling hands she picked up the phone and punched in 911. "Sorry, your call did not go through," came the robotic voice. In her panic, she had hit the wrong numbers. Now someone was pounding on her door.

Susan's whole body began shaking violently. Pulling herself together, she focused on the telephone numbers, 9-1-1. It was ringing. With a loud, splintering crash, her door burst open, and there stood the large, towering figure of Dominick Garcia. His eyes were blazing and his lips were set in a tight smile.

"No you don't, bitch," he said, yanking the receiver out of her hand, slamming it back on the set. He looked into her terror-filled eyes. "So we meet face to face at last," he said in a steely voice. "What a pleasure."

Susan stood facing him, paralyzed with fear. She saw he was in a state of fury, out of control, and knew he had come for revenge. He had fooled them. And he had waited until Charlie was gone. Now when Charlie got there, he was going to find her dead.

Garcia pulled the bottle of whiskey from his pocket and took a few sips. "Regretfully, our acquaintance is going to be short-lived." He gave her a tight-lipped smile. "Because it's time for you to die."

Susan's mind was racing in panic. If only she had a weapon. She should have grabbed a knife from the kitchen. A knife. She thought of the letter opener on the desk in her study. It was made of heavy silver, dagger shaped with a sharp point. She'd try to get it. She'd knee him in the groin and make a run for it.

"But you're not going to die quite yet, bitch," Garcia said in his steely voice. "First I'm going to fuck you over the way you fucked me over. Real bad." He let out a menacing laugh. "By the time I'm finished with you, you'll be begging me to let you die."

Susan shrank away from him in fear. He moved closer, his sour whiskey breath sending waves of revulsion through her. She needed the letter opener. She steeled herself to give him a crippling blow. As Garcia stepped close, her heart turned over, as she kneed him full force in the groin.

Garcia threw his hands down to cover himself, letting out a loud cry of pain and rage. Susan dashed to the doorway. He lunged at her, slapping her face hard. Her head reeled from the impact. He slapped her again, and then again. Her head was spinning wildly. All the color had drained from her face, and red welts stood out against her pale skin. "You shouldn't have done that, bitch," Garcia said in an icy tone, again holding his hands on his throbbing penis. "Now I want you to kiss it and make it all better."

Charlie inched along Loon Lake Road through the heavy fog, his headlights casting a dim, yellowish glow ahead of him. A deep instinct cried out to him that Susan was in danger, and he was seething in frustration. What if Susan needed him and he didn't get there in time? In spite of the low visibility, his foot bore down on the gas pedal. As Susan's house finally came into view, he saw her bedroom lights were on. She must be up there waiting for him. Yes, there she was by the window. His heart skipped a beat. Even through the dense fog, he was sure he discerned her figure in the brightly-lit room. Then his heart took a wild plunge. A second figure was moving towards her. A man? He couldn't be sure. He only saw a dark form and movement.

Charlie braked the car and jumped out, running towards the back door. A piercing scream came from inside the house. Chills raced down Charlie's spine as he frantically picked out the key Susan had given him. Turning the key in the lock, he flung the door open and dashed down the hallway, taking the stairs two at a time. When he got to the top, his heart froze as he saw Susan's splintered door. His human instinct clamored to him to charge in, but his policeman's training mandated that he first assess the situation.

Standing aside, he peered through the door opening. Susan was sprawled across the foot of the bed, her body askew, her robe and nightgown pulled up around her. A man with lowered trousers was on top of her, pinning her down. The dark-haired, sturdy looking man was facing away from the door, but Charlie felt certain it was Dominick Garcia.

Susan let out a scream. Charlie barreled into the room and flung himself at Garcia, roughly pulling him off the side of the bed. He threw him to the floor, then, with lightning speed, he slammed the back of his neck with his open hand, stunning him with a flash of blinding pain. Then he rolled him over and gave him a powerful uppercut on the chin that broke his jaw and knocked out teeth. With one solid punch, Charlie broke his nose, and blood spewed out.

"Pull up your pants, scumbag," Charlie said in a threatening tone. "I don't like looking at your disgusting little dick."

Garcia lay unmoving. Charlie kicked hard at his exposed genitals, and a loud, unearthly cry rose from the depths of Garcia's throat. "I said pull up your pants, asshole," Charlie told him. "Did you hear me this time?"

Garcia yanked up his pants and fastened them with shaky hands. He watched Charlie in terror, wondering where the next punch would land.

Charlie bent down and stared into his dazed eyes. "You're lucky I want you alive, scumbag," he said through clenched teeth.

As Charlie moved to hit him, Garcia desperately covered his face with his hands. Charlie pulled them away and began pounding his swollen face again. Blood dribbled out the corners of Garcia's mouth, and spurted from his broken nose. Finally Charlie stopped and stood up. Garcia's limp figure lay on the floor, his eyes closed.

Sitting at the foot of the bed, Susan broke into sobs. She got to her feet and moved towards Charlie, throwing her arms around him, burying her face in his chest.

"I'm so sorry," Charlie said softly.

"You got here in time," Susan answered through her sobs. "Nothing happened."

As the two remained locked in embrace, with Charlie's back to him, Garcia pulled the Beretta out of his leg holster as he inched across the carpet to the head of the bed. Then he staggered to his feet, cocking the gun with a sliding click. "Well, well. Look at the lovebirds," he sneered. His broken jaw made his speech slurred.

Charlie whirled around, reflexively throwing his arms back to position Susan behind him.

"Now you know that won't do any good," Garcia told him in a chilling voice. "The bullet will go right through you. Killing two birds with one stone, so to speak." He chuckled wildly, blood pouring from his nose. "Two lovebirds, that is."

Susan broke free from Charlie's grasp and stood beside him, giving Garcia a cold stare. "You'll never get away with this."

Garcia let out a short laugh. "I've got news for you, bitch. You're the one who isn't getting away with what you did."

"Let her go, Garcia," Charlie said in an even tone. "Take your revenge out on me. I'm the one who went after you."

Garcia laughed menacingly, aiming the gun at Susan. "But this fucking bitch started the whole thing. She couldn't keep her nose out of my business." He braced his shooting arm with his other hand, as if ready to fire. "Where's the girl?"

"She's out of here," Charlie said. "She's on her way to LA."

"Thanks for the info," Garcia answered with a bloody smile. "I'll have a friend of mine meet her at the airport."

He gave them a last cold look, his swollen eyes slits in his grotesque face. "Well, I have to go make a phone call. Time for you two to say your goodbyes."

He pointed the Beretta at Susan. "I'm shooting your girlfriend first, Lieutenant. I want you to have a chance to take a last look at her before I kill you. My gift to Internal Affairs."

BLACK DIAMOND

"Police! Freeze!"

Garcia spun and fired at the uniformed figure crouched in the doorway. The blast of a return shot resonated in the room, and Garcia crumpled to the floor, as Sheriff Wally Woods recoiled against the doorframe. Stunned by the flashes of gunfire and the deafening noise, Susan and Charlie stood looking on in shock. In the next instant, Charlie raced over to Garcia and kicked his gun away.

Susan ran towards the sheriff as he slowly crossed the room, lacking his usual springy step. "Wally!" she cried, throwing her arms around him. "Where did you come from? I thought you were out of town."

"I got back tonight," he answered with a smile. "And fortunately I was in the vicinity when the alert came over my radio. Thank goodness you had the presence of mind to call 911."

The two watched Charlie as he knelt down by Garcia, placing two fingers on his carotid artery. "He's dead," he told them. He stood and shook hands with the sheriff. "Thank you, Sheriff Woods," he said sincerely. "You saved our lives."

"Yes, thank you," Susan echoed. "We're very grateful."

"I'm glad I could be of service." His smile faded. "Of course I'm sorry I had to kill a man. But both of you are safe, so my last official act as sheriff was a worthwhile one indeed."

Susan gave him a quizzical look. "What do you mean?"

"I'm resigning tomorrow. I'll be making my last television appearance as sheriff." He smiled ruefully. "Actually, I was on my way to your house. I was going to stop in if your lights were still on. I believe I owe you a personal apology and an explanation."

With a glint catching her eye, Susan noticed Wally's badge on the floor, and went over and picked it up. Right away she saw it was dented, and realized it had been struck by a bullet. "Wally!" she cried, rushing back. "Are you hurt?"

"I'm sure it's nothing serious," he said. "The medics will fix me up. They'll be along any minute."

"Let me see," Susan demanded, working his Ike jacket off.

Wally winced in pain, and clutched his wounded shoulder. Blood seeped through his shirt, and a crimson stain was spreading down the front. While Charlie helped the sheriff to the bed, Susan dashed into the bathroom, returning with clean towels and a pair of scissors. Charlie took the scissors from her and cut the sheriff's shirt and undershirt away from his shoulder. Blood was pluming from the torn flesh wounds made by the shattered bullet. Charlie began applying pressure, as Susan fled downstairs to get the trauma bandage from her first aid kit.

"It was really lucky your badge deflected the bullet," Charlie told him.

"Yes. I guess it was my lucky day all the way around," the sheriff said. "You might say, I saved my own life today. I was all ready to board a flight to the Cayman's, but I changed my mind and came home."

The sheriff had grown weak from blood loss and shock. Blood was still oozing from his wounds, and he gratefully felt Charlie apply more pressure. He knew he could bleed to death. Here came the medics now. Sirens were wailing down Loon Lake Road.

Wally gave a weak smile. "You know, when I played ball for the town as a kid, I played clean. And I was damned proud of it. But as sheriff, I'm afraid I made some moves I'm not so proud of. So I decided to come back and pay the penalty, whatever it might be." His eyes fell closed for a few seconds, then slowly opened again. "And face the home crowd."

Charlie smiled softly. "So you're a real hero."

The next morning, while Heidi was taking Fritz for a walk, Susan and Charlie sat on the balcony outside his room at the Marble Point Inn looking out at the rippling, sunlit lake. The previous night, after the medics had taken the sheriff to the hospital, Charlie had called Heidi to tell her what happened, promising he and Susan would be there as soon as they could.

It had been quite late by the time all the police left, and when they got to the hotel, they found Heidi sound asleep. Fritz had happily curled up on the floor beside her, and Susan had taken the other bed. Charlie had gotten a room across the hall, and complained it wasn't fair that he was all alone, and that he should at least have Fritz. Susan had smilingly told him if he left her a key, she'd slip over and stay with him awhile so he wouldn't be lonesome.

When Susan woke up in the morning, she told Heidi her plans had changed, and she would be going to LA with them the next day. She was taking Charlie up on his invitation to stay with him until her house was made livable again. She would meet with the decorator later that day and make all the arrangements. Charlie had convinced her it would be good to get away for awhile, giving herself time to put her nightmarish experience behind her. It would also allow her to help Heidi get situated. Now that Garcia was no longer a threat, Heidi could stay with her friend Cheryl. After Heidi had called her from Susan's house, Cheryl's mother had phoned back to invite Heidi to stay with them for the rest of the school year.

Charlie was going to the sheriff's office after breakfast to turn in his supplemental report about the shootings. Susan was taking Heidi to buy her a swimsuit so she could enjoy the hotel's pool and spa. Heidi was also picking up a set of paints and colored pens to make the sheriff a get well card to take along when they visited him in the hospital that evening. The sheriff was doing well, but was being kept in the hospital for observation, and had postponed his television appearance until the following day.

A motorboat took off from the hotel dock, racing across the lake. Charlie followed it with his eyes, then turned to Susan and smiled. "Well, I'd have to say my trip to Marble Point was successful."

"I would certainly say so," Susan answered. "I know you're disappointed not to be taking Garcia back alive, but at least it's over. We'll never have to worry about him again."

"I agree," Charlie replied thoughtfully. "It would've been nice to get the whole Hollywood Division cleaned up, but it's a consolation knowing you're rid of the rottenest apple in the barrel."

It was four o'clock when the decorator left Susan's house. Susan had been very pleased with her, and felt confident she would do a good job coordinating all the repair work, getting new bedding, and having the same style carpet installed. Relieved that she could go off to LA with an easy mind, Susan added a few items to her suitcase and took a last look at the room in its current condition, remembering the ugly scene the night before. Now she was going to start putting the unfortunate event behind her.

Charlie had taken a walk while Susan met with the decorator. Their conference hadn't taken as long as had been expected, and he hadn't returned yet. Susan's lips turned up in a smile. She'd give Nan a call. She hadn't talked to her agent, except through the Internet, in the past two weeks. It was seven o'clock in New York, a good time to catch her at home. She walked into her study and punched in the number.

"Hello. Nan Whitcomb."

"Hi! It's Susan Muir."

"Susan! What a coincidence. I was just about to call you. I found a marvelous place for Mary, and it's only a two-hour bus ride to Marble Point. The Crooked Arrow Ranch in Bridger, about a hundred miles east of you. Mary's really looking forward to visiting."

"That's wonderful!" Susan exclaimed. "I'm glad you found a place you're happy with, and I will really enjoy having Mary come. Besides, she and Heidi will probably be the best of friends."

Nan sounded puzzled. "Who's Heidi?"

"Kind of like my adopted daughter."

"You're kidding!"

"No, I'm not kidding. And I owe it all to you. That's why I called."

"What do you mean?"

Susan laughed. "Well, it all started when you asked me to check on the Black Diamond Ranch. When I agreed, I had no idea what I was getting myself into." Prompted by Nan's questions, she went on to tell all about what had happened.

"Susan, that is incredible!" Nan sputtered. "Did all that really happen, or are you exercising your writer's imagination?"

"I was wondering that myself for awhile," Susan answered with a chuckle. "But it really happened. It's been an incredible two weeks. And now, thanks to you, I have the storyline for my next book. It's all plotted, and the characters are lined up ready to go."

"Susan, are you kidding me about all this?"

"No, I'm really not," Susan answered, laughing again. "I'm very excited about my new book. I can hardly wait to get started. I even have a title."

"Hold on a minute!" Nan interjected. "How exactly does this Charlie Martin fit into the picture? I noticed something in your voice when you talked about the dashing, idealistic lieutenant from LAPD Internal Affairs."

"Oh, Nan! You never were a dummy! He's the love interest, of course."

"Am I guessing correctly that you're the heroine?"

"Naturally. I'm not crazy enough to let someone like that get away!"

"Why, Susan!" Nan said laughingly. "I think I finally believe you. So what's the title of your new book?"

"*Black Diamond.*"

ABOUT THE AUTHOR

Joan Wolf is a graduate of the University of Pittsburgh and lived in New York City, bush Alaska, and Seoul, Korea before settling in the Bitterroots near Missoula, Montana. She lives with her husband, writer Frederick Wolf, and their German Shepherd, Bruno. Ms. Wolf is currently at work on her second suspense novel.